FOREPLAY

FOREPLAY
the ivy chronicles

SOPHIE JORDAN

wm

WILLIAM MORROW
An Imprint of HarperCollinsPublishers

HarperCollins books may be purchased for educational, business, or sales promotional use. For information please e-mail the Special Markets Department at SPsales@harpercollins.com.

FIRST EDITION

Designed by Lisa Stokes

Library of Congress Cataloging-in-Publication Data

Jordan, Sophie.
    Foreplay / Sophie Jordan. -- First edition.
       pages   cm.—(The Ivy Chronicles ; Book 1)
    ISBN 978-0-06-227987-3
    1. Love stories. 2. College stories. I. Title.
PS3610.O66155F67   2013
813'.6--dc23
                            2013017069

13 14 15 16 17   OV/RRD   10 9 8 7 6 5 4 3 2 1

To Maura and May, my champions

Chapter 1

ALL MY LIFE I knew what I wanted. Or rather, what I didn't want.

I didn't want the nightmares that plagued me to ever become reality again. I didn't want to return to the past. To live in fear. In constant doubt whether the ground beneath me would hold solid and firm. Ever since I was twelve, I've known this.

But it's strange how that thing you run from always finds a way of catching up with you. When you're not looking, it's suddenly there, tapping you on the shoulder, daring you to turn around.

Sometimes you can't help yourself. You have to stop. You have to turn and look.

You have to let yourself fall and hope for the best. Hope that when it's all over you come out in one piece.

SMOKE BILLOWED UP FROM beneath the hood of my car in great plumes, a gray fog on the dark night. Slapping the steering wheel, I muttered a profanity and pulled to the side of the road. A quick glance confirmed that the temperature gauge was well into the red.

"Shit, shit, shit." I killed the engine with quick, angry movements, hoping that might miraculously stop the vehicle from overheating further.

Grabbing my phone from the cup holder, I hopped out of the car into the crisp autumn night and stood well away from the vehicle. I knew nothing about engines, but I'd seen plenty of movies where the car blew up right after it started smoking. I wasn't taking any chances.

I checked the time on my phone. Eleven thirty-five. Not too late. I could call the Campbells. They would come and get me and give me a ride back to the dorm. But that still left my car alone out here on this road. I'd only have to deal with that later, and I already had a ton to do tomorrow. I might as well handle it now.

I glanced at the quiet night around me. Crickets sang softly and wind rustled through the branches. It wasn't exactly hopping with traffic. The Campbells lived on a few acres outside of town. I liked babysitting for them. It was a nice break from the bustle of the city. The old farmhouse felt like a real home, lived-in and cozy, very traditional with its old wood floors and stone fireplace that was always crackling at this time of year. It was like something out of a Norman Rockwell painting. The kind of life I craved to have someday.

Only now I didn't quite appreciate how isolated I felt on this country road. I rubbed my arms through my long thin sleeves, wishing I had grabbed my sweatshirt before I left tonight. Barely October and it was already getting cold.

I stared grimly at my smoking car. I was going to need a tow truck. Sighing, I started scrolling through my phone, searching for tow trucks in the area. The lights of an oncoming car flashed in the distance and I froze, debating what to do. The sudden insane idea to hide seized me. An old instinct, but familiar.

This had horror movie written all over it. A girl all by herself. A lonely country road. I'd been the star of my own horror movie once upon a time. I wasn't up for a repeat.

I moved off the road, situating myself behind my car. Not hiding exactly, but at least I wasn't standing out in the open, an obvious target. I tried to focus on the screen of my phone and look casual standing there. Like if I ignored the approaching car its inhabitant would somehow not notice me or the smoking pile of metal. Without lifting my head, every part of me was tuned in to the slowing tires and the purring engine as the vehicle stopped.

Of course they stopped. Sighing, I lifted my face, staring at a would-be serial killer. Or my rescuer. I knew that the latter was much more likely, but the whole scenario made me queasy and I could only think of worst-case possibilities.

It was a Jeep. The kind without a roof. Just a roll bar. The headlights gleamed off the stretch of black asphalt.

"You okay?" The deep voice belonged to a guy. Much of his face was in shadow. The light from the instrument panel cast a glow onto his face. Enough that I could determine he was youngish. Not much older than myself. Maybe mid-twenties at the most.

Most serial killers are young white males. The random factoid skittered across my thoughts, only adding to my anxiety.

"I'm fine," I quickly said, my voice overly loud in the crisp night. I brandished my phone as if that explained everything. "I have someone coming." I held my breath, waiting, hoping he would believe the lie and move on.

He idled there in the shadows, his hand on the gear stick. He looked up ahead at the road and then glanced behind him. Assessing just how alone we were? How ripe his opportunity was to murder me?

I wished I had a can of Mace. A black belt in kung fu. Something. *Anything.* The fingers of my left hand tightened around my keys. I thumbed the jagged tip. I could gouge him in the face if necessary. The eyes. Yeah. I'd aim for the eyes.

He leaned across the passenger seat, away from the glow of instrument panel, plunging himself into even deeper shadow. "I could look under the hood," his deep, disembodied voice offered.

I shook my head. "Really. It's okay."

Those eyes I had just contemplated gouging with my keys glittered across the distance at me. Their color was impossible to tell in the thick gloom, but they had to be pale. A blue or green. "I know you're nervous—"

"I'm not. I'm not nervous," I babbled quickly. Too quickly.

He leaned back in his seat, the amber glow again lighting his features. "I don't feel right leaving you out here alone." His voice shivered across my skin. "I know you're afraid."

I glanced around. The inky night pressed in thickly. "I'm not," I denied, but my voice rang thin, lacking all conviction.

"I get it. I'm a stranger. I know it would make you more comfortable if I left, but I wouldn't want my mother out here alone at night."

I held his gaze for a long moment, taking his measure, attempting to see something of his character in the shadowy lines of his face. I glanced to my still smoking car and back at him. "Okay. Thanks." The "thanks" followed slowly, a deep breath later, full of hesitation. I only hoped I wasn't going to end up on the morning news.

If he wanted to hurt me he would. Or at least he would try. Whether I invited him to look at my engine or not. That was my logic as I watched him pull his Jeep in front of my car. The door swung open. He unfolded his long frame and stepped out into the night with a flashlight in his hand.

His footsteps crunched over loose gravel, the beam of his flashlight zeroing in on my still-smoldering vehicle. From the angle of his face, I didn't think he even looked my way. He went straight for my car, lifting the hood and disappearing under it.

Arms crossed tightly in front of me, I stepped forward cautiously, edging out into the road so I could watch him as he studied the engine. He reached down and touched different things. God knows what. My knowledge of auto mechanics was right up there with my origami-making abilities.

I went back to studying his shadowy features. Something glinted. I squinted. His right eyebrow was pierced.

Suddenly another beam of lights lit up the night. My would-be-mechanic straightened from beneath the hood and stepped out, positioning himself between me and the road, his long legs braced and hands on his hips as the car approached. I had my first unfettered view of his face in the harsh glow of oncoming headlights, and I sucked in a sharp breath.

The cruel lighting might have washed him out or picked

up his flaws, but no. As far as I could see he had no physical flaws. He was hot. Plain and simple. Square jaw. Deep-set blue eyes beneath slashing dark brows. The eyebrow piercing was subtle, just a glint of silver in his right eyebrow. His hair looked like a dark blond, cut short, close to his head. Emerson would call him lickable.

This new vehicle halted beside my car and I snapped my attention away from him as the window whirred down. Lickable leaned down at the waist to peer inside.

"Oh, hey, Mr. Graham. Mrs. Graham." He slid a hand from his jean pocket to give a small wave.

"Car trouble?" a middle-aged man asked. The backseat of the car was illuminated with the low glow of an iPad. A teenager sat there, his gaze riveted to the screen, punching buttons, seemingly oblivious that the car had even stopped.

Lickable nodded and motioned to me. "Just stopped to help. I think I see the problem."

The woman in the passenger seat smiled at me. "Don't worry, honey. You're in good hands."

Eased at the reassurance, I nodded at her. "Thank you."

As the car drove away, we faced each other, and I realized this was the closest I had allowed myself to get to him. Now that some of my apprehension was put to rest, a whole new onslaught of emotions bombarded me. Sudden, extreme self-consciousness for starters. Well, for the most part. I tucked a strand of my unmanageable hair behind my ear and shifted uneasily on my feet.

"Neighbors," he explained, motioning to the road.

"You live out here?"

"Yeah." He slid one hand inside his front jean pocket. The action made his sleeve ride up and reveal more of the tattoo that crawled from his wrist up his arm. Unthreatening as he might be, he was definitely not your standard boy next door.

"I was babysitting. The Campbells. Maybe you know them."

He moved toward my car again. "They're down the road from my place."

I followed. "So you think you can fix it?" Standing beside him, I peered down into the engine like I knew what I was looking at. My fingers played nervously with the edges of my sleeves. "'Cause that would be awesome. I know she's a jalopy, but I've had her a long time." And I couldn't exactly afford a new car right now.

He angled his head to look at me. "Jalopy?" A corner of his mouth kicked up.

I winced. There I went again, showing off the fact that I grew up surrounded by people born before the invention of television.

"It means an old car."

"I know what it means. Just never heard anyone but my grandmother say it."

"Yeah. That's where I picked it up." From Gran and everyone else in the Chesterfield Retirement Village.

Turning, he moved to his Jeep. I continued to play with my sleeves, watching him return with a bottle of water.

"Looks like a leaky radiator hose."

"Is that bad?"

Unscrewing the cap on the water, he poured it inside my engine. "This will cool it down. Should run now. For a while at least. How far are you going?"

"About twenty minutes."

"It will probably make it. Don't go farther than that or it will overheat again. Take it to a mechanic first thing tomorrow so he can replace the hose."

I breathed easier. "That doesn't sound too bad."

"Shouldn't cost more than a couple hundred."

I winced. That would pretty much wipe out my account. I would have to see about working a few extra shifts at the daycare or getting some more babysitting gigs. At least when I babysat, I could get in some studying after the kids went to bed.

He slammed the hood back in place.

"Thanks a lot." I shoved my hands into my pockets. "Saved me from calling a tow truck."

"So no one's coming then?" That corner of his mouth lifted back up again and I knew I amused him.

"Yeah." I shrugged. "I might have made that up."

"It's okay. You weren't exactly in an ideal situation. I know I can look scary."

My gaze scanned his face. Scary? I knew he was probably joking, but he did have that certain edge to him. A dangerous vibe with his tattoos and piercing. Even if he was hot. He was like the dark vampire in movies that girls obsessed over. The one who was torn between eating the girl and kissing her. I always preferred the nice mortal guy and never understood why the heroine didn't go after him. I didn't do dark, danger-ous, and sexy. *You don't do anyone.* I shoved the whisper back, batting it away. If the right guy—the one I wanted—noticed me, all that would change.

"I wouldn't say scary . . . exactly."

He chuckled softly. "Sure you would."

Silence hovered between us for a moment. My gaze swept over him. The comfortable-looking T-shirt and well-worn jeans were casual. Guys wore them every day on campus, but he didn't look casual. He didn't look like any guy I ever saw around campus. He looked like trouble. The kind that girls lost their heads over. Suddenly my chest felt too tight.

"Well, thanks again." Offering up a small wave I ducked back inside my car. He watched me turn the key. Thankfully smoke didn't billow up from the hood.

Driving away, I refused to risk a glance back in my rearview mirror. If Emerson had been with me, I'm sure she wouldn't have left without his phone number.

Eyes on the road again, I felt perversely glad she wasn't there.

Chapter 2

I NUDGED THE DOOR open with my shoulder, my hands overflowing with a popcorn bag and bottled pink lemonade. I walked into the adjoining room and sank down onto Georgia's swivel chair. As usual, Emerson's was covered in clothes.

ABBA throbbed on the air—Emerson's signature getting-ready-to-go-out music. Whenever I heard it blaring through our thin walls, I knew preparations had started.

Setting my bottle down on her desk amid her mess of notebooks and books, I shoveled a fistful of popcorn into my mouth and watched as she shimmied into a tight miniskirt. The crazy black-and-white zigzag print looked good on her tiny frame. I winced, envisioning myself wearing it. Not a pretty picture. I wasn't a five-foot-tall, hundred-pound spinner.

"Where are you going tonight?"

"Mulvaney's."

"Not your usual playground."

"Freemont's has gotten too full of frat brats."

"I thought that was your thing."

"Last year maybe. I'm over them. This year I'm more into . . ." She angled her head, examining herself in the mirror that hung on the door. " . . . men, I guess. No more boys for me." She flashed me a grin. "Wanna come?"

I shook my head. "I have class tomorrow."

"Yeah. At like nine thirty." She shook her head with disgust. "Please. My class is at eight."

"Which you will probably miss."

She winked. "Prof never takes attendance. I'll get the notes from someone else."

Likely some hapless freshman who got tongue-tied when Emerson approached. He'd probably offer her a kidney if she asked.

Georgia entered the room, wrapped in a terry-cloth robe and holding her shower caddy. "Hey, Pepper. You coming out with us tonight?"

My hand froze in the bag of popcorn. "You're going, too?" That would be unusual. Georgia spent most nights with her boyfriend.

She nodded. "Yeah, Harris is studying for a big test tomorrow, so I figured why not? Mulvaney's is pretty cool. Beats Freemont's."

Emerson shot me an I-told-you-so look. "Sure you don't want to join us?" she asked, sliding a turquoise top over her head. It was sexy. One-shouldered and hugged her like a second skin. Something I would never wear.

"I'll leave the wild nights to you two."

Emerson snorted. "I don't know how wild we can get with Georgia here. She's practically an old married lady."

"Am not!" Georgia unwrapped the damp towel from her head and threw it at Emerson.

Emerson grinned and snagged some popcorn from my bag. She wolfed down a mouthful and then licked at her buttery fingers, nodding at me. "You're the one who should be going."

"You *should* go," Georgia seconded. "You're single. Live a little. Have fun. Flirt."

"It's all right." I shook my head. "I'll get my vicarious thrills through the two of you."

"Oh, be honest. It's because of Hunter," Emerson said accusingly as she stood in front of her mirror and applied product into her short dark hair. She tugged and arranged the strands until they stuck out at different angles, creating a wild, choppy look that surrounded her round face. She looked like some kind of cool pixie.

I shrugged. It was no secret that my heart belonged to Hunter Montgomery. I'd been in love with him since I was twelve.

A familiar ring tone trilled from my room. I thrust my popcorn bag at Emerson and rushed through the adjoining door.

Landing on my bed with a bounce, I snatched my phone from where I'd left it, glimpsing the caller's name before answering. "Hey, Lila."

"Oh my God, Pepper, you're never going to believe this!"

I smiled at the sound of my best friend's voice. She attended school across the country in California, but every time we talked it was like no time had passed. "What happened?"

"I just got off the phone with my brother."

My heart squeezed at the mention of Hunter. It was no secret that I was infatuated with him. Crazy as it seemed, he was part of the reason I applied to Dartford. Not that it wasn't a great school. When a little voice in the back of my head reminded me that there were other stellar schools out there, I chose to ignore it. "And?" I prompted.

"He and Paige broke up."

My hand tightened around the phone. "Are you serious?" Hunter had met Paige his sophomore year and they'd been glued together ever since. I was beginning to fear that she would become the future Mrs. Montgomery. "Why?"

"I dunno . . . something about them wanting to date other people. He said it was a mutual split, but who cares? The point is my brother is single for the first time in two years. Now's your chance."

Now was my chance.

Excitement hummed through me for a few seconds before dying a swift death. Then the panic set in. Hunter was free. Finally. I'd been waiting for this moment forever, but I wasn't ready. How could I get him to notice me? As far as Hunter was concerned I was his little sister's best friend. End of story.

"Oh! I have to run," Lila was saying in my ear. "I have rehearsal, but let's talk more later."

"Yeah." I nodded as if she could see me. "I'll call you later."

I sat on my bed for a long moment, the phone in my limp hand. Emerson's and Georgia's laughter drifted from the neighboring room, mingling with "Dancing Queen." It was a grim moment. The reality I had longed for had finally come. And I didn't have a clue what to do.

Emerson pushed open my cracked door. She dropped down in my chair. "Hey. I'm about to finish off your popcorn."

She shook the bag at me. Her smile slipped when she saw my face. "What's wrong?"

"They broke up," I murmured, my fingers playing about my lips, tapping against them with a nervous energy.

"What? Who?"

"He's single. Hunter is single." I shook my head like I still could not quite believe it.

Her eyes widened. "Georgia, get in here! Quick!"

Georgia appeared, towel-drying her hair. "What's going on?"

"Hunter is single," Emerson explained.

"Shut up! No more Paige?"

I nodded.

"Well. Now's your chance." Emerson bounced onto the bed beside me. "What's the plan?"

I blinked at her and held out a hand helplessly. "I don't have a plan." The plan was for him to fall in love with me. That was the dream. That's what happened in romance novels. Somehow. Some way. That was supposed to happen. I never quite knew *how* it was going to happen. Only that it would.

"What should I do?" I looked at them helplessly. "Drive over to his apartment and knock on his door and declare myself to him?"

Georgia cocked her head to the side. "Um. I'm going to go with *no*."

"Yeah. Too forward." Emerson nodded as though I'd just made a viable suggestion. "Not enough mystery. Men like a bit of the chase."

Georgia rolled her eyes and snorted. "This coming from you."

Emerson looked affronted. "Hey, I know how to play the game. When I want them to chase me, they do."

That was just it. I didn't know how to play the game. I didn't know how to do anything to entice a guy. I didn't flirt. Didn't date. Didn't make out or shack up with random guys like other girls.

I buried my head in my hands. Why hadn't I thought about this sooner? A little experience under my belt might help me win over Hunter. I was pretty sure I was a bad kisser. At least that's what Franco Martinelli told everyone in tenth grade after we made out behind the cafeteria. Well, if one kiss and a quick grope under my sweater before I shoved his hand away constituted making out.

"I don't know how to play the game," I confessed. "How am I going to attract Hunter? I haven't even kissed a guy since high school." I held up a finger and looked at my two friends desperately. "And just one guy. I've kissed one guy."

My two suitemates stared at me.

"One guy?" Georgia echoed after what felt like the world's longest silence.

"Tragic." Emerson shook her head like I'd just cited some horrible world hunger statistic. She snapped her fingers, smiling brightly. "But nothing we can't fix."

I frowned. "What do you mean?"

"All you need is a little experience."

My eyes widened. Emerson had uttered this so simply, and I guess for her it was. She had no shortage of confidence and no shortage of admirers.

"You're going out with us tonight," Georgia announced,

locking eyes with Emerson. They nodded at each other as if reaching some form of unspoken agreement.

"Yes, you are. And you're going to kiss someone." Emerson stood and stared down at me, her hands propped on her slim hips. "Someone hot who knows what he's doing."

"What?" I blinked rapidly. "I don't think kissing some random—"

"Oh, not random. You'll need a pro."

My mouth sagged. It took me a moment to recover my voice. "A prostitute?"

Emerson shoved my shoulder. "Oh, be serious, Pepper. No! I'm talking about a guy with a well-earned rep. A good kisser. Someone to, you know . . . teach you foreplay."

I eyed her uneasily. "Who?"

"Well. I was targeting him myself tonight, but I'll stand down for a good cause. You can have him."

"Have who?"

"The bartender at Mulvaney's. Annie down the hall made out with him last week. Carrie, too. They said he's wet-your-panties hot."

Georgia nodded, her eyes earnest with agreement. "I've heard some girls in my philosophy class talk about him, too."

"So, what? I'm supposed to just waltz into Mulvaney's and approach some man-whore bartender and say, 'Hey, will you make out with me, please?'"

"No, silly. Just make yourself available. He's a guy. He'll rise to the bait." Emerson waggled her eyebrows. "Pun intended."

"Stop." I tossed a pillow at her, laughing miserably. "I can't do that."

"Why don't you just come out with us?" Georgia coaxed. "You don't have to do anything you don't want. No pressure."

I gawked at Georgia. I almost expected this harebrained scheme from Emerson, but Georgia was the steady one. Practical and conservative.

"But"—Emerson held up one slim finger—"if we scope out this bartender and you like what you see, you can say hello. Nothing wrong with that, right?"

I shrugged uneasily. "Yeah. I guess so." Staring at my two friends, I felt myself buckle beneath their persuasion. "Fine. I'll go. But I'm not promising to hook up with anyone."

Emerson bounced and clapped her hands. "Great! And just promise to keep an open mind."

I nodded in agreement. No harm in that. At the very least, I could observe the way everyone interacted. Bars were one giant meat market. Maybe I would learn some dos and don'ts. Observe what it was guys responded to. It couldn't simply be short skirts and ginormous breasts.

I was a psychology major. Studying human nature was what I did. Tonight I just needed to pretend Mulvaney's was one giant petri dish. Like scientists before me, I'd observe and learn. And maybe have some fun in the process. After all, who said learning had to be boring?

Chapter 3

THERE WERE SEVERAL THINGS—OKAY, a lot of things—that remained perpetually unclear to me. The exact location of my mother, whether I preferred Canadian bacon or sausage on my pizza, and what precisely I was going to do after college with a degree in psychology.

But the one point of fact that never wavered in my mind was that I wanted to be part of the Montgomery family. I wanted to marry Hunter Montgomery.

I wanted to belong to the family that had offered me such solace growing up. The Montgomerys were everything that a family should be. Loving. Supportive. They sat down at the table for dinner every night and talked about their day. They played Monopoly together and had pool parties. They shared more than a house. They shared their lives with each other. It was everything I never had.

Before living with Gran, my life had been a series of motel rooms. I vaguely remembered a house with a tire swing in the backyard. When my father was still alive. I remembered him standing over a barbecue pit with lots of people around him. It was the Fourth of July. There were fireworks, and I was sticky with Popsicle juice. But that was all I had. The only memory of a time that wasn't crowded with the sounds of Mom crying as some guy beat on her, heard through the thin walls of the bathroom or closet where she'd hidden me.

The Montgomerys attended church together. Sent out Christmas cards with all five of them and the dog posing before a huge ten-foot tree. Ever since Lila took me home with her in seventh grade and I was given a glimpse into their life—ever since I met Hunter—I knew I wanted to be one of them.

"You sure you don't want to go back and change? You can borrow one of my outfits."

Emerson's suggestion pulled me from my thoughts. "I couldn't fit my big toe into your jeans."

She rolled her eyes at me as we made our way across the gravel lot.

Mulvaney's was a local institution, catering to townies and college students alike, but that didn't mean I had ever been there before. Bars . . . the smell of alcohol, loud drunken voices—it reminded me too much of Mom. Emerson and Georgia dragged me to Freemont's once, but I only went because it was Emerson's birthday.

There were two entrances. As we entered through the back one, we squeezed past the people in line at the food counter. The aroma of fried food filled my nose.

Emerson pointed to the whiteboard above the counter. "At one in the morning there's nothing better than the fried macaroni balls. We'll have to get some to go before we leave."

I nodded, tempted to ask why we didn't just do that now,

but Georgia gave me a quelling look, warning me not to even suggest it. Linking her arm through mine, she led me up a wood plank ramp that opened into the main room. A long bar stretched against the far left wall. The place was packed. There weren't near enough tables, so at least a hundred people milled about the room, drinks in hands, their voices a deafening crescendo that rivaled the music blaring from the speakers.

Sliding into single file, we held hands as we squeezed through the press of bodies. I ended up in the middle, a deliberate move on Emerson's and Georgia's part I'm sure. Guys tried to talk to us as we pushed past. Emerson smiled, calling hello back to a few of them.

"Hey, Red," one called to me, sandwiching between me and Emerson. I had to look down at him. He barely reached my chin.

I started to stammer out a hello when Emerson backed up and looked him over. "Red? Really? You lose points for originality. C'mon, Pepper." With a tug on my wrist, she pulled me after her. "See. Not five minutes here and you're already getting hit on."

I rolled my eyes.

"He's not what we're aiming for, but no worry. The night's still young. We haven't found who we're looking for yet." Emerson pointed at the bar. "Why don't you get us a pitcher? We'll get a table."

I craned my head to look around. "How are you going to find a table in this zoo?"

Emerson gave me an insulted look. "Oh, we'll get a table. Leave it to me."

"Here." Georgia thrust some money in my hand. "First pitcher's on me."

"The only pitcher. We don't need to buy our own drinks." Emerson shook her head like we both had much to learn and motioned for me to move on toward the bar. "Go on. And while you're there keep an eye out for you-know-who."

I watched as they disappeared into the throng, convinced now that the whole point of sending me to the bar was for me to scope out the player bartender we'd come here looking for. I worked my way through the crush, wading through bodies until I stood in line behind a pair of giggling girls.

"Yeah, that's him," a bleached blonde said to her friend. "Lydia said he was hot, but OMG . . . that's putting it mildly."

Her friend fanned herself. "If he would mess around with Lydia, he's going to think he hit the lottery with us."

Who talked about themselves like that? I couldn't help myself. A laugh escaped me. I slapped a hand over my mouth.

The dark-haired girl glared over her shoulder at me. I quickly dropped my hand and tried to look innocent, angling my neck as though I was impatient to place my drink order and not eavesdropping.

The blonde slapped her arm. "You're so bad, Gina."

Gina returned her attention to her friend. "Well, hopefully I'll get to be bad with him tonight. I call dibs." She waved a ten-dollar bill, clearly trying to gain the bartender's attention.

I shook my head, regretting every time I'd ever judged Emerson for her lack of inhibitions. Compared to these two she was a Girl Scout. Clearly they were discussing my bartender. *Wait*. When did he become *mine*? I winced. From the sound of it, he belonged to every female that passed through Mulvaney's doors.

I reminded myself that I would *not* be hooking up with anyone tonight . . . especially a bartender with a reputation for swapping DNA with the entire female population of Dartford. Thanks, but no. I couldn't imagine myself with someone so undiscriminating. I had standards. There was no way I could contemplate messing around with someone like that. Even if it was to gain some much-needed experience to win over Hunter.

And then I saw him.

The air froze in my lungs. He stepped up in front of the two girls, bracing his arms against the bar top. I heard his voice, low and deep, over the steady drone of the bar. "What can I get for you?"

I gawked, unable to blink. I had an unobstructed view of him in the space between the girls. The blood rushed in my ears, and suddenly it was last night all over again and I was on a lonely stretch of country road, the acrid smoke of my overheating car filling my nostrils as I stared at his familiar face. That dark blond hair cut close to his head. The tall, lean body that had bent over the engine of my car less than twenty-four hours ago. I could see him even more clearly now, but I hadn't been mistaken in my initial assessment. He was hot. His jaw square and strong. His features like something chiseled from marble. There was a shadowy hint of stubble on his face, and his eyes were so piercing a blue they looked almost silver.

He looked just a few years older than me. I could see that now. It was probably the way he held himself. Experienced. Capable. He wore a well-worn cotton T-shirt with MULVANEY'S stretched across one of his impressive pecs. Dimly I wondered if his shirt felt as soft as it looked. If his chest was as solid.

The girls were tittering like seventh-graders now. Gawking at him, too. I felt like someone sucker punched me. My rescuer. My bartender. Mulvaney's man-whore. One and the same.

"What can I get you?" he repeated.

"What's good?" Gina propped her elbows on the bar, no doubt flashing him some of her cleavage.

He rattled off the various beers on tap like he had done it a hundred times before, which he probably had. His gaze slid the length of the bar as he talked, assessing the crowd.

"Hmm. What's your favorite?" Gina called.

Shaking his head, he looked back down at her. "Look, I'll come back to you when you make up your mind." His eyes snapped over them to me. "What'll you have?"

My mouth parted, surprised that he was addressing me, that he dismissed them so easily. Just like that. And when they were flirting with him no less.

His eyes narrowed with recognition. "Hey. You." He nodded slightly at me. "How's the car?"

Before I could answer, Gina sent me a withering look and then turned back to him. She waved her money in his face. "Excuse me. We were here first."

Sighing, he looked back down at them, his expression a blend of annoyance and boredom. "Then order already."

She tossed her dark hair over her shoulder. "Forget it. The service here sucks. We'll go somewhere else." Turning, they shoved past me.

He didn't even watch them depart. With his stare fixed on

me, he shrugged one shoulder and flashed me a half smile that made my stomach lurch. I stepped up to the bar, trying to look confident. Like I hung out in bars all the time.

He braced his hands on the edge of the bar, leaning forward slightly. "Now what can I get for you?" His tone was decidedly friendlier than when he spoke to the other girls, and heat swarmed my face. I'm sure it was just because we knew each other—in a way—but it still made me feel special. Singled out.

I lowered my gaze, eyeing his arms. The muscles bunched. A tattoo peeked out from beneath his sleeve and crawled down his tanned bicep and forearm, stopping at his wrist. It looked like some kind of intricate feathered wing. I would have liked to study it further, but I was already conscious that I was ogling him, and I still hadn't answered his question.

"Um. A pitcher of Sam Adams." I knew Emerson liked microbrews.

"ID?"

"Oh." I fumbled for the fake ID Emerson made me get last year for the one time she dragged me to Freemont's.

He glanced at it and back to my face. A hint of a smile played about his lips. "Twenty-four?"

I nodded, but my face went from warm to scalding.

"Guess you just have one of those baby faces." He didn't wait for a reply. Still smiling faintly, he stepped away.

My eyes were drawn to his broad back. His T-shirt hugged the muscled expanse. He wore a pair of well-worn jeans, and the view from the back was almost as nice as the front. Suddenly the bar felt oppressively hot.

He set the full pitcher and a stack of cups in front of me.

"Thanks." I handed him the money. He took it and moved to the cash register.

In the moments he was gone, I tried to think of something to say. Something cute and engaging. Anything that might draw out our conversation. I didn't let myself consider why. Or that suddenly I wasn't so averse to the idea of talking to him. Flirting with him. *Flirting.*

My throat closed up, panicking at the prospect. How did Emerson do it? She made flirting look so effortless.

He returned with my change. "Thanks," I murmured, dropping it into the tip jar.

"Take care."

I looked up but he was already gone, moving on to the next customer. I hesitated, staring after him. Shaking my head, I reminded myself not to ogle. Tucking the cups under one arm, I held the pitcher with two hands and dove back into the throng. Only I didn't make it two steps before someone bumped me. The pitcher flew from my hands, somersaulting amid bodies, sloshing beer everywhere. People cried out, wiping ineffectually at their doused clothing.

"Sorry!" I apologized to their glaring faces, grateful that I, at least, had somehow managed to stay dry.

Bending, I retrieved the plastic pitcher from the plank floor just as my pocket started to buzz multiple times in quick succession.

I dug it out of my pocket and read the text.

Emerson: Found table. Still at bar? Did u see him?

Rolling my eyes, I tucked the empty pitcher under my arm and texted her back.

Me: Yes. Yes

Sighing, I squeezed back to the front of the bar and set the pitcher down on the surface. My gaze searched for him. He was serving customers a little way down the bar now, bending his lean body over the counter to better hear orders. I waited until he caught my gaze. He sent me a nod of acknowledgment. I nodded back.

My phone vibrated in my hand again. I glanced down.

Emerson: U r taking 4ever. Better be making out w/him 2 take this long

I snorted and was in the process of typing back to her when he arrived in front of me. He nodded at the pitcher. "That was quick."

"Yeah." I hastily slid my phone back in my pocket, almost as if I feared him seeing the texts about him. I smiled wanly. "I didn't make it three feet."

"Ah." He nodded in understanding, bracing his hands on the bar top again. The action stretched his shirt taut over his chest and pulled it against his shoulders. "I'll let you in on a secret. Nice girls get eaten alive in places like this."

I stared at him for a moment, his words sinking in. I moistened my lips, reaching deep inside me where some reservoir of female instincts dwelled. "Maybe I'm not that nice."

He laughed then, a short, deep sound that sent ripples eddy-ing through me. My face flushed. I smiled hesitantly, unsure if his laughter was good or bad.

"Sweetheart, you've got 'nice girl' written all over you."

The "sweetheart" made my stomach flutter. Until the rest of his words sank in. *You've got "nice girl" written all over you.* I frowned. Nice girls didn't win the guy. Hunter's ex-girlfriend flashed across my mind. No one would accuse her of being a nice girl. She was sexy, with sleek, surfer-blond hair and designer clothes that showed off her body. Sophisticated. Not your girl-next-door type at all. Not like me.

"You might be surprised," I bluffed.

"Yeah." He nodded, his gaze skimming me, and suddenly I wished I had worn something besides a shapeless sweater. "I would be."

I clamped my lips shut to stop myself from arguing with him. He thought I was a nice girl because that's how I looked. I wasn't going to change his mind with words. That was the kind of thing one proved.

He bent his arm and tapped his elbow. "Use your elbows to get through out there."

He stepped away and filled another pitcher. He set it down in front of me. I fumbled for my money in the tiny purse strapped across my chest.

He swiped a hand through the air. "Don't worry about it."

"Really? Thanks."

He pointed out into the main room. "Just remember to use those elbows, Nice Girl."

With that parting tip, he moved down the bar to the next

customer. I stood there and stared after him for a moment, contemplating our exchange. *Nice Girl*. It echoed through my head. Fantastic. That's how he thought of me. No name. Simply that.

Someone nudged me to move out of the way. Turning, I maneuvered back through the room, following his advice and using my elbows. It got me glares, but worked.

"Pepper! Over here!" Emerson waved wildly from a table.

Two guys already occupied the table. Something told me they'd had it first. Half a pitcher of beer sat in the middle. Emerson and Georgia sipped from glasses that were doubtless courtesy of their tablemates.

"Guys, this is Pepper." She slapped the arm of the guy next to her. "Troy, be a gentleman. Let her sit down."

"It's Travis." He stood and waved me into his seat.

Lowering myself into the chair, I set the pitcher down beside the other one.

"Well." Emerson scooted closer. "How hot is he?"

I poured a glass and took a deep gulp, suddenly feeling like I needed the fortification even though I wasn't a fan of the stuff. Coming up for air, I answered. "Hot."

"Did you talk to him?"

I shrugged one shoulder, for some reason keeping to myself that he was the guy that helped me with my car last night. That might lead me to explaining how he had just dubbed me "Nice Girl." I winced anew over that. He might as well have dubbed me "Undesirable" or "Leper."

"I ordered beer," I volunteered.

"Ugh, that's all? Well, there's lots of fish in the sea." She motioned around us. "We'll find you someone to hone your wiles."

My gaze skimmed the sea of people, including the two guys at our table. The one who gave up his chair squatted now, sitting on a motorcycle helmet. He watched Emerson raptly as if he was actually a participant in our conversation. Meanwhile, his friend was working hard to impress Georgia. I couldn't imagine a more hopeless endeavor than that. She had to have told him she had a boyfriend. Georgia was like that. She wasn't into leading guys on.

"Looking to hone your wiles?" Travis echoed. "I can help you there."

"Down, boy." Emerson patted his arm and I could read her subtext even if she was too kind to say the words: *You're not what we're looking for.*

"I wasn't actually talking about me. I was talking about the campus kink club."

"Kink club?" I blinked.

"Yeah. Everyone's talking about it."

"Whoa, hang on a minute. Did you say 'kink club'?" Emerson held up a hand. "Everyone can't be talking about it. I haven't heard about it."

"It's invitation only. Members are few and select."

She angled her head and gave him a pointed look. "And again, I haven't heard of it."

I grinned. Emerson's sharp blue eyes cut to me. I quickly covered my lips, trying to hide my amusement. She obviously felt slighted to only be hearing about this now.

"What's a kink club?" Georgia asked, and the words themselves seemed odd emerging in her Alabama accent.

"You know," Travis's friend volunteered. "It's just what it sounds like. A club for people who like their stuff outside the box, you know?" He drew a little box in the air as if that somehow explained everything.

"People who like their stuff outside the box," I murmured, glancing at the faces around the table. "That's not that helpful." Especially considering I wasn't even sure what everything was inside the box.

"The girl in the apartment across from mine is a member," Travis added. "She told me about it."

"Yeah?" Emerson's eyes sparkled with interest. "What's she into?"

Travis looked the three of us over. "Oh, she'd be into the three of you."

"She's gay?" Emerson looked unimpressed. "What's so outside the box about that?"

"I said she would be into the *three* of you."

We stared for a long moment. Then Emerson *ahh*ed and Georgia nodded in understanding. I still stared blankly.

Travis laughed at my expression. "As in the three of you . . . *together*. All at once."

"Oh." My cheeks burned.

Travis laughed. "Your expression is priceless."

"Kink club. Huh." Emerson looked at me thoughtfully. "You would definitely learn a thing or two if you visited—"

"Forget it," I cut her off. "It's one thing to flirt around with a bartender and . . ." My gaze swung to the two guys listening attentively, suddenly embarrassed. Still, I pushed on. " . . . and think about doing other stuff. I don't need to sink to debauchery."

Travis slapped the table, laughing again. He waved at me. "Where did you find this one? She screams 'never been laid.'"

"Oh, and you have?" Georgia snapped.

Emerson kicked Travis's helmet out from under him. He toppled over onto the plank floor. She nodded out into the room. "Get lost."

Travis stood, dusting himself. "Sorry. Just kidding." He looked at his friend. "C'mon, man."

The two waded into the mass. For a moment, the three of us sat there, silent.

"Don't listen to that ass hat," Emerson finally muttered.

I shrugged like I wasn't bothered. Seriously, what did I care what some douche thought of me? Even if his assessment did seem to echo the bartender's opinion of me. "Nice Girl" and "never been laid" seemed to kind of go hand in hand, after all.

It honestly didn't bother me that I was a virgin. What bothered me was that I was invisible to the opposite sex. And until I became visible, how was Hunter ever going to notice me?

I took a sip from my cup and glanced around the room, eyeing the crowd. Beautiful girls were everywhere, laughing, talking, flipping their hair with smooth, gliding movements. I'd never felt so apart from my environment as I did in that moment. Any one of these girls had a better shot with Hunter than I did. All because they weren't afraid to go after what they wanted. All because they knew how to talk, how to act, how to *be* around guys. And they didn't need a kink club to educate them. They figured it out and I could, too.

My gaze snapped back to my friends, resolve sweeping through me. "All right."

Emerson cocked her head to the side. "All right . . . what?"

"Let's do this," I announced. "I'll take whatever advice you dish out. I'll flirt and wear whatever clothes you pick."

Emerson perked up, sitting alert and board straight in her chair. "Are you serious?"

Georgia looked uncertain. "Are you sure, Pepper?"

I nodded and took another drink, wincing at the bitter mouthful. "Yes. Foreplay. I want to learn." I *needed* to.

Emerson clapped her hands and glanced around the room. "Yesss! Okay. Let's see. Who should we—"

"No." I held up one finger. "If I'm doing this it's not going to be with some wasted guy who's probably no better at kissing than I am." I leveled my stare on each of my friends. "Like we talked about earlier, I want someone who knows what he's doing." I inhaled a deep breath, one image filling my mind. "I want the bartender."

Emerson smiled slowly, nodding in approval. "All right then. The bartender it is."

Chapter 4

NOTHING HAPPENED THAT NIGHT.

It's one thing to decide to make a play for a guy, and another thing entirely to get up and do it right then. I'd already seen him reject two girls who threw themselves at him. Evidently he was more discriminating than the rumors implied. I didn't want to be shot down. Once that happened, I'd never have a chance with him, and for some reason I'd set my sights on him. Maybe it was the fact that he helped me that night when my car died. Who wasn't a sucker for a knight in shining armor? Or maybe it was simply that he had called me a "nice girl" and I had determined to be naughty. Maybe I wanted to make him eat those words.

We all agreed to call it a night and to return armed with a plan. Or at least a better outfit.

I actually got up in time for my morning class. Emerson's soft snores drifted through the adjoining door, telling me she wasn't going to make it to her morning class. The ever reliable Georgia was already up and gone.

I trekked across campus, admiring the turning leaves and

enjoying the nip in the crisp New England air as I walked. Just barely into fall and already every shade of orange, red, and yellow was out in full force. Last night's nip in the air still bit at my cheeks. It might even be colder. When I went home to Pennsylvania for Thanksgiving I was going to have to return with more sweaters.

I sat through botany, taking notes inside the packet the prof had handed out at the start of the semester. After class I packed up quickly, trying to beat the crush out the door.

I trucked it to the Java Hut. Normally I grab a latte before class, but there hadn't been enough time. By the time I entered the coffee shop, I was dying for a jolt of caffeine. I stepped into line. A pair of girls decked out in sorority regalia—matching sweatshirts and velour pants—chattered noisily about their weekend plans in front of me.

My phone vibrated in my pocket. I pulled it out and read the text.

Emerson: Lrge Carmel Latte Xtra Hot PLS!

Apparently she was up. Grinning, I texted back.

Me: What will u do 4 me?
Emerson: Make u so hot u will have 2 beat hottie bartender off w/stick

I laughed lightly under my breath and typed back.

Me: Why does that scare me???

Emerson: b/c you're afraid to look good and get what u
        want

Me: Not true

Emerson: So true

"Hey, Pepper!" The words kissed my cheek in a small gust of breath.

I whirled around, and my gaze collided with the target of all my pent-up desires. My heart seized inside my chest.

"Hey, Hunter." Was that breathless squeak my voice? My gaze swept over him, taking him in all at once. The chestnut brown hair carefully arranged to look artfully messy. The soft brown eyes. The dimpled cheek.

He pulled me into a warm hug. A warm, brotherly hug. The kind he always gave me. Stepping back, he nodded at my phone. "Reading something funny?"

I shoved my phone into my pocket. "No. Just a text from Emerson."

"Ah." He squeezed my arm fondly through my sweater. "How you been?"

"Good." I nodded back, too eagerly, and then felt my face warm with embarrassment. With him, it was always this way. Awkward. Uncomfortable. At least *I* was always this way. He was only ever composed, easygoing, and comfortable, while I was forever that twelve-year-old girl in awe of him, despite how nice he was to me

He stared at me for a moment before I added: "You? Last year."

I resisted closing my eyes in a long anguished blink. Apparently I could only speak in choppy fragments to him.

"Yeah. Getting my applications together. Narrowing down my top choices."

"Wow. That's great, Hunter."

"Just hoping I get in somewhere, you know?"

"Oh, I'm sure you'll get in," I gushed.

He gestured for me to move ahead in the line. The sorority girls were ordering now.

He shrugged. "Competition is stiff, and every program only has so many spots. Watch. I'll probably end up studying medicine in Uruguay."

He laughed and I followed suit, sure he was joking. Hunter had been valedictorian of his graduating class. There was no doubt in my mind that he would end up at whatever medical school he wanted to attend.

"I talked to Lila yesterday."

"Yeah. They're rehearsing hard for their holiday production already."

Words swelled inside my throat and, unbelievably, somehow found their way out past my lips. "I heard you and Paige broke up."

"Yeah," he said slowly, rubbing at the back of his neck. It was maybe the first time I'd ever seen him look uncomfortable and I instantly regretted saying anything.

"Can I help you?" the cashier cut in. My attention snapped to the girl behind the counter. I stepped up and placed my drink order. Her gaze swung to Hunter next. "What about you?"

I waved a hand. "Oh, no, we're not together."

"No, I got it, Pepper," he said, reaching for his wallet. "I'll have your house roast, medium."

"Thanks," I murmured as we moved over to wait for our drinks. Hunter motioned to a couple of plush chairs. "Want to sit down?"

"Sure." I nodded and sank into an armchair, swinging my messenger bag around me and to the floor.

"So my sister didn't waste much time spreading the news."

I shook my head. "I'm sorry. I didn't mean to—"

"Pepper, it's fine. I'm kidding. You're like family. Of course Lila would tell you." His lips twisted. "And everyone else in the northern hemisphere."

Family. *Fabulous*. He saw me as another sister. They called our drinks and he rose ahead of me, reaching the bar in two strides and returning with the three drinks.

"Guess you can't stay long," he commented as he sank back down. "Your friend's drink will get cold."

"I ordered it extra hot and it has a stopper in it. It will be fine." And Emerson would gladly sacrifice a hot drink if it meant some one-on-one time for me with Hunter.

"Well, yeah. We decided to see other people. I'll be starting med school and she has another year here. Just made sense. I mean, the idea of living without her . . . it didn't kill me, you know? And that's what I asked myself. Can I live without her in my life?" He shrugged. "I figured I could."

"I never heard it put like that before."

He winced. "I guess I sound callous."

"No," I quickly reassured him. "I think it was fair. To both of you."

He nodded and took a sip from his cup.

"So," I hedged, hoping I wouldn't sound too obvious with my next question, "you're not into long-distance relationships?" I had two more years here after this one, after all, assuming I finished on time. I hoped the right girl—*me*—could convince him that the challenge of a long-distance relationship would be worth it.

"Oh, I could. I mean, I would. That didn't factor into the breakup."

I smiled, relieved that he didn't read anything into the question. Relieved that he didn't realize I was fishing for myself.

He smiled that achingly disarming smile of his back at me. I think it was his smile that endeared him to me the most. With all his advantages he could so easily be arrogant and full of himself, but he was just so *good*. "But for that to happen it's gotta be right. It's gotta be . . . special. You know?"

I nodded dumbly, a fist tightening around my heart. Hope filled me. The hope that one day he would look up and see me as that someone special.

"Sure." I carefully sipped my hot latte. "I get that."

He leaned back in his chair. "Enough about me. What about you? Are you seeing anyone?" He winked. "Anyone I need to give the once-over, make sure they treat you right?"

My face heated and I looked down at my cup, toying with the edge of the lid. "You don't have to do that."

I didn't know whether it was a good or bad thing—him adopting a protective role. If his motives were more selfish than altruistic it would be a good thing. Unfortunately, he'd always looked out for me in the same way he looked out for his sister. It was sweet, but only served to underscore his very platonic interest in me. I wanted, *needed*, him to look at me like a flesh-and-blood girl . . . someone he protected because he wanted me for himself.

"And there isn't anyone anyway," I added.

"Yeah. Well, when you do meet someone make sure he treats you right, Pepper. You deserve that." His eyes softened, but not for the right reasons. Not because he saw *me*. His velvety brown eyes weren't softening because he was overcome with tenderness for the me sitting in front of him right now.

No. Looking at me, he saw twelve-year-old me. And the absolute suck that was my world—my past. A dead father. A mother God knows where. Growing up with a grandmother in her retirement community was a far cry from his idyllic life. He pitied me.

"Well, I guess I'll get Emerson her drink." My throat suddenly thick, I stood, securing my bag around me before bending to collect the drinks from the round table in front of me. He followed me to the door, holding it open for me.

Stepping outside after me, he gave me a quick hug, mindful of my cups. "Good talking to you. See you around, Pepper."

"Yeah, you, too." My bright smile slipped as he turned away. I watched him move down the sidewalk, merging with the traffic of students.

I stood there, blocking the entrance to the coffee shop until I couldn't make out the back of him anymore. Until he became lost from sight.

All the emotion, all the desperation I felt last night surged through me again. It came back with a vengeance. I knew what I had to do. If I was going to get him to look at me differently, minus the pity, I had to be *different*.

Chapter 5

"THERE HE IS." EMERSON shook her head. "I can't believe I gave him to you. He's so damn hot." She nudged me encouragingly and waggled one of her finely arched eyebrows. "You better climb all over that or I'm going to punch you. No backing down."

I stood several yards back from the bar, tucked half behind Emerson as I scoped out the bartender undetected. Her words didn't faze me. "You know the small matter of his interest in me, or lack of interest, might come into play."

She looked back at me. "You're kidding, right? You look good tonight. Better than most of these overdone peahens prancing around in here shaking their tail feathers his way. You've got something they don't."

"Yeah?"

She nodded. "Yes. You've got . . ." She paused, searching for the word. " . . . a freshness to you."

I winced, feeling rather as if she'd just called me a "nice girl." I couldn't seem to escape that moniker.

The bartender (I really needed to learn his name) wore

another Mulvaney's T-shirt, this one a soft-looking gray cotton with blue script across the chest. I had a flash of myself wearing that shirt and nothing else, wrapped up in his scent. Wrapped up in him. Sucking in a breath, I shook off the wicked image. Probably every girl who walked up to him entertained that fantasy—along with a few choice others that I probably didn't need to visualize. That thought made me feel decidedly un-special. I had to somehow stand out from the rest of them, and I wasn't convinced my *freshness* would do the trick.

He looked as good as ever if my memory served. Better. A body made for sin and a face that was too masculine to be beautiful, but the sight of it did something to me. Made me feel boneless and trembly all over.

"No backing down," I echoed, my resolve still there, burning hot inside me, keeping me from turning and running out of the building.

It was just the two of us tonight. Georgia was off with Harris.

"Okay," Em announced. "I think we've reconned long enough. Let's move in."

Her words sent a wave of panic washing through me. "It's crowded . . ."

"It's crowded every night. Unless you want to come stalk him on a Monday. Assuming he's even working then."

I shook my head. No. No more delays.

"Let's go then. You should feel good. You look great."

I glanced down. The jeans I wore belonged to Georgia. They were too tight, but Emerson said that was the whole point. *You've got the perfect curves. Show them off.* The blouse was

Georgia's, too. Various shades of orange and yellow. Very bohemian in style and flouncy. Emerson vowed that it went great with my hair. It was wide-necked, and every time I pulled it up over one shoulder, it slipped down the other one. Again, the whole point, according to Emerson.

As we inched toward the bar, Emerson shoved me in front of her. There were only three people working the counter, and we made certain to approach the side he was working.

I watched as he poured beer into a pitcher, admiring the flex of his bicep. His gaze lifted and scanned the bar, the way I'd noticed him do last night. Surveying, assessing the crowd. Maybe for trouble? Those pale blue eyes passed over me for a split second before jerking back.

He smiled crookedly. "Hey, it's Nice Girl. How's it going?"

"Nice girl?" Emerson hissed in my ear. "Okay, clearly you did not tell me everything about last night if he's already given you a nickname!"

I elbowed her, unsure how to respond to his greeting. I smiled. "Hi."

He handed off the pitcher, collected the money, and turned to me. "What can I get you?"

I ordered two longnecks. He glanced at Emerson. "ID?"

I watched her as she dug in her purse and pulled out her fake ID. When I looked back up it was to catch him looking at me. He looked away, giving her ID a cursory scan before moving to fetch our drinks.

"So hot," Emerson muttered near my ear as he bent to grab them from the back chest. "And he was eyeing you. Did you see that?"

I shook my head, unconvinced, but my heart beat a hard rhythm in my chest.

"Slip him your number."

My gaze swung to her. "What? Just like that?"

"Well, you'll know if he's interested by his reaction. Maybe he'll call. Or he won't. Either way, you can get this thing off the ground or move on to someone more receptive."

I bit my lip, contemplating. The only problem was that I had decided it would be him. He would be my test subject. If he wasn't receptive I didn't feel like moving on—I didn't *want* to. And where did that leave me?

Sighing, Emerson dug around in her purse.

"What are you doing?" I demanded, looking in his direction and confirming he was heading back our way.

Shaking her head, she pulled out an eyeliner pencil and snatched a thin square napkin off the stack sitting on the bar. Lightning fast, she scrawled my name and number.

I felt my eyes bulge. "Stop! No!" My hand dove for her arm, but she angled herself away from me, standing on her tiptoes and stretching out her arm.

"Here you go," she called just as my fingers clamped down on her wrist.

"Em, no!"

Too late. I watched as long, masculine fingers took the napkin from her. My gaze followed that hand up to the bartender as he set our drinks down single-handedly. Bile rose up my throat.

I heard Emerson's voice beside me as though from far away. "This is *her* number."

Her. Me. The girl with the face as red as a tomato.

His gaze moved from the napkin to me. Those silvery blue eyes fixed on me. He flicked the napkin in my direction. "You want me to have this?"

He waited, his expression blank. The ball was in my court. Without giving me the slightest indication of whether he even wanted my number, he was asking me what I wanted.

I stammered out the words. "Uh, n-yes. Well, sure. What-ever."

Lame. I felt like a thirteen-year-old girl. My face burned.

"She wants you to have it," Emerson insisted from beside me.

If possible my face grew hotter. He leaned forward, setting his elbows on the bar, his gaze fastened on me with searing intensity. "Are *you* giving me this?"

Apparently *whatever* wasn't going to work for him.

The air ceased to flow in and out of my lungs. I felt myself nod dumbly. Emerson elbowed me discreetly. "Yes," finally spilled from my lips.

He straightened. Without another word, he slipped the napkin into his pocket, took the money that Emerson handed him for our drinks, and turned away to another customer.

With one hand on my arm, Emerson dragged me away. I risked another look back at the bar, searching for him among the multitude of heads bobbing up to the front of the counter for their drink order. I spotted him. He was pouring more beer, holding the lever down. But he wasn't looking at what he was doing. He was looking at me.

"HE SO WANTS YOU."

I glared at Emerson as I took a pull from my longneck, forgetting that I wasn't a fan of the taste. I was too annoyed. "I can't believe you embarrassed me like that." As the words spilled out of me, I deliberately trained my eyes on her to keep myself from glancing at him across the room again.

"We had to get things moving. Nothing was going to happen if you just ordered, paid, and moved on."

I frowned, leaning one hip against the pool table. I refused to admit she had a point. Or that maybe he would call me now. He had put my number in his pocket, after all. Or was that just simple politeness? To spare my feelings. Maybe he'd thrown it away already.

"God." I lifted my fingers and rubbed at the center of my forehead where a dull ache was forming.

She patted my back. "I know. It's hard being a girl who actually emerges from her dorm room and talks to sexy boys."

The guy beside Emerson nudged her, bumping her hip. "Hey, hot stuff, your shot."

Turning, she lined up her pool stick and prepared her shot, earning a lot of stares when she bent over, thrusting her bottom up in the air to the appreciative gazes of nearby guys, specifically the two that had invited us to play pool with them.

The ball plunged into the pocket with a *whoosh*.

"Nice!" Ryan—or Bryan?—high-fived her, clinging to her fingers longer than necessary.

Emerson didn't seem to mind. He was cute. I could tell she thought so, too, by the way she arched her throat when she laughed.

Unfortunately, his friend seemed into me, and I didn't think he was cute. Or maybe he was. I just wasn't into him. There was only one guy here that caught my interest and I'd just humiliated myself in front of him. I had actually muttered *"whatever"* when he asked me whether I wanted him to have my number. Not exactly the self-assured femme fatale I aspired to be. Really, I should just call it a night and go home now.

"You sure you don't want to play?" He offered me a stick. I tried to view him with an open mind. After all, my phone number could be wadded up in a trash can right now. Whether I liked it or not, I might have to contemplate other alternatives in order to gain the experience I needed. A foul taste coated my mouth. Easier said than done. For whatever reason, the bartender was the only guy that I could consider kissing and touching without feeling mildly revolted.

The guy in front of me wasn't *bad*-looking. A little pudgy-soft in the middle. Probably too many beers and late-night burritos. But youth was still on his side. He had nice symmetrical features. I predicted he'd be sixty pounds overweight in ten years, but right now he was okay.

"No, thanks. You guys already started anyway."

He smiled, but looked disappointed.

For the next hour, I sat on a stool, watching as Emerson and Ryan/Bryan grew friendlier, laughing, talking, touching at every opportunity as they moved around the pool table. I made small talk with the friend. He stayed close even as he played pool, chatting me up and drinking steadily. Hopefully he wasn't driving.

The crowd started to thin out around eleven.

"Bunch of big parties on frat row," Scott—I had since learned his name—explained when I wondered aloud where everyone had disappeared to so early.

I nodded, but couldn't help sneaking a glance down the length of the room toward the bar. I couldn't resist. With the crowd dissipating, there was little to obstruct my view.

Only one bartender worked the counter, but it wasn't him. I didn't see my bartender anywhere. Was he on a break? Or did he cut out early? If he left early he could have talked to me. If he wanted to. Now I was convinced the napkin with my number was balled up on the floor. Stupid tears burned my eyes. I blinked them away furiously.

Taking a breath, I commanded myself to stop obsessing. He wasn't the end goal, after all. Hunter was. I could find someone else to help give me the experience I was looking for.

"Can I get you another drink?" Scott asked, following my gaze to the bar.

I snapped my attention back to the pool table. Ryan/Bryan had Emerson in an intimate body lock, teaching her some move. I rolled my eyes.

"No, I'm fine. Thanks."

"How about we get out of here?" Ryan/Bryan suggested, stepping back from the table and looking first at Emerson, then at me and Scott. Then again at Emerson.

The four of us leaving together? I could already see where this was headed. Emerson making out in some room with Ryan/Bryan and me stuck alone with Scott. No thanks.

Emerson and I stared at each other, silently communicating. She gave me the barest nod, understanding. I was ready to leave but not with these guys. That was the good thing about Emerson. She might be in sexual overdrive most of the time, but she never put our friendship on the back burner.

I slid off my stool. "I gotta go to the bathroom."

Hopefully that would give her time to wrap things up with her guy and swap numbers. Or not. You could never really tell with Emerson. Sometimes I thought she was really into a guy and then she would drop him for no apparent reason. She once dumped a guy after a third date because he asked for a doggie bag at dinner. She claimed he was too comfortable with her if he did that. I didn't think she cared that this made sense only to her. Personally, I thought she was scared to get too serious with a guy, but what did I know? I'd only kissed one guy in my life.

I crossed the room to the narrow hall leading to the bathrooms. They were single occupancy and there was usually a line, but not tonight. Once inside, I dropped the little hook in place, locking the door. Turning, I caught sight of my reflection and winced. As usual, my hair was out of control. I tried to arrange the russet-colored waves. Maybe it was time for a haircut. Layers or something.

Moments later, I finished washing my hands and pushed open the thick oak door, immediately spotting Scott waiting outside. At first I thought he was in line for the men's room, but the way his gaze trained on me I realized he was waiting for me.

"Hey." He pushed off the wall.

"Hey," I murmured, stepping out into the narrow hall and wishing the light was better. The shadowy space made it feel too intimate.

He moved into my path. "Why don't you and Em come back to our place?"

I shook my head. "I have to get up early." I didn't, of course. My shift at the daycare didn't start until eleven, but he didn't know that.

"Aw. C'mon." He inched closer.

My back bumped the wall, rattling the picture frames and license plates that decorated it. I held up my hands in front of me as he encroached closer. "Uh, what are—"

He swept in then, planting his lips on mine. I froze in shock. His sour tongue pushed between my lips and I gagged. I didn't know if he was just too into the kiss and didn't realize I wasn't or he didn't care. Or he was too drunk. Or maybe he thought I was going to have a change of heart after another minute of this and start returning his fervor. Whatever the case, his lips stayed firmly glued to mine, messier and sloppier than my last kiss. Damn it. You would think things would have improved since tenth grade.

I squeezed a hand out from between us. Curling my fingers into a fist, I beat him on the shoulder. He didn't budge, and that's when I felt the first thread of panic. Even as it worked its way through me, I told myself to stay calm. We were in a public place. What could happen that I didn't want to happen? Well, besides a terrible kiss that tasted of sour beer and didn't appear to be ending anytime soon.

I hit his shoulder harder with my free hand. He held me so tightly I couldn't get my other arm out from between us.

Then he was gone. Just like that.

I sagged against the wall, dimly registering that the corner of a particularly jagged license plate scratched my neck. Funny I hadn't noticed that before. I wiped my mouth with the back of my hand as if I could rid myself of the unwanted kiss and stepped away from the wall, focusing on the scene before me.

Scott was on the floor, and someone stood over him, gripping him by the front of his shirt. It took me a second to recognize the back of my bartender—to understand that *he* was here, whaling on Scott, helping me. Rescuing me yet again.

I moved, my feet covering the short distance. Peering over his shoulder, I gasped at the sight of Scott's face. He was bleeding, mostly from the mouth. You couldn't even distinguish the whiteness of his teeth amid the wash of blood. I latched onto the bartender's arm just as it was pulled back, ready to deliver another punch.

"No! Stop!"

He looked down at me, his expression feral, nothing like its usual blankness. Tension lined his jaw. A muscle ticked in his cheek. I didn't know how long he stared down at me with glittering eyes. It felt like forever before he spoke, before I felt his voice, low and deep, pulse through me. "Are you all right?"

I nodded. "Fine." I nodded toward Scott. "You can let him go."

Scott was blubbering now. I couldn't decipher his speech. It was more sobs than words.

Tightly bunched muscles eased beneath my fingers and I realized I was still clinging to the bartender's bicep. And yet I didn't release him. Not right away. I looked down at that arm as if I had to see for myself where our flesh connected. Where his tan skin met my pale fingers. My hand curled over part of his tattoo, and I imagined the inked skin felt warmer there. Unthinkingly, I brushed at the dark edge of the wing and something inside me squeezed and twisted. I dropped my hand.

He tore his gaze off me and looked down at Scott again. He lifted his other hand and Scott flinched like he expected another punch. Instead he pointed down the narrow hall. "Get out of my bar."

Scott nodded fiercely, his face a mess. I winced. It hurt just looking at him. He scrambled to his feet, mumbling, "I'll just get my friend."

Scott was almost out of the hall when the bartender called after him, indifferent to the customers who glanced curiously in our direction. "I don't want to see you in here again."

Nodding, he scurried off.

Alone with my rescuer, I inhaled into lungs that suddenly felt impossibly tight, too small for air. "Thank you."

He faced me. "I saw him follow you into the hall."

I cocked my head. "You were watching me?"

"I saw you pass by."

So yes. He was watching me.

Silence filled the air. I rubbed my hands along my thighs. "Well. Thanks again. I hope you don't get in trouble with your boss for any of this. If you need me to vouch for you—"

"I'll be all right."

Nodding, I stepped past him, took three strides and stopped. Turning, I pushed the wayward fall of hair back from my face and asked, "What's your name?"

It just seemed absurd to keep thinking of him as The Bartender. I didn't want to go back to my dorm tonight, lie in bed, and stare into the dark thinking about him—because I knew I would—and not know his name.

"Reece." He stared at me, *through* me, his expression impassive, unsmiling.

"Hi." I moistened my lips and added, "I'm Pepper."

"I know."

I nodded lamely. The napkin. Of course. With a shaky smile, I stepped out into the main room.

I was halfway to the pool table when Emerson was there, her eyes enormous in her round face. "What happened to that guy's face? It looked like a truck hit him, and he practically ran out of here."

I linked arms with her and steered her toward the exit. "The bartender happened."

"What?" Her cheeks flushed. "Like he got jealous and . . . hit him?"

I winced. "More like Scott tried to suck my face off against my protests and Reece intervened."

"Reece?" she echoed.

"Yeah. He has a name."

Shaking her head, she looked at me in awe as we stepped outside. "I think you've gotten more than his attention, Pep."

I snorted. "He was just doing his job—"

She shot me a look. "He's a bartender. How is kicking some guy's ass for getting fresh in his job description?"

"He's not about to let a customer get accosted outside the bathroom."

She looked skeptical as we weaved our way out into the

parking lot. "You just don't see it. You don't know *how* to see it. Trust me. He's going to call you."

I wasn't as naïve as Emerson claimed. He could have kept me longer in that hall, said something more to fill that awkward stretch of silence. For being such a player, he didn't make any moves on me. He didn't even smile.

No. He wouldn't call. This wasn't me being negative. I just knew.

Chapter 6

HE DIDN'T CALL THE next day, and despite convincing myself that he wouldn't, I had hoped that just maybe Emerson was right.

Naturally, I blamed her. Em's words niggled their way inside me and fed hope where there normally wouldn't be. I couldn't stop glaring at her as she stood in the center of my room, distracting me from reviewing my Abnormal Psych notes.

"Well, you know we gotta go back again tonight, right?"

"Uh. No, we don't."

She dropped down on the bed with me, landing on her stomach. "C'mon. You can't vow to do this and then not give it a hundred percent."

"I'm not training for a marathon here—"

"You are. That's exactly what you're doing." She nodded, the light catching on the many sparkly clips she'd arranged at different angles through her short dark hair. "You're training for Hunter. Look at him as your 5K."

Biting on the inside of my cheek, I considered her words.

She must have seen me wavering because she pushed on.

"C'mon. You've made an impression on him. Two nights in a row." She waggled two fingers in front of my face. "We've got to go there tonight, too. We'll round up some others to go with us this time. Georgia is going to that concert with Harris, so I'll get Suzanne and Amy from down the hall. They're always up for some fun." Her gaze drilled into me. "Say yes, Pepper."

With a sigh, I closed my notebook. "Fine. Yes."

She clapped and jumped off the bed. "I'll go get the others rounded up. You hit the shower. But don't pick out your clothes yet." She pointed a finger at me. "I'm supervising in that department."

"Of course you are," I called after her as she slammed out of my room. If she had her way, I'd leave here in fishnets.

Rising, I grabbed my shower caddy, robe, and towel, my stomach doing strange things. Butterflies, I guessed. Although I didn't know why. I had barely spoken to Reece. He might have helped me out last night (and when my car broke down), but that was part of his job. Keeping order at Mulvaney's. There hadn't been anything personal in his actions.

Still, the memory of those pale blue eyes settling on me amid the dozens of others vying for his attention made my skin tingle. And they weren't vying for his attention just because he was the guy serving up drinks. In addition to being sexy as hell, he had that strong, silent thing going for him. It was such a cliché and it shouldn't work on me. But it did. I was a sucker for it. Like every other girl to stroll inside Mulvaney's.

And this made me frown. I didn't want to be like the rest of them. Interchangeable.

He might be accustomed to making out with countless

women whose names and faces he couldn't recall the next week, but I wanted to be different. Someone not like my mother.

Someone he remembered.

EMERSON ROUNDED UP NOT only Suzanne and Amy, but a couple other girls from our floor. We totaled six, so we needed two cars. Someone decided Suzanne and I would drive—likely because we weren't big drinkers. Fine by me. I liked being in control of my own transportation.

When we got to Mulvaney's we walked in through the back door, past the food counter. My stomach growled and I remembered I hadn't eaten since lunch. Emerson pulled me along when I hesitated, looking longingly at a basket of cheese-coated French fries someone had just ordered.

"C'mon. You can eat later. I'll buy you the biggest burger on our way out."

It was jam-packed tonight again, but I spotted Reece right away in his usual spot at the bar. Was he a student, too? What else did he do? Besides half the girls that trolled through here—if rumors were to be believed. He had to have some-thing else going for him. Disappointment curled through me to think that there might be nothing more for him than this. No goals outside of tending bar.

Hunter was just one goal for me. One piece of the pie. If everything went as planned, I'd soon have a degree and a future working with children. That's what I wanted. Some-thing to enrich me, to make me feel better about the things in my life that I could never change.

"Here you go." Emerson slapped some money into my hand. Suzanne and the others were already looking for a table. "We'll start with two pitchers. I'll be right behind you to help you carry them." She shoved me in the direction of the bar.

I inched up to the bar, as close as I could get to him, already hating this moment that was starting to feel so redundant. He hadn't spotted me yet and I wanted to run, certain he would know that I was here because of him—certain he would look right at me and call me the idiot that I felt like. Or worse. He could look at me and point and say: *Hey, it's my stalker girl!*

My mother flashed across my mind. She was in a faded blue dress, strung out, her eyes glazed over as she sat on a man's lap and toyed with his hair, desperate to win him over so she could score some money for her next fix. She was always desperate. A creature without pride. The memory left a sour taste in my mouth.

Digging in my heels, I looked back at her. "I don't want to do this."

"What? Why—"

I stepped closer and spoke into her ear so she could hear me over the din. "It's just not my MO to chase after a guy. I'm sure he gets that I'm interested by now. If he's such a player, why am I doing all the chasing?"

Emerson turned her mouth to my ear. "He just hasn't had an opportunity yet. He's been stuck behind that bar. With guys it's all about opportunity. So give him an opportunity."

Shaking my head, I resisted telling her that if a guy really likes a girl he creates an opportunity. But then what did I know? Apparently nothing. Why else would I be here on a mission to learn foreplay from a hot stranger?

I slapped the money back into her hand. "You do it. I'll stand behind you so he can see me, but I'm not standing in front of him for a third night. I might as well have a sign around my neck. I think he gets the hint." I flashed her a warning look. "And do *not* embarrass me again."

Rolling her eyes, she took the money. "Fine." She pushed to the front, getting there faster than I ever could. I couldn't help noticing how much she used her elbows. I'm sure she never dropped a pitcher.

I hung back as Emerson leaned against the bar, holding up her money, the universal sign that she needed service. A few moments passed before he turned his attention her way.

When he saw it was her, his gaze skipped around, like he was looking for someone. My breath locked in my windpipe as his gaze landed on me. It was a split second, just enough to register my presence. Nothing more. No sign that he even remembered me.

He looked back at Emerson, inclining his head, communicating for her to go ahead and order. She waved her hands, obviously talking. She always talked with her hands.

Nodding, he turned to fetch the beer. I waited for his return, my breathing irregular. He handed her the pitchers, took her money, and returned her change. All without looking at me.

Disappointment flashed through me. I'd thought I'd get another glance, and then . . .

I exhaled. I didn't know what then. I dragged a hand through my hair. My fingers caught in the thick mass, and I gave up, pulling my fingers free.

I didn't know what I was doing here. Trying to be something I wasn't so I could catch Hunter's notice? I was kidding myself. If he hadn't noticed me in all these years, why would that change now?

By the time Emerson reached me, I was feeling more foolish than ever before. And she must have seen some of what I was feeling on my face.

"What's wrong?" she demanded.

I shook my head. "This is just crazy. I really don't want to be here. Not again. I'm gonna head back—"

"Aw, Pepper, c'mon." She stomped her foot, her pert features screwing tight in frustration. "Don't go."

"You stay. Ride back with Suzanne." I edged backward in the crowd. A curse rang in my ear as I stepped on someone's foot.

"Wait. I'll go with you." She looked around, searching for somewhere to leave the pitchers she held.

"No. It's okay, really. I have a statistics exam on Monday anyway. I should go, and don't give me that look. This is more than I've gone out in like . . . ever."

She blew out a breath, nodding. "Yeah. Okay. I'll see you later."

I fluttered my fingers in a little wave and turned, pushing my way through the squeeze of bodies until I was outside. I lifted my face to the crisp fall air and sucked in a breath like I'd just emerged from a deep icy pool.

Walking through the parking lot, the soles of my boots crunched over the loose gravel. I almost turned back around when I remembered the burger I had wanted. Instead, I continued walking, thinking which drive-through I wanted to hit on the way back to the dorm. I was contemplating chicken strips and Tater Tots when a hand fell on my shoulder.

With a shriek, I whirled around, my fist instinctively flying, lashing out, making contact. My knuckles grazed off a shoulder.

"Whoa. Easy there." Reece stood there, holding one hand up in the air while his other hand rubbed at the top of his shoulder where I'd struck him.

I covered my mouth with both hands. My words escaped muffled. "OhmyGod! I'm sorry."

"Don't be. I should have called out. Good reflexes. But you should work on your aim."

My hands fell from my face slowly.

I stared at him, still trying to comprehend that he was here. In front of me. It was strange seeing him out of his element. Other than that first time, I'd only ever seen him inside Mulvaney's. Here, outside, he seemed bigger, larger than life.

My head cocked to the side. "Are you"—I waved a finger between him and me —"following me?"

"I saw you leave."

"So. That's a yes."

He was watching me? He noticed me. I wasn't invisible after all.

He continued, "Look, you shouldn't be out here alone at night. Guys get a few drinks in them, see a pretty girl walking by herself . . ." His voice faded away, his implication clear.

I only heard one thing. *Pretty.*

"I'll walk you to your car," he finished.

"Thanks." I turned in the direction of my car. He fell in step beside me.

I slid him a long look. Without the distance of the bar top between us, I was fully aware of his height. I was no tiny thing like Emerson, and the top of my head barely reached his chin. He had to be a few inches over six feet. It was a new experience—feeling delicate and petite.

"I hope you don't get in trouble for leaving the bar. Are you on a break?"

"It'll be fine."

I was conscious of his arm, so close to mine as we walked. He slid one hand into his front jeans pocket.

"You're leaving early," he noted.

"Yeah." Silence fell. Feeling a need to fill it, I added, "Not feeling it tonight." At least I wasn't before. Now I was feeling it. I was feeling everything. His body beside mine radiated heat. My every nerve vibrated like a plucked wire, achingly aware of him. We weren't even touching, but it was like I felt him everywhere. It was a shock I could even talk in a steady voice.

"Not feeling it tonight," he echoed, his voice low. There was amusement in his voice even though he didn't come right out and laugh. He dropped his head back and looked up at the stars. A slow smiled curved his mouth.

"What's so funny?"

"Just thinking about that."

"What?"

He looked back down. "I can't count the nights I'm not 'feeling it,' but I still have to be there."

Have to. Interesting choice of words. "You don't like your job?"

He shrugged. "Sometimes I do."

"Are you a student, too?"

"Nope."

"Did you graduate already?"

"Just high school."

So working the bar was all there was for him. Again, there was that stab of disappointment. Which was not only judgmental of me but absurd. I wasn't considering this guy for a boyfriend or lifelong partner material. I shouldn't feel anything at his lack of ambition.

He continued. "You in college?"

I nodded.

"Let me guess. Dartford?" There were three universities in the area, but Dartford had the most prestigious reputation.

"Yes."

"Thought so. You've got 'Ivy' written all over you."

"What do you mean?"

"You look sweet and nice. Smart." We were almost to my car when he added, "And you're not a regular, but you've been here three nights in a row." Not a question. Just a statement.

Again, that he was aware of me made me go all warm and fuzzy inside. "My friend, Emerson, comes here a lot. You've probably seen her before. She's hard to miss." He neither confirmed nor denied this. "She invited me along. I don't do the bar scene all that much."

"So you've decided to start living the college experience in full then. Is that it? Last night didn't scare you off?"

I frowned. "Oh, you mean that guy by the bathroom. Should I have let that scare me?"

He didn't say anything, and I thought back to his comment on Thursday night about nice girls getting eaten up in places like Mulvaney's. "Oh. That's right. Nice girls like me should stay home."

"I didn't say that."

We stopped at my car.

The low rumble of his voice continued. "Getting mauled outside the bathroom might have turned some girls off from coming back again the next night though."

"I'm not most girls." He had no idea. I might look naïve and innocent, but my scars ran deep. It took a lot to spook me.

I fumbled for my keys, the slow burn of my temper making my hands shake.

"I might look like some nerd college girl and not one of the sexpots tripping through the bar every night, but—"

His voice cut in smooth and deep, no hint of the temper I was feeling. "I didn't say that, either."

"You're thinking it."

"You're right. You're nothing like the other girls I see every night."

"Oh, that's nice," I muttered.

My fingers closed around the hard steel of my keys. Unlocking the door and pulling it open, I looked up, ready to tell him off, but then I lost myself in those pale blue eyes until I wasn't sure what I was mad about anymore. Those eyes made everything inside me go hot and weak all at once.

"And that's not a bad thing. Trust me."

Suddenly my knees felt all trembly, and I knew I needed to sit down.

"Thanks for the walk." I started to duck inside the car, but his voice stopped me.

"Tell me something, Pepper."

It was the first time I'd heard my name on his lips.

I nodded dumbly, the open door at my back. "How old are you really?"

The question caught me off guard. "Nineteen."

He laughed, the sound loose and dark, curling through me like hot chocolate. "Thought so." His well-carved lips quirked. "You're just a kid."

"I am *not* a kid," I protested. I haven't been a kid since I spent my nights in motel bathrooms, listening to my mom getting bombed with random guys on the other side of the door. "How old are you?" I shot back.

"Twenty-three."

"You're not that much older than me," I argued. "I'm not a kid."

He held up both hands as though warding me off. His half smile mocked me. "If you say so."

I made a growl of frustration. "Don't do that."

"What?"

"Condescend to me," I snapped.

One of his dark eyebrows winged high. "Uh-oh. I made you mad. College girl is pulling out the big vocabulary now."

How did this guy get girls to make out with him? He was a colossal jerk. I could blame it on his looks, but not all hot guys were jerks. Hunter wasn't.

"Prick," I muttered as I turned to slide into my car. "Why don't you go back to serving beer and stale peanuts?"

His hand closed around my arm and pulled me back around. I looked down at his hand on my arm and then up to his face.

"Hey," he said flatly, all hint of a smile gone. My pulse skittered at my neck and I resisted the urge to press a hand there and steady the wild thrum of my blood. I wouldn't reveal his effect on me. "The peanuts aren't stale."

I might have laughed except there was no levity in his expression. His pale blue eyes fastened on my face. His fingers clung to my arm, burning an imprint through my sleeve.

Then those eyes dropped to my lips.

OhGodOhGodOhGod. He's going to kiss me.

This was it. The moment of my second—scratch that. *Third* kiss. Unsolicited or not, I had to count last night. This one was the one I had been waiting for though. The one where I would learn to actually kiss. From a guy—a *man*—who knew how to do it properly.

He inched toward me. My heart erupted like a drum in my chest. His head dipped, and then all thought of what I was about to do fled. There was no thinking. No calculated logic. Just pure sensation.

Blood roared in my ears as he closed the last scrap of space between us. It wasn't fast. Not like in the movies. No swooping head. I watched his face coming closer. His gaze moved from my mouth back to my eyes several times, studying me, watching my reaction. His hand touched my face, holding my cheek.

No one had ever done that. Well, not that I had a lot of reference, but the warm rasp of his palm on my face felt so very intimate. It made the moment so real, so powerful.

I jumped a little when his mouth finally settled over

mine. As though the contact brought on an electrical shock or something. He pulled back and looked at me. For a moment, I thought it was over, that he was finished after just that brush of our lips.

Then his mouth pressed down on mine again and there was nothing tentative about it. His kiss was confident, demanding. Pure deliciousness. Still holding my face with one hand, his other one moved to the small of my back, drawing me closer. His lips tasted mine, angling first one way and then another. As though he wanted to sample every possible direction. His tongue traced the seam of my lips and I shuddered, letting him inside my mouth. My hands gripped his shoulders, fingers curling around the soft cotton, reveling in the warm solidness of him beneath the fabric.

Then it was over. Too soon. I staggered, losing my balance. I caught hold of my open car door with one hand, blinking like I had just woken from some sort of dream. I lifted my hand to my lips, brushing them, feeling them, still warm from his lips. I focused on him, watching in astonishment as he turned and left me standing beside my vehicle.

Not another word. Not another look back.

Chapter 7

AFTER SURVIVING MY STATISTICS exam, I trekked across the quad toward the Java Hut. Even though I'd grabbed a latte beforehand, I felt like I deserved another one after that hellish test. Plus, I hadn't slept very well over the last two nights. Not since Reece had kissed me.

Emerson claimed it was a surefire sign of my growing irresistibility. Thinking of that, I rolled my eyes, getting a strange look from a girl passing me.

I ducked into the coffee shop, glad to escape the chill. I'd have to wear my heavy coat and gloves soon.

Walking across the wood flooring, I inhaled the aroma of espresso and fresh pastries. There were several pumpkin muffins and scones on display and even orange iced cookies shaped like jack-o'-lanterns.

The line was shorter than it had been two hours ago and I fell in behind a girl talking loudly on her phone. I tried to ignore her jarring tones as I stood on my tiptoes and eyed the scones several feet ahead. Deciding on the cranberry one, I let my thoughts drift back to the animated conversation I'd had with my roommates yesterday.

Emerson had insisted that Reece following me out of the bar translated into mad skills of seduction on my part. Her words, of course. I didn't see it that way. Not when he walked off after kissing me without another word. I felt like I was in tenth grade all over again. Any moment I was going to turn around and find kids whispering behind their hands about me in indiscreet voices. *Worst kisser.*

Absurd, I know. This wasn't high school. We weren't fifteen years old. And we hardly moved in the same social circles, anyway. If he did want to share that my kiss left him uninspired, who would he tell?

Georgia simply thought I should go back and see what happened next—the assumption being that something more *would* happen between us. It was that possibility that made my belly flutter like it was home to a thousand bees. I was caught between the fear that he would ignore me and the panic that he wouldn't.

"We really need to stop bumping into each other like this. People will think we're having an affair." Lost in my surging thoughts, I jumped a little at the voice close to my ear.

"Sorry." Hunter chuckled, pulling back from where he had leaned his face close to mine. "Didn't mean to scare you."

"No." I pressed a hand to my beating heart.

Hunter gave me a quick hug. I leaned into him, soaking up his warmth. Pulling back, he motioned for me to move up and order. Flustered as always around him, I tucked my hair behind my ear—a useless gesture. Only more tumbled forward. I really needed to do something with it. Maybe cut it all off. Wear my hair short and sassy and spiky all around my head like Emerson did. I almost snorted at that image. I'd never manage to pull it off. I'd look like I stuck my finger in an electrical outlet.

"Medium latte and cranberry scone," I told the smiling cashier.

Hunter quickly followed with his order and held out a credit card before I even had time to reach for my wallet inside my bag. Again.

"You don't have to pay—"

"Pepper, please." He dropped a hand on my arm, staying it from diving through my bag for my wallet. "Keep your money. You work hard for it."

My face heated, the warmth crawling all the way to my ears. I tried not to let my discomfort surface. I'm not ashamed that I work. I'll have to work forever to pay off my student loans. I'm prepared for that. I know that. It was just the reminder of how different I was from him that bothered me. We came from two totally different worlds. The fact that we both attended Dartford didn't change that. He'll graduate debt free. Probably get a convertible for his graduation present.

"Got time to chat?" he asked as we collected our drinks from the bar, inclining his head toward the alcove where several comfy chairs sat.

"Yes, I have some time."

Thankfully my voice did not reveal how nervous I felt. I hardly ever saw Hunter last year. Paige kept him busy. And now I'd seen him twice in a week.

We settled into two chairs facing out onto the sidewalk. The large glass window was decorated with fall leaves. I set my latte on the coffee table in front of me and balanced my scone on a napkin on my lap. Breaking off a corner, I nibbled at it, observing him as he drank from his cup.

He smiled at me, leaning back in his chair and setting one ankle across his knee as though making himself comfortable for a long chat. My heart thudded faster. Whatever he had to say, he clearly wasn't in a rush, and that's when it dawned on me that maybe he just wanted to . . . hang out. Maybe there was no objective. Unlike my objective. *Objectives*. Make him fall in love with me. Marry me. Bless me with 2.5 beautiful children.

The need to break our silence finally drove me to say, "Never seen you in here before. Other than the last time. And I would know. I'm in here way too much." I waved at our surroundings.

He shrugged. "Paige never cared for coffee much. She preferred smoothies."

"But you prefer coffee?"

"I'm figuring out what it is I prefer. I just pretty much let her decide for the last two years." He winced. "God, I'm making myself sound whipped, aren't I?"

I closed both hands around my cup, letting the heat from inside thaw the chill away. "It's the gentleman in you. And the fact that you were raised with a sister."

"Are you analyzing me?"

I shrugged. "It might be my psych class talking. But I know your family. It's easy to see that you're a product of your parents. Your mother raised you to be a good man, sensitive to others." Like that's not a fact that made me fall into a deep infatuation with him when I was a mere twelve.

Two years older, popular, and good-looking, he didn't have to be kind to me. When I first moved in with Gram and started school, everyone made fun of my clothes, my hair—the fact that I was obviously behind everyone else academically. When they found out where I lived, they told me I smelled like Bengay. That pretty much became my nickname. A whispered chant when I walked by.

Hunter could have looked the other way. Instead he'd stepped in and talked to me one day. Right in front of everyone. That same day, Lila asked me to sit with her at lunch. I don't think he put her up to it exactly, but she'd seen his kindness to me. I'll never forget what he did for me that day. I fell a little in love with him then and the rest of the way over the following years.

Hunter stared at me for a long moment. I looked down at my scone, crumbling off another piece between my fingers, worried that he might see some of how I felt in my eyes.

"Gentleman, huh?" he murmured. "Maybe too much. I stayed with Paige longer than I really wanted to just because I didn't want to hurt her."

I lifted a piece of scone to my mouth and chewed, considering my words carefully. "I think you can still be a gentleman and be happy, too. They're not mutually exclusive."

He cocked his head and grinned down at me. "How is anyone who hangs out with Lila so smart?" he teased.

I let out a laugh and studied my remaining scone. "I won't tell her you said that."

"Thanks. That will probably save my life. But it is true, you know."

"I'm not so smart. Just an old soul." That's what Daddy always told me. It was one of the few things I remembered him saying to me. That and to look after my mother. It stuck in my mind because after Mom dropped me at Gram's I used to wonder if my dad was looking down on me with disappointment. Did he think I'd failed him?

Suddenly aware that Hunter hadn't responded, I snuck another glance at him. He wasn't grinning anymore. He was simply studying me. And not in a way he had ever looked at me before. He studied me like he was really seeing me. "Yes. I can see that."

I tried not to fidget beneath his scrutiny.

"I'm glad I ran into you," he continued, his familiar smile sliding back in place as the pensive look melted away. "I was wondering if you wanted to ride home together for Thanksgiving next month. Unless you have other plans."

"No." I shook my head, heart hammering with excitement at this sudden opportunity. Last Thanksgiving he'd gone home with Paige. Truthfully, I had been debating flying home rather than making the four-hour drive. Especially considering how unreliable my car was.

"Great. It will make the ride go faster to have someone to talk to."

"For sure," I agreed.

"Cool." He nodded. "I don't think I have your number." He slid his phone from his pocket. "What is it?"

I rattled off my number.

"Great." He pushed a button and my phone started to ring. "Now you have mine."

I glanced down like I could see my phone through my jacket pocket. "Great," I echoed.

"Let's stay in touch." He glanced back down at the time on his phone. "Man, I'm late. I gotta go. Meeting with my tutor. Chem is kicking my ass."

"You should have picked a different major," I teased.

"They didn't offer basket weaving," he countered, his expression mock serious. Like he somehow would have chosen the slacker course if it had been available.

"As if Hunter Montgomery would be anything less than a brain surgeon."

"I'm actually interested in reconstructive surgery. Correcting birth defects . . . that type of thing."

Of course. He wouldn't want to be your standard plastic surgeon. Helping people who most needed it. That was his MO. Saving puppies and rescuing the new girl from bullies. Standing, he slung his backpack over his shoulder. He waved his phone lightly in the air. "Talk soon."

I watched him weave between tables and exit the coffee shop. He passed the window to my right and waved cheerfully at me through the glass.

Yes. We would talk soon. Before Thanksgiving. I would see him again. A couple more run-ins like this and he might start to think of me as more than a friend, more than the girl he grew up with, more than his sister's best friend. He would see me. Finally. Maybe.

Chapter 8

STEPPING INSIDE THE CAMPBELL house was like coming home. Only no home I had ever known. Mrs. Campbell greeted me, adjusting her earrings, as her two daughters raced past her and flung themselves at me.

I grabbed hold of them with a gasp, lifting both up off the floor.

"Pepper!" they cried in unison. "We missed you!"

"Hey, guys," I gasped. "I missed you, too!"

"You like our costumes?" They both dropped back down to model and twirl in the costumes.

"I ladybug," Madison announced, holding out her black tulle skirt.

Sheridan hopped several times to gain my attention. "I'm a princess!"

"You guys are awesome. These are like the best costumes I've ever seen. I didn't even recognize you until I heard your voices."

They tackled me again, elbowing each other to get in a better position. For two years old, Madison held her own remarkably well against her seven-year-old sister. I staggered, wincing as I stepped on what felt like a Barbie. I glanced down. Yep.

Mrs. Campbell closed the door after me. "Thanks for coming, Pepper. They've been bugging me all day about when you were going to get here."

I dropped my bag near the door under the weight of squirming girls and readjusted my hold on them. "I wouldn't miss a chance to hang out with my favorite monkeys."

"I'm ready. Let me just round up Michael. We've had a minor crisis today. The garbage disposal died on us." She shot a narrow-eyed look at her oldest daughter. "Sheridan might have decided to put some marbles down the sink."

Sheridan's face went pink. I rubbed her small back comfortingly.

Shaking her head, but still smiling, Mrs. Campbell waved me after her into the house. "C'mon. I made spaghetti and I have garlic bread in the oven."

"It smells delicious."

"Thanks. It's my mother's recipe," she called over her shoulder. "Michael would probably prefer to stay here and eat that than the five-course dinner at Chez Amelie tonight."

Even without the rich aroma of garlic, meat, and tomatoes, the renovated farmhouse always smelled good. Like vanilla and dryer sheets.

With Madison and Sheridan clinging, their skinny little legs wrapped around me like vines, I managed to follow their mother through the living room (avoiding additional Barbies) and into the kitchen, where Mr. Campbell stood over a guy who was half buried in the open cabinet below the kitchen sink, his long, denim-clad legs sticking out into the kitchen, various tools surrounding him.

"Michael. Our reservation is in forty minutes. We need to go. Can you please let Reece off the hook?"

My stomach bottomed out. *Reece?*

My gaze fixed on those long legs jutting out from beneath the sink. His face was beyond my vision, but I could make out the familiar flex of his tattooed bicep and forearm as he worked. My lips tingled, remembering how his mouth had moved over mine, and it took everything in me not to reach up and touch my lips.

Mr. Campbell shot his wife a pleading look and motioned to the sink—to Reece really. "We're almost done."

She looked on the verge of laughter. "Really? *We?*" She sent me a knowing look. "We had to call in reinforcements. Michael's an accountant. Not quite the handy man."

"Nice." Mr. Campbell's face flushed. "We all heard that, honey."

She shrugged. "Maybe you should take some of those weekend classes at Home Depot and stop calling up Reece every time something breaks."

Mr. Campbell pushed his glasses up the bridge of his nose even though they didn't appear to have slipped.

"Michael. We're going to be late," she reminded him sharply.

He motioned to Reece again with a swift wave of his hand. "Ten more minutes."

Reece's deep, familiar voice rumbled up from under the sink. "I'm almost done here. You can go on, Mr. Campbell."

"Thank you, Reece." Mrs. Campbell's voice was all relief. When her husband looked prepared to object, she cut him off. "Michael, get your coat."

Mr. Campbell's shoulders slumped but he nodded. He kissed both his girls and reminded them to behave. "Thanks, Reece," he called, a certain glumness to his voice as he exited the kitchen.

Mrs. Campbell turned to me. "The girls have had their baths already. We shouldn't be too late tonight. Just text or call if you need anything."

I nodded, knowing the drill by now. "We'll be fine."

"Thanks, Pepper."

At the pronouncement of my name, my gaze flew to the sink—to the guy under it—registering the way he froze. I swallowed. How many girls could be named Pepper, after all? He knew I had watched the Campbells' kids before. It only made sense that it would be me here. Pepper from the bar. The girl he kissed. The girl who less than smoothly gave him her number. Not that he had called or texted me. A knot formed in the pit of my stomach and I quickly decided this was going to be uncomfortable.

Awareness crackled in the air. He knew I was here. He knew *I* knew he was here. And the last time I'd seen him he had kissed me. He slid partway out from beneath the sink and propped himself on one elbow. His gaze locked on mine. My chest tightened as we stared at each other. His well-worn T-shirt hugged his chest, leaving little to the imagination. Under that shirt his body was firm, muscled. Stroke-worthy.

"Hey."

I snapped my gaze back to his face and found my voice. "Hi," I returned, the sound small and breathy.

Madison started bouncing her weight against me. I staggered, squaring my feet on the floor to keep my balance. "We hungy, Pepper!"

"Okay." Grateful for the distraction, I untangled myself from the girls and ushered them out of the kitchen, leading them into the hall bathroom to wash up for dinner.

When we returned several minutes later, Reece had picked up the tools from the kitchen floor and was washing up at the sink.

He glanced at me. "You can use this sink now."

I nodded as I helped Madison up into her booster seat, my thoughts churning feverishly, trying to come up with something to say that didn't reflect the hot mess I was inside.

"Are you gonna eat with us, Reece?" Sheridan asked.

My gaze shot to his as I clicked Madison's buckle into place.

"We eatin' noodles," Madison declared, slapping her chubby little hands on the top of the table as I dragged her chair closer.

"With meatballs," Sheridan added. "Momma makes the best meatballs."

"The best, huh?" Reece looked at her, considering her thoughtfully, like what she was saying really mattered. Not like other adults, who just looked through kids without really seeing them. Or talked down to them like they were some sort of sub-level human. "What are we talking about here?" He dried his hands with a dish towel and leaned a hip against the counter. "How big are these meatballs?"

Sheridan bit her lip, thinking, and then formed a circle with her hand about the size of a softball. "'Bout like that."

I grinned at the slight exaggeration.

"Oh, man. Really? That's the perfect size."

Sheridan nodded, clearly happy to have Reece agree with her judgment.

His gaze slid to me.

"Would you like to stay?" Really. What else was I supposed to say at that point?

"Sure."

The girls cheered, and I quickly moved toward the stove and the waiting bowls beside the pots of noodles and sauce. I grabbed a fourth bowl from inside the cabinet.

Turning, I jumped with a small yelp to find Reece directly behind me. The girls giggled uproariously, Madison snorting through her nose.

He held up his hands, palms face out. "Sorry. Just seeing if I could help."

I nodded, hating the way my face burned. "Yeah. Thanks. Um. Could you pour drinks? There's milk in the fridge."

He opened a cabinet—the right one; clearly he had spent some time here—and selected four cups. I smiled, noticing that he picked two princess cups with sliding lids for the girls.

He poured milk as I dished noodles into each bowl. From the corner of my eye, I watched as he set the glasses on the table. Without being told, he opened the oven and removed the heavenly smelling garlic bread from inside.

With shaking hands, I tried to focus on spooning the thick red sauce over the noodles, but I was acutely conscious of

Reece's every move. The faint sawing sound of the knife as he cut the bread into slices. The girls' silly chatter behind us. It was such a strange, domestic moment. I could almost fool myself that it was real . . . a peek into the life, the future, I wanted for myself.

"I want three meatballs!" Sheridan announced.

"Yeah?" Reece said as he carried the bread to the table. "I'm going to eat fourteen."

Sheridan giggled. "You can't eat fourteen!"

My lips curved as I poured only a small spoonful of sauce over Madison's noodles. Just enough to coat. Setting the girls' bowls before them, I went back for mine and Reece's.

"Sorry," I said, meeting his eyes as I sat between the two girls. "I couldn't fit fourteen in your bowl."

"There's always seconds."

My pulse spiked as he said this because for the barest second he looked at my mouth, and it was like he wasn't talking about food at all.

Sheridan provided a welcome distraction, tossing her head back in a fit of giggles. "You're so crazy, Reece!"

He made a funny face at her as he shook Parmesan over his noodles and then did the same over the girls' bowls. Something inside my stomach flipped over. It was an odd thing, reconciling *this* Reece with the guy from the bar.

I realized I didn't know him. Not really. But this. This *him*. It felt . . . wrong somehow. Like trying to force two mismatched puzzle pieces together. He even looked different. No longer cast in the hazy amber glow of the bar, but in the warm yellow of the kitchen. There was no way to hide the faintest flaw in this bright light, and yet, believe it or not, he looked hotter.

Sheridan stared at him with wide eyes. "Momma says you get a tummy ache when you eat too much."

"What? This belly?" He sank back in his chair and patted his flat stomach. "No way. It's made of steel. You should have seen what I ate for breakfast. My pancakes were stacked . . ." Squinting, he held his hand two feet above the table. " . . . this high."

Madison smacked a hand over her mouth, stifling her gasp.

"Sharks eat tires," Sheridan volunteered loudly, and not entirely on topic.

Madison nodded sagely in agreement. "Momma read that to us in my shark book. They found a tire in a great white's belly."

"I could eat a tire," Reece replied with utter seriousness, popping a whole meatball into his mouth and chewing.

More giggles erupted at this claim.

Smiling, I twirled spaghetti around my fork and tried not to compare this to the dinners of my childhood, when I usually ate in front of the television. If I was lucky enough to be in a motel room. Often it was the backseat of Mom's car. Either way, there was rarely a microwave handy so I ate a lot of cold SpaghettiOs straight from the can. "Eat up, girls."

The girls obliged, slurping noodles into their mouths and making a general mess. Sheridan stabbed her fork into a meatball and lifted it to her lips for a bite. She ate about half of it before it fell into the bowl with a splat, spraying sauce.

Madison proclaimed herself full after three bites, but I coaxed her into eating a little more, bribing her with the lure of bread. All the while, I tried to ignore Reece's watchful gaze, hoping I was playing it cool as I wiped sauce off chins. Lowering the napkin, I glanced at Reece, only to find him staring back at me.

Heat prickled over my face and I looked away quickly, tucking a strand of hair behind my ear self-consciously.

"C'mon." I waggled a slice of bread at Madison. "One more bite and you can have this yummy yummy bread."

Eyes glued to the bread, the toddler shoveled one more tangle of noodles into her mouth and then snatched the promised bread from my fingers.

Sheridan was another story, happily devouring her spaghetti and moving on to her second meatball. I picked at my dinner as they polished off their milk. Everything I chewed sank like lead into my stomach. It was hard to eat with Reece across from me. Watching. Eating with gusto. Apparently he had no such troubles.

"All right," I instructed when the girls declared themselves stuffed. "Let's hose you down and get in your pj's and ready for bed. I promise to read to you if you guys don't stall." I clapped once. "Chop chop."

"Two stories," Sheridan wheedled.

"Um." I pretended to think hard. "Okay."

"Three!" Madison shouted, holding up four fingers.

Sheridan pointed at her. "Ha! You can't count! You're holding up four—"

I closed a hand around the seven-year-old's arm and lowered it to her side. "I think three stories sounds perfect."

"Yay!" The girls cheered and climbed down from their seats, Madison unlocking her own booster strap in her eagerness.

"Wait. Wash hands first." I led them to the kitchen sink

and supervised as they stepped up on the stool and washed up. They raced from the kitchen.

Turning, I faced Reece. He was watching me intently, relaxed in his chair, one arm reclined along the surface of the table. "You're good with them."

"I was thinking the same thing about you."

He shook his head. "Not really. Just experienced. I grew up with a little brother who insisted on shadowing me everywhere."

"That didn't annoy you? I thought big brothers tortured their younger brothers?"

"Not so much. We got on pretty well. Still do."

"You're lucky," I murmured, trying not to let the envy creep in. But then who knew what would have happened if I'd had a brother or sister? They might not have survived my mother. I barely did.

He angled his head. "Let me guess. You and your sister are still bitter rivals?"

"No. Only child."

"Oh." The teasing tone left his voice. He studied me again. I sank back into my chair and toyed with my food like I was still going to eat it. I stabbed at a meatball beneath his close scrutiny. "Never would have guessed it. You're a natural with kids. Just a born mother, I guess." The way he uttered that, I didn't feel complimented. It was almost like the observation disappointed him.

"Thanks." I supposed someone raised in a retirement village (not that he knew that about me) wouldn't necessarily be adept at interacting with children. But I understood children like I understood the elderly. Both were usually overlooked. They lacked control in their worlds. I understood what they needed. I gave them attention. Kindness. Respect.

"I think I want to work with kids," I volunteered, and then wondered why I said anything. He wasn't interested in what I wanted to do when I graduated. He was a bartender. He wasn't Emerson or Georgia. Or even Hunter. Especially not Hunter.

The silence stretched between us, and his lack of comment only proved he could care less about my ambitions. Giving up on my plate, I used a napkin and started to clean up the spilled food on the table surrounding the girls' bowls. Good excuse to avoid his gaze.

Suddenly, he murmured, "You mean you're going to Dartford and you're not going to be a surgeon or some executive type?"

I shot him a glance. "Are you stereotyping me?"

He shrugged unapologetically.

I had no right to be offended. Not when I'd singled him out because of the category I thought he fell into. I gravitated toward him because all rumors indicated he was an unparalleled player.

"Thanks for letting me stay for dinner."

Now I shrugged. "Of course. You did fix their garbage disposal. I'm sure they would have invited you themselves."

Nice. It was like I didn't want him to think I was interested in him—when I clearly was. Only further evidence of how unskilled a flirt I was.

A loud crash followed by a squeal drifted from upstairs. I shook off the spaghetti and crumbs I'd gathered into Sheridan's empty bowl. "I better get them settled before someone loses a limb."

His mouth twitched. "Sure."

I exited the kitchen, the back of my neck tingling. I knew without looking that he was watching me walk away, considering me. If I were Emerson, I'd probably do that thing with her hips that she does. But I wasn't Em. I was just me.

Thirty minutes and three bedtime stories later, I returned to find him gone. I pulled up hard and looked around the quiet kitchen for him. As though he lurked in some corner. He'd cleared the table, rinsed and stacked the dishes beside the sink, but he was gone.

Yeah. I was just me. Hopeless me.

Chapter 9

"WHY AM I DOING this again?" I stared at my reflection in the mirror. Tinfoil sheets covered the top of my head. Emerson sat next to me, similar sheets arranged in her much shorter hair. Only where mine were highlights of various shades of gold and copper, hers were chunky magenta streaks.

She sipped from her iced coffee as we waited for our stylists to return and remove the foil from our hair. Hopefully the results wouldn't make me want to wear a hat for the rest of the semester.

Emerson lowered her drink and met my gaze thoughtfully in the mirror. "This will seal the deal."

"How's that?" I asked.

"Well. Hottie bartender kissed you—"

"Reece," I supplied, flipping the page of a magazine I wasn't really interested in. "And let's not forget he bailed on me the other night without even a good-bye. So kiss aside, I wouldn't say I'm close to sealing the deal with him."

She waved a hand, continuing. "He's still into you. He

stayed and ate dinner with you and the girls, didn't he? Trust me. He wants you."

"He was probably just hungry," I grumbled under my breath.

"More importantly, Hunter is starting to finally come around—"

"I never said Hunter was—"

"Pepper, sweetheart, he's interested. He wouldn't offer to drive home with you for Thanksgiving if he wasn't potentially even one teeny tiny bit"—she held up her fingers in the barest pinch—"interested in a *you* and *him*. A guy wouldn't suffer a four-hour car drive otherwise."

"Hmm," was all I said, taking a sip of my water. Staring at my reflection, I hoped the combination of gold and copper highlights the stylist insisted would make my hair *pop* wasn't a disaster. For what I was spending, it had better look nothing short of miraculous.

Emerson leaned over and squeezed my hand. "I'm so glad you're doing this."

"Letting you make me over?"

She shrugged. "It's more than that. This is *fun*, Pepper. I mean, I love you and you're a great study partner and all . . . and it's nice that you're always up for a movie night, but you've never been one to join me for a girls' day at the salon followed by a night out."

I resisted pointing out that my budget didn't precisely allow for trips to the salon and manicurist. Emerson had never had to budget for anything in her life. Her credit card bill went straight to her father. Maybe if I thought she was perfectly happy, I would tease her about being a spoiled little rich girl, but I didn't go there.

Not knowing what I did—that she spent most of her holidays alone in an empty house while her father spent them with his current girlfriend. And I knew almost nothing about her mother except that she was remarried, and Emerson saw her maybe once a year. She was proof that money didn't promise happiness.

Instead, I agreed. "It is nice. A little pampering now and then doesn't hurt."

"Well, if you someday become Mrs. Hunter Montgomery, I'm sure he'll make you get lots of pampering."

I merely smiled. It had never been about Hunter's money. It was him. His family. How perfect they all were. I wanted that. I needed it.

And yet I couldn't forget one steamy kiss from a bartender. It frightened me a little. Made me think there might be a little bit of my mother in me after all. She always did like the bad boys. Men that led her into trouble. That had been my father before he got his act straight and joined the Marines. After Daddy, there was no saving her.

But I wasn't my mother. I would not follow in her footsteps. I would not repeat her mistakes. I had enough nightmares to live with already. I refused to add to them.

There was no saving my mother, but I would save me.

"WOW," GEORGIA BREATHED TWO hours later when she returned to our suite to find Emerson and me raiding—collectively— our closets for the perfect ensemble. We had already gone through mine and moved on to Emerson's and Georgia's after Em announced mine a supreme failure.

Georgia dropped down on her bed, tossing her backpack to the floor. Her velvety brown eyes scanned my hair. "You look amazing!"

"Right?" Emerson nodded, preening like a proud mama, not unjustified. She was responsible for dragging me to the salon in the first place. She had made the appointments and wouldn't take no for an answer until I agreed to go. "Now we need the right outfit."

I held up a blue and yellow checkered skirt that Emerson had just forced into my hands. "Help me, Georgie. Even if I could fit into Em's clothes, they're not me. I can't pull it off." I looked back at Emerson, who was now pulling out a tiny orange tank top from her drawer. My eyes widened helplessly. "Please. Just let me wear something from my closet."

Emerson waved the scrap of orange at me.

"I'll freeze in that! It's microscopic!"

"We didn't get your hair looking sea siren worthy just so you can wear something that you would wear to class on any given day!"

Georgia held up a hand, staying the battle that was about to be waged if the militant light in Emerson's eyes indicated anything. Together, we watched as Georgia moved to her closet and started pushing hangers. "I have the perfect thing."

Hope hammered in my heart. Georgia's wardrobe screamed understated elegance. Everything looked expensive and sexy without appearing over the top.

Turning, she brandished a gray cashmere sweater that was form-fitting. I touched it reverently, reveling in the lush softness against my fingertips. "Oh," I breathed. "Are you sure?

It will probably reek of bar afterward. And what if someone spills something on it?" I was sure it cost more than I could ever afford to spend.

"Try it on," she insisted, pushing it toward me and shaking her head, dismissing my protests.

"With a decent bra," Emerson inserted.

I looked at her blankly.

"Something with underwire that gives you a little push." She motioned to her own perky B cups.

I shook my head. "What I'm wearing is fine—"

"Here." Georgia opened a drawer, pulling out a pink bra. Slamming the drawer shut, she waved it at me. "We're both a C."

Sighing, I turned my back and pulled my top over my head. Unfastening my bra, I slipped on the pink one, hooking it behind me and marveling at the silk against my skin.

Facing forward, I stared at my reflection in the mirror hanging on the closet door. The bra did wondrous things to what I had always considered fairly unremarkable breasts. Not that I had ever considered them much at all.

"Oh, my." Emerson assessed me with wide eyes, nodding in approval. I resisted the urge to cover myself with both hands. "Good thing I'm not lacking in self-confidence 'cause those cupcakes are enough to give me a complex."

I laughed weakly. "As if."

"Now try it on with the sweater," Georgia encouraged.

I slipped the incredibly soft cashmere over my head and smoothed it down my torso. It fit like a glove.

"Yes!" Emerson clapped her hands once. "He won't resist you in that. And you can borrow my black boots. At least we're the same shoe size."

"Those knee-high leather ones?"

"Yes." She nodded sagely, the light catching in her fresh magenta highlights. "Also known as fuck-me boots."

I smiled wryly. "Well. There won't be any of that going on."

"Probably not." Emerson smirked. "Especially when you can't even say it."

"I can say it," I protested, staring at Em's smug expression. Georgia looked hard-pressed not to laugh.

Still, the word stuck in my throat. In reality, I couldn't say it. It was just too, too . . . bad.

Emerson burst out laughing. "Maybe after this bartender is through with you, you'll be able to say it."

"Maybe," I allowed. "But I won't be doing *it*. At least not with him."

"Hmm." Emerson turned and started digging for shoes in her narrow closet space. "Are you sure? Nothing wrong with your first time being with someone who knows what he's doing."

"No. I want my first time to be with Hunter."

"Of course you do." Georgia nodded. "It should be with someone you love."

"Says the girl who's only ever been with the one boyfriend."

"So? What's wrong with that?" Georgia squared her shoulders. "He's the only guy I've ever loved."

"Well. How do you know you're not missing out on something better?"

A funny look came over Georgia's face. I had never really seen her angry before, but I thought this was close to it. Splotches of color broke out across her clear complexion. "There is more to a relationship than just sex."

"Yes, but a relationship sure is better when the sex is good."

Georgia angled her head. "And just how would you know? How many relationships have you been in?"

Seeing this going nowhere but ugly, I intervened. "So, Georgia, can you come out with us tonight?"

She dragged her gaze off Emerson. "No. Harris's father is in town on business and we're supposed to have dinner with him."

Emerson faked an exaggerated yawn, and Georgia tossed a pillow at her.

"Maybe you guys could meet us out afterward?" I suggested.

"Mulvaney's isn't really Harris's scene . . . "

At this, Em made a snorting sound. Georgia shot her a glare. Emerson shrugged and turned her attention back to the contents of Georgia's closet.

Georgia continued. "But we'll try to make it."

"That'd be great," I said lamely, hating these rare moments of tension between them. As different as the three of us were, we had always made it work. Ever since we'd met each other at freshman orientation, laughing, not too discreetly, when we were assigned to an upperclassman who insisted on starting our campus tour with a song she wrote.

"Well, don't be too late. You're going to miss all the excitement when hottie bartender sets eyes on Pepper."

I smiled, but it felt more like a grimace on my face. "His name is Reece," I reminded her, but they weren't listening. Both of them converged on the various cosmetic bags accumulated on Emerson's desk, sharing ideas for what type of makeup I should wear.

Chapter 10

OUR GROUP FOUND A spot near the pool tables, a choice location with a direct view of the bar.

"He's working tonight," I called over the music into Emerson's ear. Come to think of it, he'd worked every night I'd ever been there. I could only think how tedious that must be. Pouring beer night after night. I shook off the thoughts. His life ambitions weren't supposed to matter to me. I wasn't looking for anything deep and lasting with him. Just like he would never consider anything deep and lasting with me. It was a bracing reminder as my gaze narrowed in on him at the bar. *This was just a hookup.* Assuming, of course, anything happened at all.

"Is that your man, Pepper?" Suzanne whistled approvingly between her teeth. "Nice. He's like sex on a stick. Didn't know you had it in you."

I didn't bother pointing out that he wasn't my man. Call it a base urge to claim him for myself.

Right now several girls were lined up in front of him to order drinks. I'd noticed that before. That most of the girls went to his drink line. And yet he seemed all business. Pouring drinks and taking money with easy efficiency, not talking for too long to anyone. I wondered when exactly he was supposed to hook up with all the girls he was rumored to hook up with.

"Well. How you gonna play it?" Emerson called in my ear, eyeing the bar as if she were scoping out a point of entry.

I shook my head. "He hasn't seen me yet."

"Well. You haven't gone up to the bar."

"I thought I should wait for him to notice me maybe."

"That could take a while. This place is slammed."

"What do you suggest then?"

"You know me. I'm direct." She looked me over and then looked back at the bar. "I'd get myself in front of him looking all hot ASAP."

"Do it, do it!" Suzanne chanted, slamming her hand on the rough-hewn table. She leaned forward, her face flushed either from the warm press of bodies around us or the fact that she already practically consumed the first pitcher all by herself. From the glassy glint to her eyes, I suspected it was the beer.

A scuffle broke out somewhere in the corner. I turned my head at the sound of several shouts and a chair clattering to the floor. Glass broke and a girl screamed.

"Oh, oh, there's your man."

I didn't bother to correct Suzanne. We all turned and watched in appreciation as Reece and another employee cut through the crowd and dove into the melee.

"He's so hot I could eat him up." Suzanne sighed dreamily.

"Hey, back off. He's Pepper's," Emerson reprimanded her and sent me a sharp look when I opened my mouth to protest that he wasn't mine.

My gaze returned to Reece, watching his broad back as he peeled bodies apart to get to the two guys punching each other at the bottom of the pileup.

"Hey-hey, guys!" Annie descended on our table, a hot mess of corkscrew curls and breasts that jiggled dangerously close to spilling free of her halter top. She draped an arm around Suzanne's shoulders. Immediately a bitter taste coated my mouth as I remembered that Annie was the one who'd tipped her off about Reece in the first place. It was stupid. Why should I care if he hooked up with Annie once upon a time?

"Hey, you! We're here scoping out Pepper's new man," Suzanne volunteered.

"Pepper!" Annie looked me over, appraising me with her heavily lined eyes. "You've got a man? I thought the only thing you ever made out with was your calculator." She laughed at her joke, slamming a hand on the surface of the table.

My face burned.

Emerson gave her a disgusted look. "Don't be a bitch."

She rolled her eyes. "Would you lighten up? Jeez. Tell me. Who's the lucky guy?"

Emerson waved a hand like it was nothing. "You already know him." I could tell she didn't want to share his identity either. Like she felt protective of whatever this thing was I had going with Reece, too, and didn't want to involve one of his past flings.

"Yeah?" She glanced around as if she would know him on sight. "Who is he?"

"The bartender you told me about that works here."

Annie's eyes widened. "Really?" She looked me over with

new respect. "I didn't think you had it in you to be so . . . flex-ible, Pepper." She emphasized the word *flexible,* the innuendo deliberate. My face burned hotter. She might as well have called me a virgin to my face.

"What's that supposed to mean?" Emerson snapped.

"Pepper is such a goody-goody. I didn't think she'd be up for sharing him. I mean, the guy gets around, Em. He's kissed like three girls tonight already. He'll score with at least one of them before midnight. When I hooked up with him he was on break and we just used the backseat of my car."

"Ew." Suzanne wrinkled her nose. "Remind me never to sit in the backseat of your car."

I closed my eyes in a slow blink. I wished Annie hadn't said that. Now I had the image of them branded in my mind. The blood rushed to my head. The deep roar started in my ears as I thought of the kiss he gave me out by my car. It had seemed so spontaneous, almost as if it surprised him, too. Had I been one of many that night? My sense of betrayal was ridiculous. The guy was obviously experienced. I knew that. You didn't get to be that good a kisser and not have a fair share of experience.

"No way. You're so full of it, Annie," Emerson interjected.

"Seriously," she insisted. "I saw him feeling up a girl out-side half an hour ago. And he was kissing another girl over by the dartboard just five minutes ago." She jabbed a purple fin-gernail toward the corner where people threw darts.

Suzanne shook her head. "We've been watching him for the last half hour. No way."

"Yeah," Emerson agreed, looking at me as if I needed that reassurance. "She's exaggerating. We've watched him for how many nights now? If your bartender was hooking up with other girls, we would have noticed."

I nodded, the tight band around my chest loosening. She and Suzanne were right. Annie couldn't be talking about Reece. Maybe she was jealous. Or confused. I didn't know her motivation. I only knew that he could not have made out with three other girls tonight without me noticing.

Annie's gaze suddenly shifted beyond my shoulder. Her bright red lips broke out in a smile. "Well, let's just find out. There he is now."

I shook my head desperately, determined that Annie not embarrass me in front of him. "No! Really, you don't have to do that!"

Too late, she was calling hello and waving him over. Mortifying heat fired my cheeks. I felt a presence arrive just behind me. I was too horrified to look. I stared straight ahead as Annie stepped around the table, her arms opening for a hug. Her halter top only gaped wider, and I caught the barest flash of a nipple. The overwhelming urge to scratch her eyes out overcame me.

"Hey, babe!" Her voice dripped like honey. "How are you?"

Babe? I wanted to puke.

"Good. Anna, right?" a male voice asked.

"Annie," she corrected, a flash of something ugly crossing her expression at his apparent forgetfulness.

"Annie. That's right," said the deep, masculine voice.

Emerson was already swiveling around on her stool. She elbowed me sharply in the ribs and let loose a small bark of laughter, which she quickly stifled behind her fingers.

I glared at her, rubbing the offended area. She gave me an I-told-you-so look. *See,* she mouthed, *nothing to worry about.*

"So you know my friend Pepper, here, right?" Annie asked, waving at me with a flourish.

I swiveled fully on my stool, facing the inevitable—and felt my stomach plummet to my feet.

It wasn't him.

It wasn't Reece. Sure, this guy was hot. He even bore an uncanny resemblance to Reece, but it wasn't him.

"No," he said, extending his hand to me, looking me over like he was imagining me without my clothes on. I shook his hand, at a loss for words.

"Of course you do, Logan." Annie frowned, looking between the two of us and insisting, "You know Pepper."

His smile flickered for a moment. "Uh, sorry, no. Should I remember you?" I could see the wheels in his head turning, searching his memory of girls he had slept with.

I shook my head dumbly and shoved at Emerson who was laughing herself silly beside me now. "No. We haven't met before."

Logan. His name was Logan.

His fingers still held my hand in a warm clasp. "Thought so. I would have remembered someone so pretty." Slick. And with a face like his, I bet he didn't have to work too hard.

Emerson, who was still laughing, held up a hand. "Whoa, whoa, whoa. You work here? How come we haven't seen you the last couple nights we've been here?"

"I only pick up a shift here and there. Usually I work one or two days during the week, but Reece called me in when one of the guys got sick." He shrugged one shoulder, considering Em now with the same thoroughness with which he had examined me. Apparently he liked what he saw. He winked at her, his smile widening to reveal straight perfect teeth. "I was free."

Em grinned back, clearly dazzled.

"Reece?" I echoed.

"Yeah. My brother."

"Your brother," I breathed.

Annie was laughing now, holding her sides, her boobs jiggling.

Emerson looked at me a little worriedly at this new information.

"Your brother?" I murmured. Things clicked into place in my head. I'd been throwing myself at some guy who wasn't the bar's resident man-whore. Logan was the younger brother Reece had mentioned. Oh. God.

Annie wiped at her eyes, leaving streaks of mascara on her cheeks. "Oh, this is too precious. Don't tell me you were making a play for Reece. Oh, he doesn't give the time of day to anyone."

"Well, he gave the time of day to Pepper," Em retorted, angry color filling her face. "He kissed her. Maybe he's just not into skanks."

Annie flattened a hand to her impressive cleavage. "Oh, I'm the skank?"

Logan's eyebrows lifted. "My brother kissed you?" He assessed me with new interest, ignoring the hostile banter.

"Yeah." Annie waved a hand in agitation. "Don't you get it? She thought he was *you*."

I closed my eyes in a slow, pained blink, my hope fleeing that this might somehow not get back to Reece.

"What?" Now Logan looked genuinely confused. He waved a finger between the two of us. "You came here to make out with me?"

My mortification only grew. "Of course not."

Annie nodded sagely. "Your reputation precedes you."

After a long moment in which I wanted to curl up and die, the confusion cleared from his features. His grin returned, and his chest swelled. "Cool. I've got a rep."

I dropped down from my stool, feeling like the biggest idiot. "I have to go."

Emerson nodded sympathetically. "I'll go with you." With a quick good-bye to everyone—even Annie, who I would rather have slapped—we began wending our way through the bar. We had to stop occasionally for Emerson to chat with someone she knew. I shifted on my feet impatiently, scanning faces, hoping desperately that Reece wouldn't appear. I couldn't talk to him right now. I couldn't play cool and unaffected.

The crowd grew tighter. A body bumped me, and I lost my grip on Em's wrist. I felt like a buoy at sea, tossed in the current. I stretched onto my tiptoes and called for her, searching for her among the flushed faces.

Suddenly I felt her grip back on my wrist. My chest loosened. *Now we can leave.*

My gaze swung up. Reece stared down at me.

The hundred-pound weight was back on my chest, pressing down hard, trapping my breath. My face burned, flamed, the encounter with his brother still fresh. Embarrassingly so. "Hey, there," I said lamely, studying him closely, trying to gauge what he knew.

His fingers burned an imprint onto my skin. I could feel the shape of each one locked around me.

His lips flattened into a grim line. "Heard you met my brother."

My stomach bottomed out. *Great*. He knew. "Oh. Yeah. He was nice."

His pale eyes glittered at me. "Is it true? You came here looking for him? You thought *I* was him?"

I shook my head, words evading me.

"Oh yeah. When he could stop laughing, he told me all about it. That's why you've been so . . ." His gaze raked me up and down before finishing. " . . . friendly to me?"

I shook my head. "No. Of course not—"

"You wanted to hook up with my brother because you heard the rumors about him." It was a flat statement. Full of judgment.

I tried to play it off. I snorted like it was the most absurd suggestion ever and went for outright ignorance. "Rumors? What rumors?"

Those pale eyes of his turned to ice. "The rumors that my brother fucks every girl who points her ass at him."

I sucked in a sharp breath.

He laughed roughly, but there was no levity in the sound. "It's kind of funny, you know."

I shook my head, unable to imagine anything funny about this. "How's that?" I managed to get out.

He waved a hand. "All of these college girls . . . even a *nice* girl like you"—the way he emphasized *nice* clearly told me he didn't think I fell into that category anymore—"throwing yourselves at a kid in high school."

I felt my forehead crease. "What?"

"Logan's still in high school. He's eighteen."

Oh. My. God. As if this moment could get any more embarrassing. If things hadn't gotten all mixed up that first night I came here, if Logan had been working *and* receptive—if I hadn't seen Reece first and fixated all my longing on him—I could have hooked up with a high school boy. Eighteen or not . . . he was still in high school!

I shook my head as if breaking free of the vestiges of a bad dream. "I didn't throw myself at him. I just met him tonight."

"But you came here for *him*. You thought *I* was him." His gaze cut into me, merciless and deep.

As a rule of thumb, I didn't run from life when it got ugly or uncomfortable. I'd faced a lot. A father dead. A mother who chose her addiction over me. This—*him*—shouldn't be anything I couldn't handle. His opinion or judgment of me wasn't supposed to mean anything. He was just one step getting me closer to Hunter. That's all he was supposed to be.

Even telling myself this, I couldn't stop myself. The time had come to retreat.

The tide of people shifted. Bodies bumped us. His grip slipped off my wrist and my opportunity arrived. I ran, using my elbows as he'd once advised me. Plunging out the back door, I spotted Emerson with her phone to her ear.

"There you are," she said when she saw me. "I was just trying to reach you."

"Let's go," I growled, latching onto her arm and pulling her down the street toward the packed parking lot.

"What's wrong? I mean besides the obvious awkwardness

of finding out we confused your hottie for the other hottie."
She laughed. "C'mon. It's kind of funny."

I slid her a look.

She bumped me with her hip. "C'mon. Pat yourself on the back. According to Annie, Reece is the elusive one. And *he* kissed you."

"Reece just cornered me back there, when we got separated."

"Ooh." Her eyes flared. "What did he say?"

"Oh, he knew all about it."

She winced. "Awkward much?"

"Oh, yeah, and his brother. Logan? He's eighteen and still in high school."

"Oh, that's awesome." She laughed, clapping her hands. "Wait till I tell Annie."

"Yeah, Reece pretty much thinks I'm a terrible person."

She stopped laughing. "Impossible."

"Yeah. He does." I nodded doggedly, my footsteps beating out a hard rhythm across the gravel. "You should have seen the way he looked at me."

"Well then he's a jerk. Screw him. Who needs him?"

She unlocked her car and I opened the passenger side door. I sank down onto the seat with a heavy sigh.

"You can hone your skills on any guy you want."

I laughed brokenly and corrected her. "No. Not any guy I want."

I wasn't one of those girls who didn't know what she looked like when she stared at herself in the mirror. I knew I was attractive enough, but with thousands of other pretty twentysomethings around who dressed much better (and in far less clothing) than me, I wasn't anything extraordinary.

"Yes! You're the full package, Pepper. Hunter's already noticed. Hell, you don't need Reece or any other guy for that matter. Maybe it's time you just go for it, Pepper. Stop beating around the bush and go after Hunter."

Nodding, I stared out the windshield as she pulled onto the street and left the strip of bars and restaurants behind. "You're right. It was a dumb idea."

"No, it wasn't. And even if it was, I think it was my idea, so blame me."

A smile brushed my mouth. I looked over at her. She frowned as she stopped at a red light, and I could tell she was feeling bad.

I relaxed back against the headrest. "No one made me do anything. I know you credit yourself with mad skills of persuasion, but I decided to do this."

She sent me a skeptical look. "Really?"

"Really. It is possible to go against the Great Emerson."

She sniffed as she turned onto Butler, the main street that cut through campus and crossed in front of our dorm. The academic buildings were quiet as we drove past. Several upstairs windows glowed with light. I envisioned the students within, buried in their lab work. They possessed too much ambition to cut loose for a wild night at the bars. A few weeks ago I would have been one of them, ensconced in my dorm room or at the library. It was crazy to think that a phone call from Lila, meeting a hot bartender, and bumping into Hunter had changed all that. I told myself it was the combination of the three, but what did I know? Maybe it was just time for a change. To break out of the shell I'd forced myself into the morning my mother dropped me off on Gram's front stoop.

Whatever the reason, a switch had been flipped inside me.

With Reece's face running through my mind, his light-colored eyes so sharp and scornful, I felt vulnerable and shaken. It was an uneasy sensation. Reece didn't make me feel safe at all, which was everything I needed. Everything I craved. My lips tingled in memory of his kiss, and I admitted that it wasn't the only thing I craved anymore. Hopefully things would work out with Hunter and then I could have both—what I craved and what I needed.

With a sigh, I rested my head against the glass of the window. The coolness seeped into my cheek. "I'll have to go back. Apologize to him."

"To Reece?" Emerson slid into a vacant spot in front of our building. This early, it was relatively easy to score a good space. She put the car into park and swung around to face me. "What for?"

"I was using him."

She laughed. "Oh, Pepper. You're too nice. You think he cares that you mistook him for his man-whore of a brother? So you flirted with him a few times. No harm in that."

I saw his face in my mind again, the anger in his eyes. He looked like he had cared.

"I think I owe him an explanation at least. I lied . . . I denied everything and then I ran off like a coward."

Emerson shook her head and killed the engine. "You have scruples, I'll give you that."

We got out of the car. It beeped locked after us as Emerson

continued. "Men use girls all the time and never apologize. My own father is at the top of the list. He's the king of players, even at fifty-four. I went through half a dozen nannies because he usually ended up sleeping with them and then fired them afterward because things got too awkward." Emerson fumbled for her door key. "And don't let me get started about my mother and the prize shit she married. And my stepbrother." Her shoulders shook with a visible shudder. "I won't even go there."

We stepped into the harsh fluorescent lighting that buzzed like an incessant gnat. I studied her almost warily as she punched the UP button on the elevator.

She rarely talked about her father, and her mother was a dead subject. I didn't even know she had a stepbrother. This gave me new insight into her and confirmed what I'd always suspected. There was more beneath the surface. She was more than the carefree party girl who fooled around with a different guy every night.

I wasn't going to push her to talk. After my father died, there had been a string of loser guys in my mother's life. She never hooked up with the decent, settle-down types. Some of her boyfriends were so mean that I learned to be grateful for the ones who didn't see me at all. The ones who looked through me like I wasn't there.

Yeah. Em could keep her secrets. I had mine.

As we stepped inside the elevator, her eyes swung my way, the brilliant blue there as hard as I've ever seen. "You don't owe him anything, Pepper."

"Maybe," I allowed. But I still had to see him again.

Chapter 11

"HEY, GRAM, HOW'S IT going?" I sandwiched my phone between my shoulder and ear as I kicked off the khaki pants that were regulation for all Little Miss Muffet Daycare employees.

"Oh, Pepper, dear, when are you coming home?"

It was the same question she always asked. Even though I wrote the dates of my breaks on the calendar beside the fridge, she never referred to it.

"Thanksgiving week. I'll be there the Wednesday before. I have to work that weekend." I winced at my reflection in the mirror as I unbuttoned my blouse. The tightly constructed braid had deteriorated hours ago. It hadn't held up well against wrangling toddlers. I tugged the band loose from the already unraveling mess.

"They need an accurate count for Thanksgiving dinner."

I shook my head at her reprimand, but said nothing. "Well, RSVP for two." Dinner was usually catered by Hardy's, a local cafeteria that did a decent roast turkey and dressing. The seniors packed into the hall as early as 10 A.M. I would be the only one in the room under the age of seventy. But at least I didn't have to worry about my grandmother cooking a huge meal anymore.

My first Thanksgiving with her she insisted on cooking everything herself. She was going to fry the turkey. Fortunately, a daughter visiting her mother next door to us noticed Gram setting up the fryer outside and came to investigate, stopping Gram seconds before she dropped a *frozen* turkey into the pot of boiling oil and burned down our house—and us.

"I will. Just two?"

I hesitated. She had never asked that before. "Yes."

"Because Martha Sultenfuess's granddaughter just got engaged. You don't have a boyfriend yet, do you?"

"Isn't Mrs. Sultenfuess's granddaughter in her thirties?"

"Is she? I thought you were about the same age."

"I'm nineteen, Gram."

Rosco started yapping in the background. I could picture the Yorkie standing at the screen door, begging to be let out. "Your father married when he was nineteen."

I fell silent, stunned she had even said that. Was she honestly holding up my parents' marriage as some sort of example I should follow?

I took a deep breath and reminded myself that Gram had always been a little flighty. Once, in eighth grade, I opened my lunch sack to find a can of green beans, a bottle of prune juice, and the remote control inside. That had gotten a lot of laughs and earned me a few unpleasant nicknames. But lesson learned. I packed my own lunches after that. By my freshman year, I took care of her more than she took care of me. Leaving home for college hadn't been the easiest decision, but I'd forced myself to do it. I couldn't devote my life to her. She didn't want or expect that from me.

Now, at seventy-nine, there was no predicting what she would say or do. The latter was a very real point of concern for me. I worried that she would soon need to move into a full-scale nursing home. I hated to consider it. And so did Gram. The first and last time I mentioned it to her, she started crying so hard I hadn't had the nerve to bring it up again.

I'd watch her over Thanksgiving and decide if we needed to revisit the conversation.

"I'll meet someone someday," I assured her. For some reason the image of Reece flashed across my mind. What would Gram think if I brought home a pierced, tattooed bartender? She'd probably think I was a lot like my mother.

"Well, I won't be around forever, Pepper. I'd like to see you settled before my time comes."

"Oh, Gram. You're going to live forever." It's what I always said whenever she brought up dying.

She laughed. "God, I hope not."

I fell silent at this. I didn't want to think about losing her. When Gram was gone, I'd be truly alone. Emotion welled up in my throat. When I first went to live with her, the thought of losing her terrified me. I'd already lost everyone and everything. No one ever stayed. I assumed I'd eventually lose her, too. It took a few years for me to accept that she wasn't going to abandon me. I used to freak out every time she caught a cold. When she broke her leg and had to stay a few days in the hospital, I couldn't eat or sleep until she was back home.

"I gotta go study, Gram." I managed to get out without sounding too choked up.

"All right. You be a good girl." Gram said that at the end of every call. *Be a good girl.* If she only knew that I was on a path of sexual exploration.

After hanging up, I finished changing clothes. Dressed in comfy sweatpants and a Dartford Uni sweatshirt, I fell back on my bed with my copy of *Madame Bovary.* I was almost finished with it, which was good considering I had a test in World Lit tomorrow.

Highlighter and pen in hand, I lost myself, following the exploits of Madame Bovary and vowing never to become a slave to my credit cards. It was bad enough that I had school loans. As I continued to read, I felt an uncomfortable similarity between Madame Bovary and myself. Just like me, she was so committed to an idea of what she thought her life should be.

Shaking my head, I told myself my infatuation with Hunter wasn't shallow and unhealthy. He was good. Kind and reliable and safe. He was all of those things. I was no Madame Bovary.

"Hey, there."

I looked up at Georgia leaning against the doorjamb. She was in her running clothes. Earbuds dangled from around her neck. "Hi. How was your run?"

She fell onto the bed beside me. "Brutal. Paying for my weeklong junk food binge. I really stress-ate while studying for my finance exam."

Em breezed into the room then. "You should major in studio arts like me."

"You still have to take your core classes," I reminded her.

"And I'm almost through with those." She shrugged one slim shoulder. "I'm into the stuff I enjoy now. Which is definitely not finance." She made a face and shook her head at Georgia.

"Maybe if I was a genius artist, I wouldn't need to major in business."

Em flashed her a smile. "You're sweet. I hope my stuff ends up in a gallery someday, and I don't end up teaching middle school art."

"As if that would happen." Georgia laughed. "Daddy will save you."

Some of Emerson's smile faded, and I couldn't help remembering what she had shared about her father. I guess Georgia wasn't aware of that or forgot about it.

Deciding to change the subject, I asked, "What are your plans for the night?"

Emerson brightened. "I'm all yours."

"Harris has a project to work on."

"Yay!" Emerson clapped. "Let's go out. Just the three of us."

"There's a new Thai place over on Roosevelt. It's supposed to be really good. We could try that," Georgia suggested.

I nodded. "That sounds good . . ."

"And that new Bourne movie—"

"We can watch a movie anytime," Emerson pouted.

"We can go to a bar anytime," Georgia returned.

I inhaled. "I want to go back to Mulvaney's."

My friends fell silent for a moment. I knew from Georgia's uncertain expression that Emerson had filled her in on everything—specifically my humiliation at discovering Reece wasn't the bartender I had hoped to hook up with. No, that was his kid brother. The embarrassment of that still stung.

"You want to go back?" Georgia asked. "Are you sure?"

"Yeah. I need to talk to Reece."

Emerson stared at me, and I braced myself, expecting her to remind me again that I did not owe him an explanation. Thankfully the words never came, because I couldn't leave this alone. I didn't want him to think I was like every girl to walk through those doors, drawn by rumors of Logan and ready for a taste. He'd thought I was different before. That's what bothered me the most. He no longer thought there was anything special about me.

"Then we'll go," Emerson finally said, her expression unusually solemn. She moved toward my closet. "Okay. What are you going to wear then?"

"Something hot," Georgia supplied.

"Of course," Emerson replied, sliding hangers one after the other. "We're going to make him regret he ever let our Pepper go."

"He didn't let me go exactly. I ran away."

"That's because he was being a jerk. So you wanted to use him to increase your sexual prowess? Big deal. What guy isn't eager for a no-strings-attached hookup?"

Reece, apparently.

"I think the key here is that his ego was wounded," Georgia explained. "Pepper thought he was his brother."

"Well. Then you need to make him forget why he was so offended." Emerson paused, and turned around, studying me. "Wait. I'm assuming that's what you want to do. Are you still hot for him? Is he the one you want to show you the ropes?"

I should be accustomed to Emerson's directness by now, but she could always catch me off guard. I stared from her to Georgia, who looked so calm and self-assured. Like she already knew the answer.

"Yeah." I nodded, feeling my cheeks warm up. If I was going to get lessons on foreplay, I wanted it to be from him. I hadn't been able to forget that one kiss. I certainly wasn't about to renew my search and go after some new guy. A stranger. It was either Reece or no one. I would just have to wait and hope I attracted him in my own fumbling way.

"All right then." Emerson looked at me with understanding. Only what she understood, I wasn't too sure.

"I still want Hunter," I said, making sure there was no confusion.

"Of course. Of course." She nodded, and then turned back to the closet. Propping her hand on a slim hip, she studied the contents a moment longer before she pulled out a pair of dark jeans. "Georgia? What top do you think?" She lifted an eyebrow, waiting for advisement.

"Blue cowl-neck sweater. Right side of the closet."

"Thanks." Nodding, Emerson went off to search in their room.

"You know, Pepper," Georgia said, crossing her Lycra-clad legs, "the world won't end if you end up with someone besides Hunter."

Everything in me tightened, resisting the idea. "But I want Hunter. I always have." I'd always wanted to be a Montgomery. "And for once it doesn't seem like such an impossible thing."

"I never thought it was impossible. Especially not now that he's single. He'd be lucky to have you. Any guy would." She uncrossed her legs. Pressing her knees together, she scooted to the edge of my bed and looked at me earnestly. "But sometimes the thing you want isn't what you really need."

"You sound like a fortune cookie," I teased, but her words created a hollowness inside me. I couldn't explain why I wanted Hunter. I just did. I just knew he was it, that thing I had been reaching for since . . . since forever.

Like she could read my thoughts, she asked, "Why does it have to be Hunter?"

The question pried too deep. It brought to mind my mother and a stuffed bear, two things I could never get back. "Oh, I don't know." I cocked my head and sharpened my gaze on her. "Why does it have to be Harris?"

She blinked, startled by my quick retort. I sighed and glanced to the window, regretting my defensiveness.

"I've been with Harris since high school," she answered evenly.

I nodded. I wasn't trying to imply her relationship with Harris was somehow lacking. What did I know about relationships? From everything I had seen, Harris was a great guy.

"I guess what I'm trying to say is that you've been here going on two years now without a date. And you never dated in high school. Maybe you should go out with other guys rather than pinning all your hopes on Hunter."

The words were hard to hear . . . especially considering how accepting Emerson and Georgia had always been of my determination to have Hunter. Suddenly I felt cornered. I drew my knees up to my chest and scooted back on the bed until my spine aligned with the brick wall.

"They haven't exactly been lining up to ask me out, Georgia."

"Because you haven't wanted them to. Guys need a little encouragement, and you haven't exactly been putting out an 'I'm available' vibe."

I crossed my arms, unable to deny that but still not liking to hear it. "Well, I am now, aren't I?"

She angled her head. "With this bartender? He's supposed to count? I thought he was just a hookup."

I buried my head in my hands and groaned. "Yes. No. I don't know."

"I found it!" Emerson sailed back into the room. She jerked her thumb over her shoulder. "Now hurry up and shower!"

Georgia smiled. I grabbed my shower caddy and robe, content to leave the quasi-serious talk behind.

Emerson did a little dance. "We're going to break some hearts tonight!"

Just as long as it wasn't my heart.

THE BAR WAS ITS usual meat market for a weekend night— meaning standing room only. Clusters of guys and girls milled around, talking and drinking. But their eyes were always moving. Scanning. On the hunt. As soon as we entered, guys made eye contact and tried to engage us in conversation.

Emerson stopped just inside the front room, where the

aroma of fried pickles enticed me even after the dinner we'd just had at the new Thai place. "What's your plan?"

I glanced from her to the hot press of humanity all around us. Even as cold as it was outside, the faces were flushed from the warm room. And perhaps the free-flowing alcohol had something to do with it, too.

I stood on my tiptoes, trying to see to the bar. "I think I'm just going to walk right up to him."

Emerson arched an eyebrow. "That's direct. And not exactly you."

"No point delaying." Not after the last time I was in here. I wasn't going to fake memory loss. I ran away from him. He was probably finished with me now.

"Good plan." Georgia nodded. "No games."

We made our way toward the bar. I glimpsed Reece through the shifting cracks between bodies as we got in line. I stood on tiptoe, trying to gain a better view, catching only the curve of his head, the dark shadow of his closely cropped hair.

Gaze still on him, I spoke to my friends. "I can handle it from here."

"You sure?" Em didn't sound convinced.

"Yeah." For some reason, even though they knew everything that had transpired up until now, humbling myself before Reece was something I didn't want to do in front of them.

Emerson scanned the crowded room and pointed. "There. We can get that table."

A quick glance revealed that the table was occupied by two guys who were already ogling Emerson in her miniskirt. Georgia followed her through the throng, leaving me in line. I waited patiently, creeping forward until I stood at the counter.

Reece's back was to me. I watched the dark fabric of his T-shirt stretch as he bent and then straightened. When he turned around, his gaze landed on me. He stilled for a moment, his light blue eyes sharpening. "What are you doing here?"

I moistened my lips and looked self-consciously at the people squished on each side of me, not happy about publicizing our conversation but not seeing any other choice.

Ignoring everyone else, I spoke over the din. "I wanted to see you."

He lifted a dark eyebrow—the one with the piercing—as he filled the pitcher. "Yeah? Funny, considering the last time we talked you ran off like someone shouted 'Fire.'"

He handed off the pitcher and collected money from a customer, a girl who looked me up and down like I was something dirty stuck to the sole of her shoe.

I glared at her until she moved on and then looked back at Reece. "That wasn't exactly a conversation."

"No?"

"It was more like an inquisition."

His lips curved in a twisted semblance of a smile. "Call it whatever you like. I've got you pegged now, *Nice Girl*."

I bristled at this, especially the way he said it—like the last thing he considered me to be anymore was nice. "You don't know me." No one did.

"Yeah. The spoiled little college girl didn't like what she was hearing so she ran away."

Okay, maybe that was partly true. But I wasn't spoiled.

Ultimately, he was calling me a coward. Weak. A small

voice whispered through my mind like a chill wind: *Isn't that what you do? What you've done all your life? Ever since Mom dumped you? Run. Hide. Bury yourself away from the world. Obsess over a boy who doesn't know you exist. At least not in the way you want to exist for him. Pretend you belong to a family that isn't yours.*

My eyes started to burn from the cruel barrage of thoughts. I sucked a breath into my squeezing-tight lungs and held my ground, refusing to run away again just because the conversation wasn't going my way. "I came here to apologize."

He stared at me for a long moment, ignoring the girl who stepped up in front of him, money clutched in her hand. She stared at him expectantly, but he continued to look at me. She finally moved on to another bartender.

I twisted my fingers together until they were numb and bloodless. "I'd heard rumors about your brother. I had a description of him . . . and just assumed it was you that first night. Maybe I wanted it to be you. After you helped me with my car that night, I wanted it to be you," I admitted with a single nod.

He continued to stare at me, doing nothing to ease my embarrassment.

I kept talking. "It was dumb. I'm sorry. I came here looking for . . ." I couldn't say it. It was just too mortifying.

He crossed his arms over his chest, waiting. It was an intimidating pose. No one approached him at the bar looking like that. They took one look at him, looking at me, and swerved for another bartender. Maybe I should have turned away, too.

Except I had come here to do this.

"I—" Stopping, I gathered my breath, my courage, and plunged ahead: "There's this guy I've liked forever, and I'm not exactly experienced, but I thought it would help if I could gain some experience from someone who knows what he's doing. You know. If I could be better at . . . at stuff. The intimate stuff. All the girl-guy action." I released my fingers and motioned between me and him.

There. I'd said it. And it sounded every bit as bad as I thought it would.

I met his gaze head on, hoping the fact that I was shaking inside didn't show on the outside.

He revealed nothing. It was as though my words made no impact on him whatsoever. He was like some kind of stoic, hard-faced soldier staring down the enemy. Only that enemy was me.

Finally, he spoke. "So you're saying you're looking for a fuck buddy?"

I felt as much as saw a guy beside me swing his attention toward me. "Sweet." He leaned in, his shoulder brushing mine.

"W-what?" I stammered. "No!"

Reece swung his hard stare on the other guy. "Get. Lost. Now."

The guy held up both hands defensively and backed away.

I inhaled again, fighting for composure. I'd said enough. I apologized. I did what I came here for. I could leave now. "I just wanted to say I was sorry."

Turning, I moved back through the bar, making a line for the table where Emerson and Georgia waited. I hoped they didn't want to stay. I just wanted to go home. The embarrassment was still there, but like a Band-Aid ripped off, the sting was already fading. Hopefully by tomorrow I wouldn't feel it at all. All of this would be a dim memory. My time hanging out at Mulvaney's had come to an end. For some reason, that idea gave me another sting.

The girls spotted me and waved me over, their eyes bright with questions. They paid very little notice to the guys working so hard for their attention as I explained how the conversation with Reece had gone. Suddenly Emerson's gaze drifted just beyond my shoulder. Her eyes grew huge in her face.

I swiveled around at the exact moment Reece reached me. I opened my mouth and started to say something over the pulsing din of the bar. I'm not even sure what I meant to say because his hand wrapping around mine shoved every thought out of my head. Speech was impossible.

Chapter 12

His strong fingers surrounded mine while his gaze scanned my face, scrutinizing me, searching me in a way that made me squirm.

The room throbbed noisily in my ears. A glass broke near the bar and he didn't even look that way. Without a word, he turned, pulling me after him. I marveled at how bodies seemed to part for him. He didn't even use his elbows. He simply cut through the crowd.

"Where are we going?" I shouted at his back, recovering my voice.

He didn't even glance behind him. And yet I knew he heard me. His fingers tightened ever so slightly around my hand.

A horrible thought seized me. As we passed the long length of bar and stepped onto the ramp that led into the smaller back room where food was served, I gave voice to it. "Are you throwing me out?"

As mortifying as that would be, he could do that. He worked here, after all. Would he? Had it come to that?

We approached the counter where a girl in the classic Mulvaney's T-shirt scrawled orders onto a notepad and then stuck the slips of paper behind her onto a spinner for the cooks.

The line for food was much shorter than the line for drinks, but a few people waited there already, eager for a burger to go with their beer. We bypassed them. Reece lifted the countertop and pulled me after him. The girl taking food orders looked up.

"Mike's in charge," he told her.

Her gaze flicked from him to me and her mouth sagged open in a small O of surprise.

We walked through the kitchen, past the two fry cooks with nets over their heads. Reece stopped in front of a pantry door. He pulled out a set of keys, unlocked it, and pulled the door wide open.

Peering inside, I didn't see the shelves of supplies I expected. A set of stairs stretched up ahead of us. He pulled me in behind him and locked the door.

My heartbeat quickened. Blood rushed to my ears at the proximity of him. At our sudden aloneness. Instantly the sounds of the bar were muffled, like someone had just lowered the volume on a remote control.

A light glowed from the top of the stairs, saving us from total darkness. Not that we lingered long at the bottom of the stairs. He pulled me after him, his warm fingers still folded over mine.

Our steps thudded on the wood stairs, reverberating in the narrow space. The steps abruptly cleared to a wide open room. Wood floors, brick walls. Some interesting framed photographs were scattered here and there. On the walls. Leaning against a bookcase. The area was large, equipped with a bed, office space, and living area. A kitchen occupied the far right corner. A dark couch sat in front of a big screen. Otherwise not too much decor. Typical guy pad, I assumed. Not that I had been inside many. He released my hand and sank down onto a chair. I watched dumbly as he unlaced his boots.

"You live here?" I managed to get out.

"Yeah." Just that. A single monosyllable. The first boot hit the floor. He didn't look up at me as he worked on his second boot.

"Just you?" Duh. Did I think all the bartenders slept up here?

He shot me a quick look. "I own the place."

"Mulvaney's? You own it?"

"It's been in my family for fifty years. I'm Reece Mulvaney. My dad ran it until two years ago. Now I do."

"Oh." I don't know why that changed anything, but suddenly it did.

Suddenly I felt *more* uncomfortable. He'd grown up in this place. He'd seen it all. Everything. All manner of silly, horny college students traipsing through the doors. I thought of my earlier confession to him. That I'd come here looking for experience. *God.* He must think I was the silliest of them all.

I buried my hands in my tight pockets, watching, waiting for him to say something else. To explain what it was he was thinking. What we were doing here.

What *I* was doing here.

He stood back up in one fluid motion. He moved like some kind of jungle cat. Effortless and graceful. His eyes settled on me intently, glowing in that strange way, like lit from within.

He approached—not fast, but with easy strides.

He stopped before me, leaving only an inch between us.

I couldn't breathe. The air left me, but I couldn't draw it back in. I fixed my gaze on his chest, suddenly too overcome with nerves to look up at his face, and that posed a whole new problem for me. Because I could only think how broad, how hard his chest looked. I could only gawk at the golden skin peeking out of his collar.

Then his hands were on my face, his palms cupping my cheeks, his fingers burrowing into my hair. My scalp tightened and tingled. He forced my face up. I saw a flash of his pale blue eyes before his head descended, and everything else was lost except this. Him. His lips on mine. Blistering hot.

There was just his mouth, his hands gripping my face, my head. His tongue stroked my bottom lip. I gasped and he took advantage, sweeping inside, and I was full of the taste of him. I leaned forward, melting into him. His hard length against me made me feel giddy, boneless. Sensation overwhelmed me. There was no mistaking his power, his strength. It radiated from him in waves, and as heady as all of that—all of *him*—was, it also frightened me a little. Like one of those rides at the amusement park that dropped you from the sky and then jerked you back up a second before smacking to earth. I felt far from safe right now.

I broke for air, panicked and gasping. "Wait, please." My voice trembled as I looked toward the stairs, assessing my escape options. My eyes did a quick scan, confirming what I already knew. I was totally at his mercy up here.

How insane was this scenario? I let him lead me upstairs to this room. I didn't do that. That wasn't who I was.

"What?" His voice was steady, his hands still cupping my face, each of his long fingers a searing imprint.

I fought the dark cravings that urged me to throw myself back at him and continue kissing. I gulped a breath, commanding myself to think this through and ignore the little voice in my head (that sounded a lot like Emerson) urging me to jump his bones.

Avoiding his gaze, I inspected his loft like I might find a solution in the large space. My attention strayed to the bed. And stayed there. The activity in the bar was a low, steady drone beneath us. Like the rumbling from the belly of a beast. For all that it reminded me that there were people below us, we might as well have been on a deserted island. We were well and truly alone. It was just me and him. Us.

He must have read some of my anxiety. His hands flexed on my face. I snapped my gaze back up as his head dipped. He kissed me, capturing my bottom lip with his teeth. My belly did another dive. His teeth released my lip and he licked the tender flesh.

I whimpered.

His lips moved against my mouth, talking. "Don't worry. I don't do virgins."

And then he was kissing me again, his tongue sweeping inside my mouth, his hands diving through my hair and holding my head, angling me for the hot pressure of his lips, giving me no chance for speech. As if I could form coherent words.

Only two thoughts pounded through me. *Oh, shit, is it so obvious that I'm a virgin?* And: *Why is he bothering with me at all if there's no chance of sex in this for him?*

All that quickly became irrelevant, however. His mouth consumed me, obliterating everything else. The kiss went on and on. His tongue explored me, tasting until I grew more confident. I touched his tongue with the tip of mine. He made a low growling sound of approval and wrapped an arm around my waist. In one move, he lifted me off my feet just enough so that he could walk me across the loft. The tips of my boots skimmed the floor. I gave a little squeak. My hands clung to him, arms wrapping tightly around shoulders that tensed and corded.

When he stopped, his arms loosened around me. I slid down the length of him, my feet returning to the floor. My head, however, remained lost somewhere in the clouds. Or, more precisely, lost somewhere between the taste of his mouth and the sensation of his body against mine.

Suddenly the warm rasp of his callused hand against my cheek disappeared.

He backed away.

I bit back a moan of disappointment and stopped myself just short of reaching for him and pulling him back by the front of his shirt.

With his eyes trained on me, he sank down on the bed, leaving me standing in front of him. I shifted on my feet, unsure what was happening now and trying for all I was worth to look sophisticated and at ease. Pointless. He had called me out as a virgin, after all. And I had admitted I came here looking for experience. That kind of outted me.

His pale eyes gleamed in the dim, red-gold light from the floor lamp.

Deciding to act, I stepped forward to follow him, but he shook his head at me, those eyes of his glittering like shards of glass. Leaning back on the mattress, he propped his elbows on the bed, looking deceptively casual.

"Take off your clothes." The request was anything but casual, and yet he uttered it as though he were asking me to pass the salt.

An odd strangled sound rose up in my throat. I fought it, pushed it back down, and tried for speech that sounded half-way normal. "What?"

He angled his head to one side, studying me. "You wanted to learn foreplay. Isn't that why you came here looking for my brother?"

My face heated at that reminder.

"Well, you got me." He announced this like he was some-how second best. Which was ridiculous. Logan was hot, but he looked like he belonged as a lead in a boy band. Reece. Reece was something else entirely. "Now. Take off your clothes."

My hands trembled. If not for his reassurance that he didn't *do* virgins, I'd be running for the door. Probably.

I moistened my lips and my stomach tightened at the way his eyes followed the tiny movement. He missed nothing. Swallowing, I asked, "Isn't that kind of skipping foreplay and getting right to it?"

"I'm the one with the experience. Are you going to trust me?"

It was my turn to look him over, splayed so deliciously upon the bed, so effortlessly hot. Like picking up virgins from the bar and bringing them up here was something he did all the time. I didn't think that was the case, but the green monster of jealousy still crept up on me. I didn't want to consider whether he had done this before. That he had reclined there on his bed and invited other girls to take off their clothes for him. Even though the presumption of his experience was what brought me to this moment, I wanted to think I was the first to see the inside of this room.

"Should I trust you?" I lifted my chin in an attempt to look braver than I felt. "It's not as though I know you." But I did. At least a little. I knew he was the kind of guy who helped a female stranded alongside the road. I knew he was good with kids. He was also the kind of guy to get offended when he was mistaken for his man-whore of a brother. He had scruples.

"We're not going to do anything you don't want to do," he explained. "Taking off your clothes . . . looking sexy doing it." A corner of his mouth lifted. "Well, that's a hell of a turn-on. And isn't that what you want to learn? How to turn a guy on? A particular guy, right?"

Hunter. Yes. My mind leaped upon the memory of him. My purpose. The reason I was here. That was it exactly. I nodded.

"Good. Then what are you waiting for?"

What was I waiting for? I bit my lip, trying to decide. Logic and the hot pulse of desire in my veins urged me on. *Yes. Just do it. Pretend the fear is gone, and live for once.*

"Here." He sat up on the bed. "I'll match you move for move," he offered. Because guys like him were shy about getting naked. Right. As though that would somehow make me feel better about stripping off my clothes in front of him.

He reached behind his head and gathered a fistful of shirt. In one tug he pulled the dark gray fabric over his head.

An invisible band tightened around my chest. Holy sexiness. My gaze devoured him. Bronzed skin. Washboard abs.

My mouth watered and dried simultaneously. I could see now that the tattoo that covered his arm snuck down onto his chest, the fauna design covering his left pectoral. There was also some kind of script stretching down along his rib cage. Words I couldn't make out from where I stood.

"That's just ridiculous," I breathed, awe and lust swirling through me like some heady elixir. I didn't even realize I said the words aloud until they filled the space between us, making that band around my chest squeeze tighter.

One corner of his mouth lifted, curling up ever so slightly. "Tip number one: Don't call a guy ridiculous when he undresses in front of you. It might give him a complex."

I could never imagine Reece having a complex. Not the way he looked.

I scanned the lean chest and flat belly cut with sharply defined muscles. I couldn't stop ogling him. The waistband of his jeans hung low, revealing a thin strip of black waistband that belonged to his briefs.

"Your turn . . . I mean, if you're done staring."

I doubted I would ever be done staring at him.

I dragged my gaze from that delicious chest back to his face. His voice sounded different, rougher and deeper, a low rumble that caused a physical reaction in my skin. His eyes looked different, too. The pale blue was smoky, like a fog drifting in off the sea. He stared with a deep intensity that had my hands shaking as I reached for the hem of Georgia's sweater.

I can do this.

I pulled it over my head quickly, before I lost my nerve. A quick glance down confirmed I wasn't wearing my usual white cotton bra. *Thank God.* The pale pink satin cupped my breasts high. His gaze crawled over me, assessing, and I felt naked even though I was still wearing the bra. Come May there would be girls sunbathing on the quad in skimpier bikini tops than this.

"Nice," he said softly.

"Thanks."

"You don't need to stand there like you're facing a firing squad." The rumble of his voice did nothing to ease my nerves. In fact, I might have jumped a little at the sound.

He scooted to the edge of the bed and stretched out an arm, reaching for me. His fingers curled around my wrist and pulled me forward, that half smile still there, hugging his lips. I moved into him with halting steps, both relieved and oddly disappointed that he was cutting short my striptease (but mostly relieved).

All that bare, firm-looking skin drew my eyes again. I couldn't stop drinking it in. He looked edible. He should go around without a shirt on all the time. Scratch that. The guy would cause a riot.

He let go of my wrist, leaving me standing between his splayed thighs. His body radiated warmth as I stood between his legs, hovering close, looking down at him, my fingers itching to settle on the naked curve of his shoulders and feel all that solidness, that warmth, to trace the tattoo crawling over his chest and shoulder.

"Keep going." His voice slid like velvet over my skin.

I swallowed. "What?"

"As pretty as the pink looks against your skin, I want you to take this off." He fingered a single strap, barely touching me.

Okay, so he wasn't letting me off the hook, but the idea of removing the bra sent a ripple of panic through me. He was eye-level with my chest! I wasn't sure I could handle him that up close and personal.

I wanted experience, but wasn't this diving into the deep end? Couldn't we wade in a bit first? Start out with the kiddie pool?

His lips twisted. "You're thinking too much. I can tell. Stop."

"Is this what you do with other girls that you don't intend to sleep with?" I hardly recognized my voice. It sounded so small and breathless.

"This is what I'm doing with you." His hands settled on my waist, twin burning imprints on my skin just above the waistband of my jeans. "C'mon. Let go."

Maybe it was the challenge in the low rasp of his voice—or simply the truth of his words. I was thinking too much. I reached behind me and undid the clasp, wondering how, in one week, I'd gone from a girl with one bad kiss to my credit to this. Alone and half naked with a hot guy way out of my league.

Stop thinking, Pepper.

I held the cups of my bra close to my chest, stopping it from falling.

This has nothing to do with thinking. It's just instinct.

He studied me, looking from my face to my arms pressed tightly in front of me, saving me from total exposure.

He lifted one hand. Watching me intently, he slid one loosened strap free, his fingers grazing my skin, soft as a whisper. The thin scrap of satin fell soundlessly off my left shoulder.

A shiver raced through me. Goose bumps broke out over my flesh and everything in me tightened.

It was just a tiny thing. One strap that afforded no real protection, but it was like a barrier dropped. He moved to the other strap. Another whisper-brush of fingers against the curve of my shoulder. More shivers.

It was just my arms now, clutched before me, holding the pink cups in place. He continued to watch my face as he set both hands to my wrists, circling them with long, sure fingers. Slowly, firmly, he pulled them away from my chest. The bra dropped.

Despite how warm I felt—how warm he made me feel—a cold draft slid over me and I shivered. My nipples reacted, the peaks hardening. Or maybe that was just him. His stare roved over me, those eyes a glittery shade of blue, impossibly bright in the dim room.

It was the most exposed I had ever been. I didn't even strip off my clothes in front of other girls. I had been that girl in that locker room who dove into bathroom stalls or dressed hurriedly with her back to everyone. This was a big, huge, never-before-happened event.

There was nowhere to hide.

His hands settled around my rib cage. It wasn't my breasts, but he might as well have touched me there. I still jumped. His thumbs rested below the undersides of my breasts. So close but not touching.

He drew me in, pulling me down onto the bed. The mattress met my back. He curled against me, one muscled arm beside my head, one of his legs sliding over my hip, pinning me. I sucked in a tortured breath and held it. It was too much. Too soon.

"You're beautiful. All peaches and cream." His hand skimmed my stomach. The sensitive skin there quivered under his warm palm. My lungs ached, holding in my breath, but I couldn't make them function.

I brought my hands self-consciously to my chest. He was quick to act, peeling my hands free. With a bracing breath, I held them stiffly at my sides, wanting to be brave. Wanting to be someone that reveled in this and didn't feel like a scared virgin even if that's just what I was.

Heat crawled up my neck, bursting across my face. I waited, expecting to feel his hands there, on my breasts, groping like any other boy would do, but his touch never came.

He brought his face closer to mine, his lips brushing my ear with warm breath. I leaned up, seeking that touch. "You need to relax. You're supposed to enjoy this."

"O-okay." My voice wobbled.

"Rigid and afraid isn't exactly a turn-on."

"I'm not turning you on then?" I blurted, mortified, feeling like I had somehow failed. I was here to explore, to learn, and I was doing an abysmal job.

"Oh, I'm turned on. Don't worry about that." His hand threaded through my hair, pulling it clear of my neck. "I'm just talking in general terms. If you're messing around with someone else . . . he might like for you to be more responsive."

As he spoke, his mouth settled at my cheek, just beside my ear. *Someone else.* The words rattled around inside my head like loose marbles. I couldn't think of anyone else right now.

Couldn't imagine anyone but him and the way his mouth felt on my skin. The way his palm rested on my stomach, his fingers splayed wide, the blunt tips curled ever so slightly, lightly brushing my quivering flesh.

In this moment, I could forget all my fears. I could even forget the fact that I was exposed and vulnerable in a way that I had never been before. In a way I had never *let* myself be with anyone.

I squirmed on the bed, dying inside, waiting for his next move, waiting for him to touch me. Both hoping he did and hoping he didn't.

His mouth hovered over my ear, his breath fanning hotly against the hypersensitive whorls. He made me ache for more. "He wants you to be just as hot for it as he is."

Again, he referenced my supposed future lover, the guy I was doing this for. The insinuation of Hunter into this moment actually bothered me. He wasn't here. Reece was. I didn't want to think of Hunter right now. I only wanted to feel.

I turned my face to look directly at him, our lips not quite touching. "Is that what you're doing? Making me hot?" I didn't know where the question came from. It sounded throaty and seductive in my voice.

"You tell me. Am I?"

I swallowed and started to tell him yes, he had long since succeeded in that regard, but just then he bit down on my earlobe and I arched off the bed with a cry, unexpected pleasure knifing through me.

He made a deep sound of approval, and then he touched me.

It was one startling sensation after another. His mouth on

my ear. His hand cupping my breast. I gasped at that, at the full heat of his palm caressing my flesh. "You feel so amazing. I love your tits."

My head rolled on the bed and I grabbed his shoulders, forgetting my shyness. I curled my fingers around the solid muscle, my nails biting into the supple skin, silk on steel. It was a heady thing to touch him, to feel his strength, the muscles that contracted at the dig of my fingers.

And then he found my nipple. I sobbed as he traced the tip, teasing me. I writhed on the bed, the ache tightening between my legs. I wriggled, looking for a way to ease the squeezing clutch of heat.

His mouth found mine in a desperate fusion of lips and tongues. I kissed him back, my earlier uncertainty gone.

His lips broke from mine and his mouth went for my breast, claiming it with none of the teasing lightness of his fingers. He took me in his mouth, enveloping me in warm, wet heat.

I choked, the sound not quite speech, but something on the verge of words.

Suddenly my phone went off. I stiffened. He continued like he didn't hear it. His mouth continued to devour me like I was some rare treat. Like we were the only two people in the universe. With no people in the bar below us. No phone going off in my pocket.

The ring tone soon died, and I quickly forgot to even wonder who was calling me. Although it was an easy guess.

Then a text vibrated in my pocket against the weight of his hip. We ignored it. Even the second time. And the third.

At the fourth, he lifted up with a growl. "They're not going to stop."

Sitting back, he slipped his hand into my pocket for my phone. I bit the inside of my cheek at his hand there, so close to the apex of my thighs. Even after all the intimacy of the last few minutes, that felt beyond intimate.

He pulled my phone free. Instead of handing it to me as I expected, he started typing.

"What are you doing?"

Finished typing, he tossed it on the bed above my head. He came down over me. I gasped at the sensation of his bare chest against my skin, pressing down on my nipples, moist from his mouth.

Words shivered from my lips: "What did you tell them?"

His breath fanned my lips. "That you're staying the night with me."

Chapter 13

OH. MY. GOD. HIS words shot a hot thrill right down my spine. A sensation only magnified as his lips smothered mine. He settled his body between my thighs and I marveled at the fit of him there, so natural, so right. His hands went for my waistband. He slipped his fingers inside, the backs gliding into my panties and low against my navel.

As much as the touch sent a jolt of sizzling awareness through me, a frisson of panic rose inside me, too. Moaning against his mouth, my fingers locked around his wrist and tugged.

He obeyed, slipping his hand out of my panties, and instantly I was overcome with a sense of calm. He meant what he'd said earlier. He wouldn't do anything I didn't want. This knowledge gave me a heightened sense of power. I could do anything. Kiss him. Touch him. Explore him as I wished with no fear that he would demand more from me than I wanted to give.

The last of my reservations melted away. I ran my hands through his hair. It was like silk against my palms. I felt the shape of his skull, the tender skin at the back of his neck. I deepened our kiss, pushed my lips harder against him, tasting him with my tongue. He groaned in approval, muttering, "I like your hands on me."

And I liked feeling him, too, reveling in the freedom to do so, feeling all that sleek skin stretched over hard muscle and sinew. My palms skated over his broad shoulders, down the slope of his back and up again, loving the velvety texture of his short hair, the scrape of stubble on his face.

"Fuck, you're sweet," he ground down against my lips roughly, his jaw flexing beneath my fingers.

He slipped his hands under me, gripping my bottom and grinding himself into me. I felt his erection. His hardness, the arousing shape of him. Need clenched deep inside of me. He began a rocking motion and I ripped my lips free, gasping raggedly. His breath filled my ear, just as harsh as my own.

He removed a hand from behind me and placed it between us, rubbing between my legs. I cried out, lifting my hips up into the pressure of his deft strokes. He slid his fingers over the denim concealing me, increasing the pressure with each glide. The base of his palm bore down, pushing at some magical place. I started to tremble. Clutching his arms, I rocked my hips into him.

"Oh, God." *OhGodOhGodOhGod*. I closed my eyes and bit my lip to stop myself from being too loud. He was making me come. Like this. So easily. With my jeans still on.

"Let go. It's okay," he rasped. "I want to hear you."

I released my lip and let sound escape. I cried out sharply, arching under him, thrusting my hips up and out. I didn't even sound like me. I was some creature ruled by desire and wild sensations. I closed my eyes to the unbearable ache building inside me. My internal litany burst from my lips. "OhGodOh-GodOhGod!"

A low, rough chuckle left him, brushing my bare throat. His head dipped and his mouth closed over a nipple. Bright spots exploded behind my eyelids. I screamed, my nails digging into his shoulders. I shook in his arms, shudders rolling over me. I went limp, my body boneless.

He eased me back down and curled around me, spooning me with his larger body. His erection was still there, prodding my backside, reminding me that he hadn't reached his own release.

As the delicious sensations faded from my body, awkwardness crept in. I held myself still for a moment, thinking, wondering what to say.

What did one say after her first orgasm? *Can I have another, please?* I turned my face into the bed, muffling the snort at my own joke.

He got up, and I held myself still on the bed, fiddling nervously with a lock of my hair, debating how I should handle this moment. There was a soft click and the room plunged into pulsing darkness. I heard a rustle and then felt a soft blanket drape over me. He returned, sliding under the blanket, his strong arm wrapping around my waist, pulling me into his chest. Moments passed as I waited for something else to happen. Is this the part where he tried to push me into having sex? His erection was still there, right behind me, distracting and exciting, building the clenching ache back to life between my legs. I squeezed my thighs, pressing them tightly together in an effort to assuage the almost painful throbbing there.

Nothing. Not a word. Not a move.

His erection became less insistent, and eventually his chest eased into a steady rhythm against my back. Unbelievable. He was actually asleep.

I held myself tense, a board in his arms. I doubted I would ever sleep.

That was my last thought before darkness rolled in.

I WOKE WITH MY legs tangled with the longer, heavier legs of a man. A definite first.

My face burned, and various other parts of my body, as memories of the night before flooded me. I tensed instantly, all my senses alert, reaching out, listening, feeling for my surroundings. A light spattering of hair covered the masculine limbs, creating a delicious friction against my smooth legs. It was a wholly alien experience. I inhaled and caught the musky aroma of the cedar bed, and something else. Something already familiar. It was him. I knew his scent. The soap and musk and salt to his skin. I'd never known another person's scent before. Well, save for Mom and Gram. Gram was a combination of laundry detergent and Bengay. Not an unpleasant odor. Mom was cigarette smoke and sour alcohol.

I turned my head on the pillow and peeked to my right. A murky blue suffused the room, seeping in through the blinds. I studied him in the pale wash of dawn. He slept with one arm flung above his head, the other tossed out carelessly at his side. At least he no longer hugged me like some kind of favorite pillow. I was free.

With his guard down he looked younger. My palm itched to touch his face, to feel the rasp of stubble against my palm. I had an unfettered view of the ink crawling along the side of his torso, moving over finely cut muscle and sinew, stopping only a couple of inches beneath his armpit. I peered at the words in the dim light. *Lead me to the rock that is higher than I.* Was that biblical? My brow creased, more confused than ever that those words somehow held special meaning for him. Enough that he would permanently etch them onto his skin. It revealed a new side to him, a softness, depths I never suspected existed.

Suppressing the urge to touch him, I untangled my legs from his and eased from the bed, quickly scanning the floor and finding my top and bra in a ball several feet away.

As I dressed, I watched him, certain he would wake and level those smoky eyes on me at any moment. My heart beat a wild rhythm in my chest as I slipped on my last boot, bouncing lightly on my other foot.

Standing, I carefully retrieved my phone from the bed and backed away, pausing at the top of the stairs. My gaze swept along every decadent inch of him nestled in the sheets like he was the subject of some kind of sexy cologne ad. I sucked a breath into my too-tight chest.

With one hand braced on the wall for support, intense relief that he hadn't woken rushed through me. But that wasn't all I felt. Unease skittered through me, settling in the pit of my stomach like bubbling acid. It somehow felt wrong slipping away like this. Without a word. Like a thief in the night. A betrayal. Which was silly. One-night flings happened all the time. No strings. No commitments. And it wasn't like we had sex. We didn't need to stare at each other and suffer an uncomfortable conversation full of lies and promises to call. This wasn't about that. He knew why I followed him up here last night. Why I dropped my guard and let myself do all those unbelievable things with him. We both knew. I wasn't that girl he had to worry about sticking around and making a nuisance of herself, infatuated and desperately convinced he was the love of her life.

Still, I hovered, arguing with myself, convincing myself it was okay to leave. I couldn't imagine waking in the bright light of morning with last night between us. What would I say? I got what I came for. And he . . . I frowned, suddenly unsure what he had gotten out of the whole experience. I hadn't slept with him. He hadn't even . . .

My cheeks flamed hot, which only pointed at how inexperienced and awkward I still was. I couldn't even complete the thought. I shouldn't blush at my own thoughts, and yet here I was, face burning simply thinking about how he got me off and then I hadn't returned the favor.

I tore my gaze away from him and quietly moved down the stairs, shooting Em a text to come and pick me up. I needed to get home anyway. I had work today. And I needed to study.

I winced. Was I actually feeding myself excuses? As if I didn't know the truth?

As if I wasn't running scared.

THE INSTANT I CLIMBED into Em's car, the inquisition began and continued all the way back to the dorm. Apparently I would get no respite. Not that I expected I could keep any of last night to myself.

Emerson fell onto my bed when we entered the room. She hadn't bothered changing from her pajama bottoms and pink tank. She kicked off her slippers and curled her feet under her. Her short hair fell soft and smooth around her pixie face, free of product. She must have showered after Mulvaney's last night. Her face was squeaky clean. Not a spot of makeup. She looked adorable and closer to fifteen than twenty.

She shook her head at me and there was a touch of awe in the motion. "I never thought I'd see you come through that door at seven A.M. after a hookup. I mean I've done plenty of walks of shame, but you? Nuh-uh."

I waved a hand. "Please."

She lifted her face and shouted into the next room, "Georgia! She's back!" Her eyes beamed brightly with approval. "I feel like we need to go out for pancakes or something to celebrate."

"It's not my birthday, Emerson."

"Uh." One of her dark eyebrows arched. "It kinda is."

Georgia shuffled in, looking like she had been awake for a while. She was always an early riser. She eyed me up and down as if looking for signs of injury. "You okay?"

"Yeah. Fine." I nodded.

"Told you she was okay," Emerson said. Her gaze swung to me. "She was worried. That text . . . he sent it, right?"

I nodded again.

She grinned. "God. That was so hot."

I smiled weakly, dropping down in my chair. Georgia lowered herself onto the bed, shoving Emerson over.

"Well. Dish," Emerson demanded. "How was it? How was *he*?"

"It was . . ." My voice faded, suddenly uncomfortable with sharing, and that left me a little confused. It was just a hookup. It wasn't supposed to be anything special. Okay, I had covered bases one, two, and three in my otherwise base-free existence. That was special. True. But Reece . . . *us* . . . well, there was no *us*.

My friends watched me, waiting expectantly.

"It was nice," I finished. "He was . . . he was nice."

Emerson flinched. "Nice?"

"Hmm." I nodded again.

"That bad?" She tsked. "Sorry."

I blinked. "What? No. No. He was fantastic. He . . ." I floundered again.

Georgia studied me carefully.

Emerson tossed a small accent pillow at me. "*Nice* is code for *sucks*. Now tell us already!"

"Em, she doesn't want to."

Emerson looked at Georgia with a baffled expression. "Oh, come on. This was her first hookup. And he's smokin'." Her gaze swung back to me. "You can't hold out on us." Her eyes grew wide. She leaned forward, her voice dropping to a whisper. "Ohhh. Did you and he?" Her fingers did some funny little dance that ended with them interlocked.

"No!" I tossed the pillow back at her.

She caught it with a laugh. "Well, give us something then."

"Suffice it to say, a much more experienced woman sits before you."

She blew out a heavy breath. "Fine. You're not going to give us anything juicy. Can you at least tell us whether you're going to see him again, or do you feel suitably educated now?"

It was like her question triggered my need to run. I rose from my chair and moved to gather some fresh clothes. I had to be at work in an hour. "Um. Not sure." I sorted through my selection of khaki work pants, averting my eyes.

"You don't know?" A hint of concern tinged Georgia's voice. "Don't tell me he gave you the brush-off this morning. What a jerk."

I rolled my shoulders in an awkward shrug. "Ah, he might have still been sleeping when I slipped out."

"What?" Em's voice came out a squeak. "No way. He's waking to an empty bed?"

I faced my friends again, my clothes and shower caddy in hand. "Yeah." Even I detected the uncertainty in my voice.

Georgia and Emerson shared a look.

"Was that wrong?" I whispered.

"A bit harsh, Pepper." This from the girl who never spent the night with a guy—or let him spend the night.

"Why?" I looked at them searchingly, my stomach churning uneasily.

"Not even a good-bye?" Georgia asked.

"Wow," Emerson murmured. "Didn't take you for a use-'im-and-lose-'im kind of girl."

My face flushed hot. "It wasn't like that."

Georgia looked at me in sympathy. "That's what he's going to think when he wakes up."

I bit my lip, the acid stirring in my stomach boiling over. "I just didn't want to face him. And no"—my gaze shot to Emerson—"*not* because last night was bad. I was just embarrassed, I guess."

"It'll be fine. He's a guy. Probably won't think twice," Emerson assured me, and that actually annoyed me a little. I was a walking contradiction. I didn't want him to feel slighted, but I didn't like the idea that he might not care that I had vanished from his bed, either. Ugh. This was confusing as hell.

Shaking my head, I headed for the door. "I have to shower for work."

"Hey, even if he is insulted it's a nice change. Let the guy feel abused for once," Emerson called out.

"Thanks," I tossed over my shoulder, wondering what had become of me. When had I turned into a girl who shacked up with a hot bartender and then bailed on him before he woke up? It felt tawdry. Too much like the past that I was running from.

Chapter 14

IT WAS ALMOST ONE in the morning when the Campbells got home and paid me for the evening. Driving down that lonely rural road, I couldn't help thinking about Reece. Especially as I passed the spot where my car had choked and died on me. Where we first met.

My phone rang where it sat in my cup holder. A quick glance revealed it was Emerson. I answered it, keeping one hand carefully on the steering wheel. Immediately, the loud noise of music and blaring voices greeted me.

"Hello?" I said loudly.

"Are you done yet?" Her voice came back just as loudly in my ear, her tone exasperated. "You work too much, girl."

This from the girl who never had to work. I rolled my eyes. "Yeah. I'm on my way home."

"Meet us out! I'm with Suzanne."

"Nah, that's okay. I'm headed home."

"Party poop! You-know-who is here."

My chest squeezed at the singsong taunt. "It's okay. I'm tired."

"So lame! C'mon. Don't you want to go another round with him? He looks really hot . . . and you should see this skank falling all over herself to get his attention right now. You need to get up here and claim your man!"

I didn't bother explaining that he wasn't my man. Clearly Em had tossed back a few too many tonight. I doubted she would even register the words. "Is Suzanne driving you?"

"Yes, Mom. And she's dry as a whistle. Got her ID confiscated last week by a bouncer at Freemont's." She started laughing at this. I heard Suzanne in the background call her a name.

"Be good," I called. "I'm hanging up now."

Emerson started making booing sounds. Smiling, I hung up. I was still smiling as I entered the city limits. The smile started to slip as Em's words played over in my head. All I could see in my mind was Reece, serving drinks while girls fawned over him. Suddenly I wasn't driving toward home anymore.

With no clear objective in mind, I was headed toward Mulvaney's.

MULVANEY'S WAS CROWDED AS usual, but a lot of people were already leaving, spilling out the doors into the dark, cold night. I glanced at my phone, confirming that it was just thirty minutes until closing. They'd probably already announced last call. I knew it was kind of pointless arriving this late, but I was here. Out of place in my oversized university sweatshirt, jeans, and sneakers. A far cry from the girls freezing their asses off in their itty-bitty outfits.

I wore my hair back in a loose braid. My face was makeup free, but I didn't care. I wasn't here to get picked up or impress anyone. And yet I didn't pretend I was here for Emerson, either. I loved the girl, but I wasn't up for partying with her and Suzanne. I just wanted to see him. I didn't need him to see me. Actually I didn't *want* him to notice me at all. Seeing him was some kind of deep, compulsory desire that I had to feed.

I steered clear of the bar and located Emerson, smack in the middle of a group of guys. Naturally. She flung her hands in the air and squealed when she saw me. She tossed her arms around my neck and hugged me like she hadn't seen me in a week and not just this afternoon.

"You're such a sappy drunk," I muttered into her ear, uncomfortable with the attention she was drawing to me.

She pulled back and wagged a finger at me. "I'm not drunk."

I looked at Suzanne, who was clearly sober and looked annoyed over that fact. "Yeah, she's had a few."

"Okay, okay, okay, okay. Here's the deal. Here's the deal." Oh, yeah. Definitely drunk. She always repeated herself when she had too much to drink. She waved both hands in the air. "I just saw him at the bar." I winced at her volume. Even as loud as the room was, her voice rose over the din.

"Sshh." I dragged both her hands down, but she continued talking in that too-loud voice.

"I've been keeping an eye on him though. And that skank in the red top? I wanted to take care of her for you, but Warden here wouldn't let me."

I shot Suzanne a thankful look. "I think it's time we headed home."

Suzanne gave a single nod of agreement. The guys lurking close groaned in disappointment. Emerson joined in with their groans and gestured widely. "Aww. They want me to stay."

"I'm sure they do. Sorry, boys." I slid an arm around Emerson's waist.

As we moved across the main floor, I couldn't stop myself. My gaze skipped to the far right, scanning the bar. No sight of Reece. A booming voice shouted out last call, and more bodies started moving toward the back doors. We moved slowly, caught up in the sluggish current.

Emerson's voice jarred me, overly loud in my ear. "Oh! Hey! Hi there, Reece. Look, Pepper. It's Reece."

My gaze swung forward. Reece stood in front of us, looking down at me, his expression empty.

"Hello," I said dumbly.

His gaze skimmed me and I recalled the way I looked. No makeup. Messy hair. Sweatshirt stained with applesauce. Awesome.

"What are you doing here?" Not the warmest greeting. Was I banned from the bar now?

An awkward silence fell between us, which was only more noticeable because there was so much noise around us. But there we stood, saying nothing.

I shifted my feet, acutely conscious of Emerson's and Suzanne's avid gazes swinging between us like they were watching a tennis match. "I—am I not supposed to be here?" Instantly, I regretted the question. I really didn't want to hear him proclaim that I wasn't welcome here, and the decided lack of warmth in his gaze told me that's what he was about to do.

He crossed his arms over his chest, sending the feathered wing of his tattoo rippling as if caught in flight. The sleeves of his shirt pulled taut against his biceps. Something fluttered inside me as I recalled just how those biceps felt under my clenched fingers.

He looked me over again and my cheeks stung hotter, recalling that he knew exactly what I looked like beneath my less than flattering clothes. Well, at least what the top half of me looked like. "Last I remember, you were in quite a rush to get out of here." He cocked his head to the side and continued, "Or was that just my bed you were in a hurry to escape?"

I sucked in a hissing breath.

"Ohhh. Damn, Pepper!" I glared at Em. She shrugged and looked at me apologetically. "I told you that was harsh."

Did she really just out me? My gaze swung back to him. And did he really just say that?

"Hey. It's okay." He held up one hand, palm out. "I mean I knew I was being used, but I didn't realize I wasn't worth a good-bye."

Apparently finished with me, he pushed back through the crowd toward the bar.

"Your mouth is hanging open," Suzanne said beside me.

I closed it with a snap.

"Dude." Emerson stared after him. She swung her head around to look at me. I waited, thinking she was going to offer up some profound piece of advice. All I got was: "He's so hot."

I snorted. "Yeah, you've said that before."

"And you played him? Wow. I just wanted to drag you out

of your shell. I created a monster. How did you get to be such a tramp?" She covered her mouth with her fingers in an attempt to stifle a giggle.

Rolling my eyes, I tightened my arm around her waist. "You suck drunk. C'mon. Let's get you to the car."

She rested her head on my shoulder as we exited the bar. "I love you, guys," she chirped. "You're like the best people in my life. You two and Georgia."

I sent her a long look, wondering if tonight's drinking binge had something to do with the phone conversation she'd had today with her mother. I'd entered the room as she was hanging up. Emerson's complexion was usually porcelain pale. She looked like a little Irish pixie with her brilliant blue eyes, dark hair, and flawless, milky skin. But in that moment bright red flags stained her cheeks.

I didn't know what they talked about, only that Em's lips had looked tight at the corners. When I asked if she was okay, she had looked suddenly cheerful and quickly changed the subject.

Emerson fell like dead weight into the passenger seat of Suzanne's car. I looked up at Suzanne over the roof. "Can you get her home all right, Suze?"

She nodded, flipping her sleek dark hair over her shoulder. "We'll be fine."

Emerson perked up in her seat. "Where you going?"

"Just going to talk to Reece."

"Oh, talking," she said, her voice heavy with exaggeration. "Is that what they're calling it these days?"

Sighing, but with a smile, I looked back at Suzanne. "Sure you can handle her?"

"Don't worry. I'll tuck her in. And if that doesn't work I can always smother her with a pillow."

"Hear that? She wants to kill me! Don't leave me with her!"

Rolling my eyes, I shut the door on Emerson's still talking face.

I watched them pull out of the parking lot before heading back to the bar, pushing against the rolling exodus of people. I sidestepped a blonde shivering in her too-short miniskirt.

By the time I stood in the main room again, the place was almost empty, the footsteps of the remaining people thudding heavily over the plank flooring. Reece was easy to locate. He stood at the bar, talking to two other bartenders. They nodded, listening to him as he instructed them on something.

I observed this new side of him, seeing it now. Appreciating it. The authoritative edge to him had always been there, I just hadn't acknowledged it. I'd seen it but hadn't considered he might actually be in charge of the place. How did a twenty-three-year-old come to be in charge of a bar? It seemed like a big responsibility. He said it had been in his family for three generations, but where was his father? Or mother? Why weren't they operating it?

I crossed my arms. Mostly because I didn't know what else to do with them, but maybe because I also thought I could disguise my stained sweatshirt. I really should have considered my wardrobe tonight. A part of me must have known I could end up here.

I felt awkward standing there, shifting on my feet, waiting for him to see me. One of the bartenders, an older guy with a handlebar mustache, noticed me watching the three of them. He nodded in my direction. Reece turned and looked at me. Instantly, his expression hardened, the ease that had been there slipping away. And that hurt a little, knowing that I had done that.

Was it only the other night that he had kissed me and said those things that made me feel special? So not like a girl unaccustomed to kisses and hot boys with sexy grins. He made it natural . . . being with a guy. Being with him. He made me feel beautiful.

His mouth flattened into a thin line. He took a step toward me, stopping for a moment to speak to the other two bartenders before lifting up the bar top and crossing to where I stood.

"You came back."

"I'm sorry."

Whatever he expected me to say, I don't think it was this. He blinked. "Why are you apologizing?"

"I should have said good-bye. It was rude." I shrugged, uncomfortable beneath his intent gaze and decided to just go for honesty, no matter how much of a flake it made me sound. "I'm not familiar with the rules that go with hooking up. Sorry. I messed up." I gazed at him, waiting.

He continued to study me. The harshness ebbed from his expression. His mouth relaxed somewhat. He looked more baffled than anything else as he stood there looking down at me like I was some manner of strange species.

"Well. I just wanted you to know that. Good night." Turning, I walked away.

I didn't make it five steps before his hand fell on my shoulder. I turned around.

"You didn't mess up. I like that you don't know what the rules are for hooking up."

"You do?"

"Yeah. You're not—" He paused and ran a hand over his scalp, chafing his close-cut hair. My palms tingled, remembering how soft that hair felt against my palms. "You're different. I didn't like waking up and finding you gone."

I didn't move. Didn't speak as his admission sank in and made my face heat up.

"Oh," I finally managed to get out past the lump in my throat. I couldn't help wondering what could have happened if I'd stayed. If I had been there when he woke up. What would he have said? What would we have done? Would we have picked up where we left off before we fell asleep?

His hand reached out and toyed with the bottom of my sweatshirt. "I like this."

"My sweatshirt?" I laughed nervously. "I'm wearing applesauce." I motioned to the smear on my chest.

"It's a good look on you."

"Now I know you're lying."

"No." He gave my sweatshirt a small tug, inexorably pulling me toward him, bit by bit, and it was like the other night again. His presence was overwhelming, the heat that emanated from him. The blue of his eyes that seemed to turn to smoke when he looked at me. I was under his spell. Maybe I had never ceased to be. I'd been spellbound since our first kiss and especially since the night I spent in his loft. Maybe this was what had brought me back here in the middle of the night. Maybe I was hoping to repeat the experience.

"I'll never lie to you, Pepper." That soft utterance blew through me like a sonic blast. Crazy, but I heard more than his vow to be honest. The words were full of the expectation that there would be a him and me, an *us*. That we were really doing this. Whatever *this* was.

"Hey, bro! Still crashing with you tonight?" Reece's head snapped in the direction of the voice. I followed his gaze and spotted Logan carting a tub of empty glasses. His eyes brightened when he saw me. "Oh, hey. Pepper, right? How's it going?" His gaze slid between me and his brother and suddenly he looked all too pleased. "See you found the brother you were really after. Too bad for me."

Embarrassed, I mumbled a greeting and took a step back from Reece, tucking a stray hair behind my ear. His hand fell from my sweatshirt.

Reece scowled at his brother. "Yeah, after you finish busing everything to the kitchen."

"Cool. See ya, Pepper." With a wink, Logan headed for the kitchen.

"It's late." My fingers pushed at the hair that was already tucked behind my ear. "I gotta go."

"I'll walk you to your car."

"Do you walk every girl that leaves this bar to her car?"

He fell in beside me. "First off, most girls don't leave alone. They're with a group. Secondly, you're not every girl to me." He paused and my chest tightened as those words sank in like ink staining my skin. "And I think you know that."

The air rushed from my lungs. I couldn't think of a single thing to say. We stepped outside into the chilly night and started walking across the gravel lot. The closer we moved to my car, the more I thought about the last time he'd walked me to my car. Our first kiss. And then that led to thoughts of the night in his loft, which consisted of a lot more kissing. And touching. I rubbed my suddenly perspiring palms against my thighs.

At my car, I unlocked the door. With a smile that felt strange and too tight on my face I faced him. "Thanks."

He examined me for a long moment beneath the parking lot lights.

"So you just came here to apologize to me, Pepper? That's all?"

I swallowed. "Yes?"

Why did the word come out like a question? And why did he look at me like he didn't believe me?

"I thought you might have wanted to continue where we left off." He slid his hand into his pocket and rocked back on his heels. "Pick up a few more tips maybe."

There it was. The elephant in the room. No pretending it wasn't there anymore.

"I think what we did was—" I stopped short of saying "enough." Because did I really want it to be? Why not stretch this out a little longer? I'd only get better at the kissing and all the other stuff, right? Foreplay. That's what I was after. Besides, it was weeks until Thanksgiving break and uninterrupted Hunter time. Even as a voice whispered through my head that this could get complicated, I ignored it. I wanted more. Plain and simple.

"Well, what's left to learn?" I asked, mostly because I didn't want to appear like an overeager puppy desperate for a treat. Even if I was.

He laughed then. The sound was low and deep and swirled through my belly like hot cider.

Fending off the delicious effect of his laughter on me, I demanded, "What?"

"Oh, there's plenty left to learn. That question alone shows just how much you still don't know." He fell silent and considered me again. "I guess the question remaining is how far are you willing to go short of sleeping with me?" His mouth curved in a slow smile. "You're still not up for that, right?"

I blinked. "No. I c-can't. Not that."

He chuckled softly. "Don't look so scared. Just checking."

My face felt like it was on fire. I shifted on my feet and dug the tip of my car key into the fleshy pad of my thumb. I moved my gaze to somewhere over his shoulder, staring blindly into the deep night. It was too mortifying. I couldn't look him in the eyes as we discussed whether or not I wanted more lessons in foreplay from him and just how far I was willing to go.

Rather than answer him directly, I asked, "Isn't your brother staying with you tonight?"

Yes, I wanted more. Yes, I was willing to go farther, but it didn't seem like it would happen tonight.

"Yeah. He is. Guess our timing is off."

I nodded, moistening my lips as I moved my gaze to his chest, to the curvy script that spelled out MULVANEY's on his shirt. Easier than gazing into those brilliant eyes that seemed to have the power to hypnotize me.

Gravel crunched as he stepped closer. A hand dropped to my car door, partially caging me in. I followed the long stretch of his arm, scanning the inked-up skin until I was staring into his eyes again.

"Unless," he began, "you're inviting me back to your place."

Holy hell. He wants to come home with me?

"You want to go to my dorm room?"

"Unless you have a roommate." His lips quirked in that sexy half-grin. "That might make things awkward."

"Um, I actually don't. I have suitemates. I'm in the single. I have the room to myself."

My words hung between us. The air crackled, alive with tension and something indefinable. And yet I recognized it. It happened around him a lot, buzzing over my skin like an electrical charge.

"That's convenient," he murmured.

I moistened my lips. It felt as though we had been staring at each other forever. Another second and I might splinter from all the tension.

"So." He arched an eyebrow. "Are you inviting me?"

"Oh." A short, nervous laugh burst from my lips. "Yes. Yeah. I guess I am."

He smiled then, and I melted right there. I gripped the edge of my door to stop my knees from buckling.

He leaned forward, that one arm still close, partially caging me. "Okay. I'll follow you."

"Okay," I repeated, grinning like a fool.

He lowered his arm from my car and walked backward, still looking at me as he moved. "Wait here. I'll bring my Jeep around."

"Okay," I said again, wishing I could come up with something better to say. Something clever and flirty.

I released a shaky breath as he turned and jogged away.

Chapter 15

DROPPING INTO THE DRIVER'S seat, I waited, watching his tall frame disappear in my rearview mirror. My fingers tapped the steering wheel anxiously. Giving my head a fierce shake, I released a little shriek inside the safety of my car, getting it out of my system. Lifting my hands, I pressed them against my flushed face.

Yanking down the visor, I stared into my eyes, the green brighter than usual, and addressed myself firmly, "All right. Pull yourself together, Pepper. You're a big girl. You asked for this. You're not doing anything hundreds, thousands of women aren't doing tonight." I was probably doing less considering I wasn't even having sex. "No. Big. Deal." Even as I spoke the words, I continued to shake in my seat.

The lights of Reece's Jeep soon flashed behind me and I put the car into reverse and backed out.

He followed me out of the lot and down the strip. I cut through campus, driving between the familiar red brick buildings lining Butler, past the quiet quad with its grassy lawns and empty benches. I managed not to total my car, which was somewhat miraculous considering I couldn't stop glancing in the rearview mirror to watch the dark shadow of Reece inside his vehicle.

We found two spots near each other in the parking lot. Taking a deep breath, I gathered my backpack from the passenger seat and climbed out, grateful that I'd at least gotten all my studying done at the Campbells'. Reece was already waiting for me, looking relaxed and at ease with a hand buried halfway in his pocket.

"Are you all right leaving the bar?" it occurred me to ask.

"I called my brother. He can close up."

"Oh. Good."

He fell into step beside me as we headed toward the dorm. I glanced at his bare arms. "Are you cold?"

"I'm fine."

"It's a short walk," I volunteered unnecessarily. "We're almost to the door." Apparently nervousness made me spew gibberish.

I swiped my card and entered the dormitory. At the elevator, I pushed the UP button and sent Reece a small smile as we both stood in awkward silence. I tried to appear more confident than I felt. Fat chance. He knew what I was. What I wasn't. I trained my gaze on the descending floor numbers, watching each one light up. *Seven. Six.* He knew what I didn't know. *Five.* What I needed to learn. *Four. Three.* Everything. *Two.*

I quit my study of the flashing numbers as two girls spilled noisily into the building. They clearly had a few drinks in them from the way they hung on each other.

I didn't know them, but they looked familiar. But then so did everyone else who lived in the building. I was sure we had passed each other in the halls or shared an elevator before. The blond one had maybe even loaned me a quarter in the laundry room.

Their giggles and shrill voices died when they saw me standing there with Reece. They exchanged wide-eyed looks and compressed their lips as though it was killing them to hold silent. The doors slid open with a *ding* and muffled *whoosh*. Reece waited for all three of us to step in ahead of him and I swear they tittered like thirteen-year-old girls.

Rolling my eyes, I pushed for the fifth floor, wishing we had just taken the stairs. It was habit that I avoided the stairwell this late at night. It was too dark and smelled like sweaty socks on a good day. Plus, I just didn't like the sense of isolation in the stairwell. Like I was inside a tomb. Small spaces and I never got on well. Too much of my childhood spent in closets and bathrooms.

When the girls got off on the third floor, they didn't wait for the doors to close before they started whispering indis- creetly and looking back at us.

"God," I muttered. "It's like high school. Some things never change."

"Some things do." He slid me a long glance as we stepped off at my floor. "I didn't spend the night with too many girls in high school."

I arched an eyebrow. "No?"

He grinned. "No. That came later."

"I bet." I unlocked my door and moved into the pitch-black

of my room, my steps automatic, moving from memory. I flipped on the lamp at my desk and dropped my bag onto the chair. The room's adjoining door was ajar, as usual. I peeked inside the murky space. Emerson's shape was visible beneath the covers of her bed. I could even detect her soft snores. I closed the door between our rooms (probably a first) and turned the lock.

Whenever Georgia wanted to be alone with Harris, they hung out at his place. She even spent the night there on occasion. I couldn't help smiling at the thought of Emerson waking up to a closed door. She wouldn't know what to think.

I faced Reece, smoothing my hands over my thighs, the soft denim somehow normalizing me. Lifting my chin, I braced myself for his first move.

Only he wasn't even looking at me. He was studying my room, turning slowly, his gaze exploring my private sanctum like he was viewing something interesting. My bedspread with its overly large purple flowers. A poster of Mickey Mouse's ears, just the shadow of them set against a star-speckled night. He took it all in, and so did I—seeing it through the eyes of a stranger. His eyes. My gaze skimmed the bed, the poster, the stuffed Pluto resting against my pillow that had seen me through so many years. It was a poor substitute for Purple Bear, but it was the first gift Gram had bought me so I treasured it. It was a little girl's room, I realized. Or at least it would appear that way to him.

I searched for something good about it. Everything was tidy and organized. Textbooks neatly piled on my desk beside my laptop. No clutter. I hated having a bunch of stuff I would only have to cram into my car at the end of the year and then find a place to store while back home at Gram's for the summer.

He stepped up to my desk. Three pictures sat there. One of me and my dad blowing out the candles on my first birthday cake. I'm on his lap. There are a bunch of bodies pressed behind us, none of their faces visible in the shot, and I always liked that. Liked not knowing which one was Mom. If one of them even was. The photograph was of just me and Dad. The way it would have been if some land mine hadn't taken him from me and left me with her instead.

Even though it was my birthday cake, Dad was the one blowing out the candles. Probably because I wouldn't. Instead, I watched him with this wide-eyed, bewildered look on my little round face. Like he was performing the most amazing feat I had ever seen in my short life.

The second photograph was of me and Gram at my high school graduation. Tucked into the edge of that frame was a strip of four photo booth snapshots of me, Emerson, and Georgia taken at the mall last spring. It was on the same day we had decided to sign up for a suite together. We were making the requisite crazy faces. In every pose Em looked like she was making love to the camera. Like Porn Goddess was the only expression she could make.

The last picture was me with Lila and Hunter at their family's annual Fourth of July barbecue last summer. His girlfriend had been lurking somewhere nearby, but the photo had been snapped when it was just the three of us. Reece's hand went unerringly to this photo and picked it up off the desk. "Is this him?"

"Who?"

"The guy." He looked at me and then back at the photograph, his expression thoughtful.

I blinked, startled that he would guess so accurately, and uncomfortable talking about Hunter with him. At least in any detail. It was enough that he knew I was doing this to attract someone else. Did I have to share everything with him?

He must have taken my silence for confusion. Or he'd become impatient. Either way, he tapped the glass over Hunter's face. "He's the one you're doing this for. Right?" He waved the frame between us.

I gave something between a nod and a shake of the head. "How did you know?"

"You have only these photos here. I'm guessing these are the most important people in your life." I glanced at the frozen faces of my father, Gram, Emerson, Georgia, Lila, and Hunter. He was right. These people were everyone to me.

"And," he continued, "you're glowing here." He looked back down at me with Lila and Hunter.

I moved forward and took the frame from him and set it back on the desk. "I was a little sunburned that day. That's all." I don't know why his words embarrassed me or why I felt the need to deflect them, but I did.

Moving forward had placed me closer to him. Only an inch separated us. I held my ground though, determined not to step back like proximity to him scared me. That would be silly considering I had invited him back here for one reason alone. Playing coy now would just be ridiculous.

Lifting my chin, I smiled, hoping it passed for a come-hither look. I wanted him to kiss me. Touch me. That would be easier than all this talking.

But instead of getting on with it, he moved his attention to the picture of me and Dad. "This is your father?"

I sighed. "Yes."

"You're cute. Your hair was really red then."

"What little I had, yeah."

His gaze trailed over my hair. "You have plenty of it now." His attention returned to the photo. "Guess you didn't get the red hair from him though."

I frowned. Unwelcome memories nipped at the edges of my thoughts. Why was he asking so many questions? That's not why I brought him here. We both knew what he was here for.

I took the picture from him and set it back down. Turning, I moved to the bed and sank down on it, propping my hands on the mattress behind me. Crossing my ankles out in front of me, I answered him. "No. That would be from my mother. She had the red hair."

Hopefully the "had" would put him off from asking more about her. There was a reason a photo of her did not grace my desk. There was a reason she wasn't included among those people that were most important to me. He was smart enough to figure that out. Without saying anything more about her, he should be able to understand this much about me. With that small bit of information, I'd told him more than even Emerson and Georgia knew.

"My father is dead," I suddenly volunteered. I'm not sure why. I didn't have to. He wasn't prying about Dad right then. It was probably to distract him from the subject of my mother.

It was less painful to talk about my father getting blown up in Afghanistan. Sad but true. Neither qualified as makeout conversation, but one was the milder poison at least. I would rather him look at me like a poor little orphan than the way he would look at me if he knew the truth about my mother.

"Sorry to hear that. So it was just you and your mom?" He wasn't going to let it go about her apparently.

I stared at him, certain my frustration was visible. My feet twitched out in front of me. "My mom is gone, too." Not exactly the truth but not a lie, either. "My grandmother raised me."

Now the pity was there. A definite softness entered his eyes as he gazed down at me. But at least it was the orphan type pity and not the other kind. The other kind was so much worse. This I could deal with. The other pity did something to me, made me feel like I was ruined and past saving.

"Let's talk about something else," I suggested, wondering what it would take to get him to stop talking altogether and make the first move. Maybe I needed to make the first move. Assuming I could suck up the nerve to do that.

"Yeah." He ran a hand over his close-cropped hair. "Guess this conversation is a bit of a buzz kill."

Right up there with butchered bunnies and starving children. "Yeah. I was thinking that."

Smiling in an I-know-I'm-a-sex-god manner, he approached me with his loose, unhurried stride. Like some sort of jungle cat. Deceptively relaxed, when I knew he could spring into action at any moment.

Watching him, my cheeks warmed. I had felt those muscles, their flex and power against my hands. I had even seen him tear apart that guy outside the bathrooms at Mulvaney's without breaking a sweat.

He stopped in front of me. My crossed feet jutted out between his legs. He took my hand, the slightly rough pads of his fingers curling into my palm.

"Tell me about the guy in the photo. That should put you in the right mood."

I gulped. Was he kidding? I only needed to look at him to get in the right mood. The intimacy of his hand around mine was more than enough.

"Hunter? We've known each other forever."

He scooted my legs apart and knelt between my thighs. His hands closed around my knees. I watched him, breathless. Shaking from the inside out. His grip seared me through the denim.

He arched an eyebrow. "I'm listening. His name is Hunter."

I sipped air past my lips. "His sister, Lila, is my best friend."

He continued. Watching me, his hands skimmed over the tops of my thighs and slipped beneath my sweatshirt to settle on the waistband of my jeans. "Go on."

"They always made me feel like a part of their family. I think I spent more time at the Montgomery house than my own. They're this really great family. Barbecues. Family trips to Disney, you know? That kind of thing."

Those warm hands of his kept moving, inching up under my sweatshirt to graze over my belly. His thumb dipped to flick open the snap of my jeans. His attention trained there. I froze, swallowing down my words.

He glanced up at me. "Uh-huh. Keep talking."

Sucking in a breath, I continued. "I've never even been to

Disney World. They still go as a family. Like every year." *God.*
I was just babbling now. Was I actually talking about Disney
World?

He lifted my sweatshirt, pulling it over my head in one
swift move. It hit the floor.

I sat in my bra in front of him. I glanced down, verifying
the color. White with a little yellow bow nestled between my
breasts.

I shivered. Sure, I had been practically naked with him
before, but this felt different. Maybe because we were here, in
my room. Or maybe because I was just still so new at this. Still
so in awe of him that I couldn't stop myself from quaking like
the big virgin that I was. Or maybe it was the way he was looking at me. Like I was the last female on earth.

"You were saying? Disney?"

"They go there together. The Montgomerys. They're good
people." My voice didn't even sound like mine. It was more like
a strangled croak. "Hunter is a good person. He wants to be a
doctor."

He flattened his palm just below my bra, his fingers splay-
ing wide, almost covering my stomach completely, fingertips
brushing my ribs. "Sounds like a saint." He cocked his head,
assessing, staring at me, consuming me with his eyes.

All I could think was: *I hope not.* A saint would never look
at me the way Reece was right now, and I wanted that. *Needed*
that. His other hand slid around to palm my back. He traced
my spine, caressing each and every bump of vertebrae. He
made me feel feminine, small, and delicate. Like something to
be worshipped.

Suddenly he shifted both hands to grip my torso. I was air-borne for the barest moment as he launched me back on the bed. I landed on my back with a small yelp. Thank God he didn't want me to keep talking about Hunter. I couldn't speak coherently. Not anymore. Not even five minutes ago.

Rising, he unlaced my shoes and tugged them off. Each one hit the floor with a thud.

He eased down, coming over me, propping his elbows on either side of my head.

His face was so close. I felt his square jaw, reveling in the scratch and bristle. He held himself still and I let myself continue to explore his face, tracing the arch of his eyebrows, down over the bridge of his nose, the well-carved lips.

They moved against my fingers as he spoke. "As long as you look at him like that he'll be yours."

I pulled my hand back slightly. "How am I looking at you?"

He settled himself deeper between my thighs. One hand slipped between my back and the mattress. With one flick, he unhooked my bra and tugged it free. "Like you want to eat me."

"Oh."

His head lowered. I shuddered as he pressed one kiss to the tip of my breast. *Ohhh.* Then the next. I ran my fingers over his head. His mouth closed over my nipple, pulling me into the wet warmth of his mouth. I gasped and surged against him.

I clawed at his shirt, twisting the fabric, wanting to feel him, skin to my skin.

He sat up, reached behind him and pulled it over his head, and then came back down over me. This time we were chest to chest. His hardness to my softness. His mouth met mine hungrily. It wasn't sweet or gentle or easy. He kissed me deep and hard. I kissed him back, running my tongue along his, licking at his teeth.

He bit my lip, tugging it between his teeth. I moaned, lifting up for him. He evaded me and I growled, chasing his mouth until he let me have it again with a satisfying collision of lips and tongue. My hands swept over his shoulders, gliding down his smooth back. The flesh rippled and undulated under my hands.

He pulled back and stared down at me, his blue eyes so deep and penetrating they glowed almost silver. His breath crashed on the air as his gaze roamed me.

"Reece," I whispered and my voice sounded almost like a plea.

"I want to see you. All of you."

"I—" My voice broke, unsure.

"You can trust me."

I nodded, believing that. He wasn't the problem. The issue was me. My fear.

He moved quickly, sliding down the length of me. His hands went to the waist of my jeans, fingers working expertly. The zipper sang briefly. He slid my jeans off with ease. He did it better than I could have. Like he stripped jeans off girls all the time.

"Now these are hot."

I glanced down and winced at the white cotton panties with tiny yellow kittens on them. Not exactly sex goddess material.

A sound strangled in my throat, part laugh, part groan. "I really need to shop for some sexier lingerie."

"Nuh-uh. These are hot. And I promise they make an impression." He pressed a slow, savoring, open-mouthed kiss right above the edge of my panties, below my belly button. My nerves sparked and jumped like they were shot with electricity. His hand drifted lower, palming me between my legs, and I was panting now. Embarrassing little whimpers that I couldn't stop.

"Pepper, let me touch you." The rough catch in his voice was probably the sexiest thing I ever heard. He could have asked me anything right then—with that voice, with his hand between my legs—and I would have agreed.

I nodded, hair flying around me. His hand was inside my panties before I even blinked.

His fingers slicked through me, parting me. He made an almost animal growl as he eased a finger inside me.

I sat up, arching off the bed with a sharp cry. Shudders racked me. He pushed at that spot, the one he'd found before, with the base of his palm.

"So wet." I barely heard his whisper as I held tightly onto his hard shoulders. He buried his mouth against the crook of my neck and pressed a kiss there as he pulled out and buried his finger back inside me again. Deeper. More intimate, stretching me. I cried out, clenching around him with muscles I never knew I possessed. My arms wrapped around his shoulders, clinging to him like a buoy at sea as ripples eddied over me.

We stayed like that for an endless moment. An immense lethargy stole over me. His hands slipped from my panties and he pulled me against his side, holding me. As sated as I felt, I was alert and awake, not yet willing to fall asleep.

I cuddled closer to him, glad for this moment where it was okay to touch him, to let him touch me. It wouldn't be like this tomorrow. Maybe ever again.

I took the opportunity to ask what had been nagging at me ever since I learned he was running Mulvaney's on his own. "Is it just you and Logan?"

Silence met my question and I darted a look up at his face. He stared down at me, considering me.

"Logan is still in high school, right?"

"Yeah. He's a senior. He only picks up a shift here and there. He plays baseball. Hoping he can get a scholarship."

So Logan must live out in the house near the Campbells' place. With their parents. I pictured it. Some quaint old farmhouse like the Campbells owned. With a pond. And ducks. Maybe his mother wore an apron as she fed them leftover toast. An idyllic family scenario. I knew I was romanticizing his life. Okay, him. I just couldn't stop myself. I always did that when I met people. Imagined their perfect lives. Normal lives.

"It's just you living above the bar then?"

"Yeah." His hands traced a delicious pattern on my arm.

"What about your parents? They don't mind?"

"My mother passed away when I was eight."

"Oh. I'm sorry." I moistened my lips. "And your dad?"

"He's in a wheelchair. Going on two years now."

"God, I'm so sorry. That must be hard." So that was why he was running the bar all on his own? His dad no longer could. I wanted to pry more information out of him, but he looked so hard all of a sudden. So unapproachable. Apparently I had touched on a subject he didn't like talking about. I could understand that. I had my own ghosts that I kept firmly behind closed doors.

Still, I wanted to say something. Offer him some comfort. I sat up on an elbow to stare down at him, hugging the blanket to my chest as I smoothed a hand over his chest in a small circular motion.

"Don't look at me like I'm something noble," he said quietly, frowning, his blue eyes suddenly like frost. "I'm the one that put him there."

This time I felt my mouth fall open. Heard my gasp. My hand froze on his chest.

"That's right. Now you know what kind of guy I am. I work the bar because my old man can't. Because it's his legacy and it's the least I can do for him after crippling him." He made a sound in the back of his throat. Part growl, part snort of . . . something. Disgust maybe? With me or himself, I wasn't sure.

I shook my head. "I—"

"You shouldn't be wasting your time on me." He rose abruptly and grabbed his discarded shirt. Shrugging it over his head, he continued in a hard voice, "This was fun, but I think you've had enough foreplay lessons, don't you? You're more than ready for your Polo-wearing frat boy."

I watched him, his lean body leaving the circle of light cast by my lamp until he fell into shadow near my door. Part of me wanted to call him back and assure him that he was wrong. But wrong about what? That I wasn't wasting my time with him? That tonight wasn't somehow enough? That he actually couldn't have done what he said and harmed his father? I knew next to nothing about him. I couldn't say any of that.

I let my instincts kick in. The same instincts that helped me survive after my father died, when it was just me and Mom. I watched him exit my room and close the door behind him. Clutching the blanket close to me, I got up and locked it.

Chapter 16

"WAIT. HE SAID HE put his father in a wheelchair?" Georgia demanded over a stack of pancakes at our favorite waffle house a few blocks from campus. Her fork cut into a link of sausage and then swirled it in syrup. She pulled the glistening meat off her fork with a snap of teeth and chewed, staring at me as though concentrating on something complicated.

Emerson shuddered and sipped her coffee, carefully adjusting her leopard print sunglasses on the bridge of her nose and angling her face away from the window to the right of her. A barely touched bowl of oatmeal sat before her, which I made her order, insisting she would feel better with some food in her stomach. "How can you eat all that?"

"I can eat like this because I run five days a week and I don't get piss drunk," Georgia replied, cutting a perfect, bite-sized triangle out of her pancake stack. "Now. Back to the bartender. Did you ask him what he meant by that?"

I toyed with my hash browns, stabbing at them. "No. He was in a hurry to leave after that admission, and to be honest, I was kind of in a hurry for him to go, too."

"No joke." Emerson sighed. "The hot ones are always sociopaths."

"Really?" I looked at her across from me in the booth. "Always?" I glanced at Georgia for help. *"Always?"*

Em cringed, touching her forehead. "You're too loud. And if not sociopaths, they're at least damaged."

"Now you tell me that. If that's the case, why were you in such a hurry to hook me up with the hottest guy you could find then?"

"Did you want to hook up with someone homely with no skills in the bedroom? I thought the point was to get you some experience."

"Ignore her." Georgia batted a hand in the air. "She's moody because she's hungover. Hunter is hot and *not* damaged. The same can be said for my boyfriend."

Emerson muttered something into her coffee mug that sounded suspiciously like "Are you sure about that?"

Georgia shot her a look. "Funny."

"I'm just saying you never know what's really inside anyone."

"Well, that's a cheerful thought." Georgia shook her head and reached for her juice. "Listen, I doubt he meant it like that. Maybe his father injured himself on the job, working long hours to support the family and Reece blames himself. You know, something like that. The guy obviously didn't *hurt* his own father or he'd be in jail. And if he was that malicious, why would he feel obligated to run his father's business?"

"Maybe he wanted the business for himself all along," Emerson supplied.

"Gosh, you're full of optimism this morning," Georgia snapped.

"Sorry, I just don't want Pepper hurt, and he's starting to sound like someone capable of doing that."

Georgia took a sip of her juice and seemed to consider this. As did I. We made out twice, and each time he made me come without any expectations for himself. He could have hurt me plenty of times.

Georgia swirled more sausage in her syrup. "I just think she needs to find out what he meant."

"Yeah," I murmured. In the light of day, my flight instinct had diminished. Now curiosity had hold of me. What really happened to Reece's father? A guy who stopped to help a girl stranded on the side of the road wasn't the type who would put someone in a wheelchair. Especially not his own father. "I want to know."

Emerson muttered something into her mug again.

"What?" I demanded.

She leveled her blue eyes at me over the rim. "You know what they say. Curiosity killed the cat."

EVEN THOUGH I HAD decided to see Reece again and get to the bottom of his confession, it took me several days to get around to it. Partly because of my wavering resolve and partly because I was busy. Between writing a paper for World Lit, studying for my Abnormal Psych exam, and working two shifts at Little Miss Muffet's, I hardly had time to sleep.

It was probably for the best anyway. I needed a little space to remember why I began this whole thing with Reece. It was purely curiosity that refused to let me put him behind me for good. At least this was what I told myself after I turned in my paper and found a parking space in the parking lot at Mulvaney's. Upon entering the bar, the tantalizing aroma of chicken wings assailed me. Apparently it was ten-cent wing night. The place was full of stocky rugby guys. A few girls sat at tables loaded with baskets of wings. They, too, looked like they might belong on the men's rugby team.

I stepped into the open space of the main room, and it was like the last time I stood there all over again, when everyone had funneled outside after last call and the space felt wide and cavernous. There was no sign of Reece at the bar, but I recognized the older bartender with the handlebar mustache. He recognized me, too, apparently. He waved at me. "Hey, Red, what can I do for you?"

"Is Reece around?"

"Not today. He's sick."

"Sick?"

"Yeah. Called me in this morning. Asked if I could cover for him." He shrugged a bone-thin shoulder. "I said why not? Tuesdays are slow." He motioned to a basket full of chicken bones at his elbow. "I can get all the wings I want and watch TV here just as well as at home." He nodded to the television positioned high in the corner above the bar. Without the usual din, I could actually hear it.

"What's wrong with him?"

"Didn't say. Just sounded like death warmed over. Hope I don't catch it." His eyes glinted at me with a knowing light.

"Hope you don't, either." He winked and it was enough to know he thought Reece and I were more than friends. He assumed we were the type of friends that might share a few things. Including a virus.

With overly warm cheeks, I waved good-bye. "Thanks."

I headed back the way I entered, hesitating near the food counter. A few guys stood in line. The same girl who'd watched me and Reece go into his room the other weekend took orders. I hovered there for a moment, staring back into the kitchen as if I could somehow see up into his room.

Oh, what the hell?

I moved, unlatching the half door that led into the kitchen. The girl behind the counter started for a second and looked at me, a protest forming on her lips. When her gaze focused on my face, she hesitated, clearly recognizing me.

"Hey." I sent her an easy nod, acting, hopefully, like I had every right to waltz through the kitchen.

"Uh, hey," she said back, still looking uncertain. I felt her stare on my back as I strode deep into the bowels of the kitchen, where the sound of food frying in hot grease filled the air. None of the cooks paid me any attention.

Hoping the door was unlocked, I tried the handle, releasing a breath of relief when it opened. Closing it behind me, muffling out the sounds of the kitchen, I climbed the stairs. At the top, I slowed and called out.

"Who's there?"

"Pepper."

A groan met my response. Not the most heartfelt welcome. Ignoring that fact, I stepped onto the top floor.

The sight of the bed, the sheets all rumpled around him, hit me like déjà vu. It was so much like my last glimpse of him the night I'd snuck away. Especially considering the amount of his bare skin visible. A quick glance revealed that he wore a pair of athletic shorts. Grateful for that, I inched toward the bed.

"I heard you were sick."

"Dying, to be more specific," he croaked, his arm flung over his face, hiding all but his lips. Lips that looked ashen and leached of color. "Go away."

"What's wrong? Besides the fact that you're dying?"

"Let's just say that the toilet and I are suddenly on a first name basis."

"How often are you throwing up?"

"I don't know . . . think it's slowed down."

Without replying, I moved to his fridge and peered inside. Pulling out a liter of Gatorade, I poured him half a glass and dropped two ice cubes inside.

Walking back to the bed, I lowered myself to the edge beside him.

He peered out at me beneath one arm. His eyes were red-rimmed, the whites of his eyes bloodshot. His blue irises stood out in stark relief. "I said go away."

"Here. Try a sip. You don't want to get dehydrated." I held the cup to his lips.

He shook his head and pushed it away. "I can't keep anything down."

"Maybe you have food poisoning."

"I ate the same thing as someone else last night. She's not sick."

She. I don't know why, but this single word jarred me and twisted my stomach into knots. Which was just wrong. I had no claim on him. I *wanted* no claim on him.

I set the glass on the nightstand and touched his forehead, wincing at the burn of his skin. "You have a fever, too."

"You shouldn't be here." This time his voice had decidedly less bite to it. "You'll get sick, too."

I shook my head. "I never get sick. Second year working at a daycare. I have an iron constitution."

"Must be nice." His eyelids drifted closed.

I frowned at him. I had to work in a few hours, but it didn't feel right leaving him like this.

"Do you have a thermometer? Have you checked your temperature?"

He cracked open his eyes. "I'm fine. I'll be fine. You can go. I don't need anyone to take care of me. Been doing it for years." His eyes drifted closed over those brilliant blue eyes.

I sat there for a moment, staring at him. His chest eased into slow and even breaths and I knew he was sleeping again. I brushed a hand over his forehead. He still felt too hot. I wasn't totally unaccustomed to caring for sick people. I'd lived with Gram for years, after all. I'd seen what could happen when people didn't get medical care in time. Yes, he was young and strong, but one never knew.

Rising, I crept out of the loft and exited back through the kitchen again.

Five minutes later I was at the drugstore around the corner. Grabbing a hand basket, I filled it with a thermometer, Pedia-lyte, Sprite, and more Gatorade. I tossed in Tylenol in the hopes that he could keep some of that down, too, and then added sal-tines, Jell-O, and a couple of cans of chicken noodle soup for when he was feeling a little better. An employee helped me find those little frozen head packs. If he couldn't keep the Tylenol down, I could press that onto his forehead.

Ten minutes later, I was walking back into Mulvaney's. I gave a quick nod to the cashier. A smile touched her lips as she scanned the bags in my arms.

When I reentered the loft, it was to find the bed empty. Then I heard him in the bathroom.

"You okay?" I called out.

Several moments passed before he surfaced, wiping his mouth with a small hand towel. "Gatorade not such a good idea."

I winced. "Sorry."

His bloodshot eyes scanned me standing there with white plastic bags dangling from my fingers.

He flung the towel back into the bathroom with a sharp move. My gaze drank in the flex of sinew and muscles in his arm and torso. Even sick, he looked strong and powerful and sexy as hell. I blinked hard, shoving the totally inappropriate observation away. Now was not the time. And really, after his admission the other day, I wasn't sure there would ever be a time for those kinds of observations anymore.

He took several dragging steps toward the bed. "You came back." Not a question.

"Yeah."

"And you went shopping."

"Yeah. Just got you some things you might need."

I moved into the kitchen area and put the cold things away,

sticking the two little ice packs for his head into the freezer. Tearing open the thermometer's package, I read the instructions and then approached him.

He watched me through slit eyes, eyeing the device like it might bite him. Or maybe that was just me in general. "You bought a thermometer?"

"Yeah." Sitting on the edge of the bed, I held the button down and glided the roller along his forehead. Pulling my hand back, I read, "A hundred and two point four. We should get some Tylenol in you."

He motioned to his now empty cup. "I can't keep anything down yet."

I nodded. "Okay." Rising, I fetched a washcloth from the bathroom and ran it under cold water. It would do until the ice packs were chilled enough. Sitting on the bed again, I positioned the cloth on his forehead. Moving away, I gasped when he grabbed hold of my wrist. Even sick, his grip was strong.

His blue eyes drilled into me. "Why are you doing this?"

I shrugged uncomfortably. "I don't know."

He shook his head once like that wasn't good enough. "Why are you here?"

His fingers shifted, the tips sending hot little sparks up my arm. He should look ridiculous with the blue washcloth covering half his face, but he didn't. He looked human and male and all too vulnerable right then.

"Because you need someone."

It was the simple truth, but the words hung between us, and I realized they sounded like so much more than I intended them to be. His fingers slid from my wrist, and he expelled a heavy breath—like he suddenly remembered that he was sick and couldn't deal with this—with me—right now. His eyes drifted shut again. Almost instantly, he was asleep.

"YEAH, SORRY TO GIVE such short notice, but I can't leave her alone. She's too sick." I paused and listened as Beckie commiserated and assured me it was okay. "Thanks for understanding. I'll see you Saturday."

I hung up the phone on my manager, feeling a little bad about waiting until the last minute to make the call, but it had taken me the better part of two hours to decide that I couldn't leave Reece alone. Or I wouldn't. Either way, I had resigned myself to the role of nurse, even though he hadn't asked it of me. Even though he didn't *want* it of me.

"I'm guessing I'm the 'she' you were talking about?"

I swung around to meet Reece's gaze head-on. "You're awake."

He pressed down on the mattress and lifted himself up on the bed, propping his back against the pillows bunched up at the headboard. "How long was I asleep?"

"Almost two hours."

He sighed and scrubbed a hand over his face. "And I didn't get sick. That's good. Maybe I can try that drink now." He glanced to his left and, seeing that the empty glass was gone (I had since washed it), swung his legs over the side.

"No. Don't get up." I hurried into the kitchen, poured him a small glass of Gatorade, and shook out two caplets of Tylenol.

When I returned he took the pills from me and set them

on his tongue, chasing them with a cautious sip. "Thanks." He set the glass down on the nightstand. "You really don't have to miss work for me."

"Too late. Besides"—I motioned to his kitchen table where my books were spread out—"I got some studying done." I had retrieved my backpack from my car after he fell asleep.

Nodding, he eased up onto his feet, instantly towering over me.

I held out a hand as though to steady him, even though all that bare inked skin made my pulse jump a little, made me remember the other night. Both nights. Here and in my dorm. They seemed more like a dream now than real. My body tangled up with his—all lean lines, hard angles, and curving muscles. His hands touching me in places no one had before. My gaze skimmed over his body. And there was that dangerous edge to him with half his torso inked up. Like he belonged in a prison yard lifting weights with other convicts. Not with me.

I lowered my hand from where it hovered over his bicep and moistened my dry lips. "What are you doing? You should stay in bed." On your back. Weak and sick and far less intimidating.

His mouth lifted into a half-grin. "I'm going to take a shower. I'll be okay, Mom."

I blushed. I did tend to be motherly. Emerson and Georgia always said so. Ironic considering I never had that kind of mother. But when you grew up in a community where people, including your own guardian, were often sick, it went with the territory.

I watched as he moved toward the bathroom, the light play of muscles beneath the golden skin of his back mesmerizing me. His strides were much less swift and sure than normal. At the bathroom door, he paused and looked back over his shoulder. "You can stay. If you want to." He glanced back at the table where all my books were spread out. "Study here."

I nodded, my heart doing a crazy little flip. He turned back around and closed himself in the bathroom. The sound of the shower soon hummed through the door.

My heart still felt foolishly light as I found fresh sheets in a chest near the bed. Stripping off his old sheets and replacing them with his new ones, I was plumping his pillows when he emerged from the shower ten minutes later. He paused, scrubbing a towel over his head. "You changed my sheets?"

I rose to face him and had to fight a smile. He looked almost confused.

"You were sick . . . thought you might like fresh sheets."

He stared at me solemnly. Like he was trying to figure me out. My smile faded. Because that would never happen. I could never let it happen. God, first I'd have to figure myself out, and that was a constant struggle.

Just when I thought I knew what I wanted in life and who I was, I'd get a call from Gram depressed about Daddy. She'd talk about how everything went to hell when he married my mother. How he should have married Frankie Mazzerelli, his high school sweetheart, who was now married to a pharmacist and had four kids. And if it wasn't Gram, I'd have one of my nightmares, and it would be like I was ten all over again, hiding in the shadows and praying for an invisibility cloak. That had been my fantasy. Other little girls dream of castles. I dreamed for invisibility.

I didn't know anything then, and I was still trying to figure myself out. So far I'd changed my major three times, finally settling on psychology. Like becoming a therapist and helping others with their problems might somehow help me work my way through mine.

There was only one irrefutable truth in my life. Only one thing I knew. Hunter was good. Hunter was normal. And I wanted that. Correction: *Him*. I wanted him. That I knew. That was the plan.

"Thanks," he said. "For doing this. Being here."

"Want to try and eat something?" I moved into the kitchen. "I got chicken noodle soup. Jell-O. Crackers."

"I might be ready for a little Jell-O."

I removed one of the small cups from the fridge and handed it to him. He opened a drawer and selected a spoon. Leaning against the counter, he studied me. "Did you eat already?"

"I grabbed a late lunch and snacked on some crackers while you slept. I'm fine."

He peeled the foil lid off the cup. "They could make you something downstairs. It's wing night."

"That's okay."

He spooned a small bite of strawberry Jell-O into his mouth. The muscles in his jaw feathered as he moved it around, savoring it slowly.

"I didn't think I'd see you again. Why'd you come?" he asked as he focused on spooning another bite.

I couldn't see his face to properly judge his thoughts, but I thought he sounded almost relieved that I had proved him wrong. Was he glad I was here?

"After what you said that night, I'm not surprised you thought that."

He looked up then, his gaze cutting deep. "So why are you here?"

At least he didn't pretend not to understand my reference. "What did you mean, you put your father in a wheelchair?"

"Just what I said."

"So you . . . hurt him? Deliberately?"

His lips twisted into a harsh smile. "You want me to make it sound less *wrong*. You want me to tell you I'm something else. Something that isn't broken. Is that it, Pepper?" He shook his head and tossed the empty plastic cup into the garbage can. "I'm not going to lie to you and convince you that I'm someone good and shiny like your guy that's going to be a doctor."

He pushed off from the counter and moved toward the bed again.

"That's not what I'm doing."

"Yes, you are. I can see it in the way you're looking at me with those big green eyes."

My hands knotted into fists at my sides. "I just want to know the truth."

"What does it matter?" he said over his shoulder as he pulled back the covers on the bed. "We don't need to be sharing each other's life stories. We don't need to know any truths about each other. What we're doing together doesn't need to be complicated."

I blinked as his words washed over me. He was right, of course. I didn't need to know who he was.

"Would you kill the light?" he asked, sighing as he crawled back into bed.

"You're going to sleep."

"I'm still wiped. So. Yeah." He lifted his head. "Are you staying?"

I glanced from him to the table with my stuff spread out. "I think I'll go."

He held my gaze for a long moment before nodding once and dropping his head back down on the pillow. I started to gather my stuff up when his voice stopped me.

"Or you can stay. Whatever you want to do."

Did he want me to stay? It almost sounded like he did. I hovered, unsure. Gradually, I set my books back down on the table and moved toward the bed. Kicking off my shoes, I climbed in beside him.

I eased toward him. His body radiated heat in the bed. I relaxed, inching closer, burrowing the tip of my nose against his back, savoring the clean smell of his skin, fresh from the shower.

His voice rumbled through his back toward me. "Hey, your nose is cold."

I grinned against his skin. "How about my feet?" I wedged them between his calves.

He hissed. "Get some socks on, woman."

I laughed lightly. "You're feverish. Maybe it helps."

Rolling over onto his side, he faced me. His bright eyes seared me, probably sending my temperature soaring, too. His hand found my arm, fingers stroking up and down leisurely. Seductively. Even sick, he was seducing me. He probably didn't even realize it. It's just what he did. Who he was. How he affected me.

His eyes drifted shut. Without opening them, he murmured, "I like the sound of your laugh. It's real and genuine. A lot of girls have this fake laugh. Not you."

"I like your laugh, too," I whispered, feeling pulled in, cozy in the cocoon of his bed.

"Yeah?"

I flattened my palm over his chest, enjoying the sensation of the firm flesh, even warm as it was. He sighed, like my cool hand offered him some relief.

"I laugh more since you came around," he said quietly, his lips barely forming the words.

He did? I frowned. He must not have laughed at all before, then, because I didn't think he was particularly jovial.

I held him through the night. And he held me back, tucking my head beneath his chin.. His arms surrounded me and kept me close to his overly warm body. Almost like I was some kind of lifeline. I felt the moment his fever broke around one in the morning. Confident that he was on the mend, I finally relaxed and fell asleep.

Chapter 17

THE REMNANTS OF HALLOWEEN were in full evidence as I carefully maneuvered down the hall toward my room, stepping around orange and black Silly String. I could already imagine the look on Heather's face when she woke up. Our RA would probably call a special floor meeting over this. I sighed, not looking forward to it.

Speaking of Heather. I was four doors from my room when a guy suddenly slipped out of her room. Holding his shoes in one hand, he closed the door carefully, like he didn't want to make a sound. As he turned, we came face-to-face. I blinked up at him. "Er, Logan?"

"Hey, Pepper," he whispered, running a hand through his artfully disheveled hair. The action only made the dark blond hair stick out more wildly. Just like his brother, he was probably hot on his worst day. "Fancy seeing you here."

"Yeah. I live here." My gaze flicked from him to Heather's door—RA, grad student, and twenty-four. "Does she know you're in high school?"

He grinned crookedly, bending to tug on his shoes. "I don't think she cares."

I snorted. "I bet."

"Hey, you have a car, right?"

"Yes. Why?"

"Well, Heather drove last night. I was going to call someone for a lift back to Mulvaney's . . ."

I smirked. "Why don't you ask Heather?"

"Oh, I don't want to wake her."

"Right." Readjusting my laundry basket on my hip, I started for my room. "Let me just drop this off and grab my keys."

"Thanks." He followed behind. When I glanced back it was to catch him looking nervously over his shoulder—as if he was worried that Heather was going to come after him.

I dropped off my basket and grabbed my keys, a smile twitching my mouth. "C'mon, Romeo."

He grinned unrepentantly as we walked to the elevator. "I'm no Romeo. There's no one girl I'm pining for."

I nodded. "This is true."

"Now my brother on the other hand . . ." His voice trailed off as he eyed me knowingly.

I shook my head, warmth crawling over my face and reaching all the way to my ears. "I don't know what you're talking about."

"You two have been seeing a lot of each other."

I shrugged one shoulder uneasily. "I wouldn't say a *lot*." Sure, I had seen more of him than any guy before, but Logan didn't know that.

We stepped into the empty elevator. Two girls were already

there, talking. Their gazes slid over Logan appreciatively before they continued with their conversation. A conversation I couldn't help listening to—especially when I heard the words *kink club*. Em would want me to tell her everything I overheard. She'd been on a mission to learn more about it ever since we first heard of its existence. She thought it an insult that she somehow hadn't landed an invitation yet.

"Yeah . . . Hannah got an invite," one said. "Apparently she knows someone who's already a member. And you know Hannah, she's always been into the freaky stuff . . ."

I couldn't help sliding a look to Logan. Clearly, he was listening, too, if the interested expression on his face signified anything. He was probably wishing he could meet this Hannah.

Stepping off the elevator, I teased, "You want to ask them for Hannah's number?"

He chuckled as we stepped outside into the brisk morning. The wind cut sharply at my face and I wished I had taken the time to throw a jacket and scarf over my sweater. "She does sound interesting, but no thanks. I'm more of a traditionalist."

I didn't bother pointing out that sleeping with a different girl every week didn't exactly qualify as traditional. We slid into the car and I turned on the heat as soon as I started it.

"So," I began as I pulled from the parking lot. "Your brother know where you are?"

His smile shifted into something smug and catlike. His stare turned knowing, and I had to fight the urge to fidget.

"Why don't you just ask me what you really want to know?"

"W-what do you mean?" I stammered.

"You want to know everything about my brother. Admit it."

"I don't want to know everything." *Just the key parts.*

"Well, I can tell you that he's seriously into you."

"How can you tell that?" I demanded before realizing that I should maybe try to act like I didn't care either way.

"There haven't been a lot of girls. I mean, clearly he's no me." I snorted and rolled my eyes. He flattened a palm to his chest and winked. "But there have been a few. Nothing like you though."

"And what am I like?"

"You, Pepper, are the kind of girl a guy brings home. Which is why I guess Reece never got involved with your type before. We don't have much of a home to bring girls home to. Our old man is a piece of work. Even before his accident, he was bitter and foul-mouthed. Hell, I don't know what flew faster—his fists or the empty beer bottles he threw at us."

My hands clenched around the steering wheel. A familiar sour feeling rolled through me. It sounded like his childhood was no better than mine. A different poison, yes, but poison was poison. "He sounds great."

"Yeah. A real prince."

"You mentioned an accident." Reece hadn't called what happened to his father an accident. He blamed himself. "What happened?"

"He wrapped his truck around a tree. Broke his spine."

A car crash? How was that Reece's fault? I moistened my lips. "Reece said something. It sounded like he thinks he's responsible."

Logan looked at me sharply. "He said that to you?"

I nodded.

Logan swore. "It wasn't his fault. The old man blames him,

but it's bullshit. Reece didn't come home for spring break to work, and Dad wrecked his truck driving home after closing up. In his mind, if Reece had been there he wouldn't have been driving that night."

My mind reeled as I pulled into Mulvaney's parking lot. I guessed we all had our crosses to bear. Except Hunter. He only ever knew a loving family. Parents that stood by their children and protected and supported them. "That's not right."

"Nope," Logan announced, a tightness in his voice hinting that he had a lot more to say on the subject of his brother dropping out of school and sacrificing his future. "I wouldn't have done it. I'm more selfish, I guess. Once I graduate, I'm out of here. Gonna live my own life. Hopefully, Reece will, too. He won't have me to worry about anymore at least."

"You think he'll go back to school?"

He shook his head. "No, he enjoys running the bar. He didn't at first, but it's in his blood. Our grandfather opened it and made it what it is. The business had been in decline with Dad. Things have picked up since Reece took over. He's been talking with different banks about opening a second location. My dad will flip his shit. He doesn't like change. But I doubt that will stop Reece. He's determined."

I pulled up to the back door, wishing I had driven slower. Everything Logan said revealed a new side to Reece, confirming that he was more than I first assumed.

Opening the door, Logan hesitated. "Thanks for the ride."

"You're welcome."

His eyes, so like Reece's, fastened on me. "My brother is a good guy, you know."

I nodded, unsure what to say to that.

"I heard you came over and took care of him when he was sick." I nodded once, warmth flushing my face. "He deserves someone like you."

Embarrassed, I tucked a strand of hair behind my ear and looked out the windshield. "That's nice of you to say, but you don't know me at all, Logan." I wasn't someone who was going to save his brother. Even if I wanted to, it wasn't in me to save anyone. I could barely save myself.

"Maybe I can see you better than you think."

"I don't think so."

"All right then. Fine. Maybe *I* don't." Something in his voice pulled my attention back to his face. His pale eyes cut into me. "But Reece does. He sees you. He wouldn't be wasting his time with you otherwise."

My fingers tightened on the steering wheel. "You're making a lot of assumptions here. It isn't like that between us. Reece and I are barely friends."

He laughed a little then, shaking his head like I'd said something incredibly funny. "Keep telling yourself that." Climbing out of the car, he ducked his head to look back inside. "See you around, Pepper."

He slammed the door shut, and the sound reverberated on the air for a moment as I watched him disappear into the bar. Muttering to myself, I put the car into drive, deciding I probably needed to take a little break from hanging out so much at Mulvaney's.

Chapter 18

THE FOLLOWING DAY REECE stood at my door. The vestiges of Halloween still lingered in the hall behind him. Heather insisted the culprits come forward to clean it up themselves, and so far no takers. For a moment I felt uncomfortable, remembering my conversation with his brother. I was pretty certain Reece wouldn't appreciate him sharing everything he had with me, but then I doubted Logan had confessed our little chat to him—primarily his matchmaking efforts. The realization that Reece likely knew nothing of that encounter eased my tension.

He carried one of those little white boxes from Em's favorite bakery.

I pointed at it. "What's that?"

"A cupcake."

I arched an eyebrow. "What kind?"

"Red velvet." Oh my God. He was bringing me cupcakes?

He held the box out to me. "Thanks for coming over the other day and taking care of me."

I accepted the box and waved him in. He sat at my desk.

I sank down on the bed and lifted the lid. Peering in, I salivated at the glimpse of cream cheese frosting. "This looks so good." Lifting it from the box, I peeled back the wrapper and bit into it with a moan.

"That good?"

"Want some?"

"No. I'm fine."

I angled my head at him. "Seriously? It's the size of a cantaloupe. Share it with me."

With a half smile, he joined me on the bed. Later, I would wonder if maybe that had been my intention all along. To get him on the bed with me.

I held the cupcake up for him, thinking he would take it from my hand. He took a bite with his strong, white teeth instead. My eyes flared. "That's like half the cupcake."

He chewed, his thumb catching a bit of icing on his lip and licking it. "You asked me to take a bite. I'm a guy. I can't help it if I take big bites. The rest is yours."

"Hmm." I gave him a look of mock reprimand and took another bite—dainty compared to his.

"I meant what I said."

I swallowed before asking, "What?"

"Thanks for staying and looking after me."

"Oh." I took another bite, shrugging as I chewed, feeling awkward under the intensity of his stare. "Anyone would have—"

"Don't do that."

"What?"

"Make light of what you did. Who you are. The truth is

that I can't think of another person who would have fussed over me the way you did. Not since my mom died." He nodded slowly. "You're a sweet girl, Pepper."

My face warmed at his praise and my stomach got all fluttery. I swallowed the last bit of cupcake and flinched when his thumb swiped the edge of my mouth, pulling away a bit of icing that he took into his own mouth. I watched him, riveted. "Isn't it supposed to be the kiss of death when a guy calls you 'sweet'?"

He looked at me. The moment stretched thickly until he answered, "Not if you're so sweet all I can think about is getting you naked and tasting every inch of you again."

A breath shuddered from my lips. Sucking in a deep breath, I rose up on my knees and straddled him. My hands lifted, hovering in the air before I brought them down on his shoulders, feeling the firm flesh, corded and taut with sinew beneath his shirt. His hands fell on my hips, gripping gently. We stared into each other's eyes. He wrapped a hand around the back of my neck and pulled my head down until my mouth met his.

I tasted cupcake as he kissed me slow and deep, unhurried. The kiss went on and on, languid and delicious. He broke away and pulled off his shirt. Next his hands flew to the hem of my sweatshirt. I lifted my arms to help him yank it over my head. My bra followed. Losing my clothes was becoming a habit around him.

He pushed me back on the bed. Without touching me, he surveyed me in the bright light of my room like he was memorizing me. Heat inched over my body as I imagined all the imperfections he was seeing. With a whimper, I tried to push past him, embarrassed at the intimacy, too overcome at the sensations coursing through me.

"Wait." His hand flattened on my belly, urging me back down. He slid down my body. My heart thumped a painful beat in my chest as I trembled and squirmed, waiting for his next move. I snuck a peek at him. He looked up at me, his chin brushing my belly, his large hands burning two imprints on my hips as his deep gaze pulled me in and sucked me under. "Are you going to trust me?"

"Yes." I stilled under him as I realized I meant it. "I do."

He grinned slowly and took my hands. Lacing his fingers with mine, he pressed them flat into the mattress, palm to palm at my sides. "Good."

He then proceeded to kiss me. All over my body. Moist, open-mouthed kisses on my belly. My rib cage. The valley between my breasts. His mouth loved me everywhere. I sighed, writhed, quivering under his attention. *OhGodOhGodOhGod*. There was no embarrassment anymore. Just him. His mouth on me.

He unzipped my jeans and dragged the zipper down, exposing the front of my panties. I surged when he pressed a kiss right *there*. The moist heat from his mouth seared me straight through the thin layer of cotton. His name slipped past my lips on a breath.

He came up then and kissed me hard, the only point of contact our mouths. Meshing lips, tongues, and teeth. He drove me wild. I kissed him back, matching him in heat and pressure. My arms strained, still pinned at my sides by his hands. I whimpered against his mouth and pushed at his palms, my fingers linked in a bloodless grip with his, desperate to be free so that I could touch him.

Then I felt it. The unmistakable hardness of him against the inside of my thigh, scalding through our clothing. I parted my thighs wider and squirmed closer, bringing him directly against me. I lifted my pelvis and thrust my hips, grinding into him.

His lips broke from mine in a hiss. "Shit. Are you sure you've never done this before?"

"Please . . . my hands . . . I want to touch you."

His fingers laced tighter with mine, and I felt his strength as our palms pressed flush together. "Not sure that's a good idea."

His breathing was harsh, mingling with my own ragged breath. Every part of me throbbed, ached. "Please. You've touched me so much . . . let me touch you."

He shook his head once, hard.

My voice cracked a little. "Why not?"

This close I could make out the dark ring of blue, almost black, around his irises. "Because you're like candy in my mouth. I'm already too worked up for you."

"But you said I can trust you."

"You can." His eyes cut into me, intense and stark—like he was willing for me to believe in him. "I would never hurt you."

"Then let go of my hands."

After a moment his grip on me loosened. I was free. I filled my hands with his chest, caressing the carved muscle, the ridiculously cut abs. His head dipped, fell into the crook of my neck as if he was gathering strength from some hidden reserve found only there.

My hands dipped farther south, hesitating only a moment at his jeans. My fingers slid inside the waistband. Before I lost my nerve, I unbuttoned him and dragged down the teeth of his zipper just like he had done to mine.

His head lifted and his eyes gleamed bright with warning. "Pepper . . ." His voice was strangled.

My gaze flicked to his and then back down, intent on my goal. "I never touched one before."

I tugged open his jeans, pulling them down less than gracefully. It proved especially difficult with him on top of me.

"Fuck it." He flipped off me onto his back. Lifting his hips, he yanked off his jeans himself. Then he was all mine.

Smiling, I leaned over him, my attention moving from his face to . . . south.

He filled out the front of his boxer briefs impressively. I rested my hand over him, feeling, measuring the outline.

He said my name again, part plea, part groan. I ignored him, curiosity, the rush of blood in my ears, overriding the sound.

I flexed my fingers and the bulge grew under my hand. It was emboldening. Before I could change my mind, I delved inside his briefs and wrapped my fingers around him. His head fell back on the bed. "Pepper."

"It's softer than I thought it would be." I bit my lip, reveling in the length of him in my grip.

He laughed hoarsely. "Sweetheart, I'm hard as a rock."

"I mean your skin." It was like silk over steel. My hand moved awkwardly, fumbling for a moment before settling into even strokes.

His hand fell over mine, stalling me. "Pepper, you have to stop."

I looked up at him. "Isn't this part of my education?"

The tendons in his throat worked like he was battling for control. I guess it should have worried me, but I only felt empowered. Gratified. Not for a moment did I think he would lose control and cross the line. He had my trust.

"You don't have to—"

"I want to."

His grip eased off my hand. I was able to move again, glide my fingers over him.

"All right," he agreed in a thick voice. "Then you should probably call it what it is."

I glanced up at him quizzically.

"Say it. Dick. Cock," he supplied. "Don't be afraid of the word, Pepper."

My hand stilled. My face burned. I shook my head. "I can't say that."

"But you can touch it? Say it. Cock."

The word sat heavily on my tongue. My hand resumed its movements as I said it slowly, savoring the naughty word, feeling bold and wicked. "Cock."

The blue of his eyes paled to a pewter. His chest rose and fell with a sharp breath. As if that word alone on my lips aroused him.

My gaze moved from him—his cock—to his face. I didn't know what fascinated me more. The sight of my hand moving over him or his expression. His eyes were closed. He looked almost in pain.

"Pepper . . . Pepper, stop." He tensed under me.

I ignored him, squeezing and moving my hand faster.

"God," he gasped and shuddered, the muscles and sinews in his chest and stomach rippling as his body reached climax.

His breathing gradually evened. He flung an arm over his

head. After several more breaths, he muttered, "That wasn't supposed to happen."

I rose up over him and smiled. "You had a plan?"

He moved his arm from his face and peered up at me. He tucked a strand of hair back behind my ear. "With you nothing seems to go according to plan."

Still smiling, I rose to my feet. Snatching up a hand towel, I tossed it to him and then got one for myself.

He wiped himself clean. Standing in my unzipped jeans, I felt some of my earlier embarrassment creep back in. Opening the door to my closet, I picked out a T-shirt and shrugged into it. I stood there then, shifting on my feet and playing with the hem of my shirt, unsure what to do next.

He sat up on the edge of my bed. He hadn't bothered to put his jeans back on. Clad only in his boxer briefs, he was the embodiment of sex. Gold-skinned. Lean and cut. His six-pack was more like an eight-pack. Ridiculous. The tattoo crawling up his arm and down the side of his torso was the cherry on top of it all.

I swallowed against my suddenly dry throat. "What now?"

"Well. If this was just a fling, we'd say good-bye at this point."

"Oh." I nodded. But this wasn't a fling. It was less than that. It was us pretending. Playing at something more.

He settled a hand on his knee and studied me in that unnerving way of his. "Do you want me to stay over?"

"Do you want to stay?"

The crooked smile reappeared. "If you want me here, say it. That's what would happen if this were more than a fling. If we were really into each other."

If we were really into each other. The words jarred me. Stung a little with the taste of him still fresh on my lips. But it was a necessary reminder that this was fake.

I inhaled. "Yeah. Then you should spend the night. Yes."

I told myself to be confident. After what we just did—what *I* just did—it shouldn't be that hard.

"You don't sound too excited. Remember, not such a turn-on."

I needed to approach this clinically. This wasn't personal. It was an experiment. He was a hot, experienced guy offering to guide me through the art of foreplay. I already felt more knowledgeable. I could kiss adequately now. I could do *more* than kiss now. I might not be a master of foreplay, but I was more than capable. Thanks to Reece I was ready for Hunter. My belly clenched thinking about that, wondering if I would like making out with Hunter half as much.

I gathered my night bag from the shelf by my closet with shaking hands, rattled by the realization that I was enjoying my time with Reece far too much. I was enjoying him. This had not been the plan. "I'll be right back."

I dove across the hall and washed my face and brushed my teeth, scrubbing until I tasted the coppery tang of blood in my mouth. Stopping, I rinsed my mouth out. Lifting my face, I stared at my reflection, marveling at this girl I had become. Someone about to share her bed with a guy who wasn't Hunter. It was hard to conceive.

When I entered the room, he was under the covers, look-ing relaxed with one arm tucked under his head. I turned out the lamp, plunging the room into a wash of gray. The light creeping in through the blinds saved us from total blackness.

I kicked off my jeans. He held back the covers for me, and the shadow of his lean body looked so delicious and inviting against the stripes of my sheets.

I slipped in beside him. A sigh escaped me as he pulled me flush with his body, spooning me. The warm, smooth skin wakened my nerves all over again. His maleness, his size, his strength made my breath shaky.

Electricity buzzed along my nerves. Those parts of me that were heavy with aching a little while ago warmed back up all over again.

His arm wrapped around my waist, his hand resting on my stomach. He pulled away for a second to gather my hair and drape it over my shoulder so it wasn't in his mouth. I felt his breath on the back of my neck. *God.* The aching was back. I squeezed my thighs together as if I could assuage it. How was I supposed to sleep?

"This Hunter guy—" he started.

"Yes?" I asked in a small voice.

"If he runs out after you mess around, then it doesn't mean anything to him. *You* don't. Understand?"

I winced, reminded that I had done that to him the other night. "I'm sorry that I—"

"I'm not saying this to make you feel bad for bailing that first night, Pepper. I'm just telling you because I don't want some guy, Hunter or anyone, to ever use you."

His breath fanned my nape. I knew his lips were close. Unable to help myself, I rolled onto my side and studied him in the gloom, our noses practically touching.

"Thanks for doing this." I almost added "thanks for caring," but that might be assuming too much. I swallowed those words back.

He laughed lightly. "I'm not totally selfless here, Pepper. I enjoy you. Clearly." His hand brushed my cheek, the fingertips a soft graze. Flutters erupted in my belly. My cheeks burned hotter thinking about my hand wrapped around him.

"I enjoy you, too." I kissed him then, and this time it was different, slow and sweet and tender. Of course it didn't stay that way. None of our kisses ever did. It built, deepened. Blood rushed in my ears. I cupped his face and wrapped an arm around his neck, aligning my body to his. After a moment, we broke for air.

Panting, he rested his forehead against mine. "We should try to get some sleep."

I laughed a little at that. Sleep wasn't happening. At least I couldn't see how.

"Come here." He tucked me against him, pulling my head down to his chest. I listened to the faint drum of his heart. His hand threaded through my hair, his fingers softening when he hit a snarl. "You have beautiful hair."

I smiled against his chest and then turned my face slightly, self-conscious that he could feel my silly grin against him. That he would know how pleased I was at the compliment. "I can spot you a mile away with this hair. It's like candlelight. A thousand different colors."

"A poet bartender," I murmured, settling my hand against his upper chest.

"Sweetheart, every bartender is a poet."

"I guess you get to see quite a bit of the world from behind the bar."

"I see enough. I saw you."

Still smiling, I started to relax against him. The glide of his fingers through my hair began to lull me. "Tell me more," I encouraged, my voice sleepy and soft.

His voice rumbled through his chest. "You just want to hear me say that you're beautiful, is that it?"

I swatted his arm. "Noooo."

"You know you are. You don't need to hear me say it."

My smile slipped. "Why would I know that?"

"Uh. Look in the mirror. Watch the eyes that follow you when you walk into a room."

I didn't know how to respond to that. The idea oddly discomforted me. My fingers traced lazy circles on his chest.

"Hunter won't be able to resist you. I don't know how he has so far."

I stilled against him, my fingers freezing.

Anger flashed through me. Why did he have to bring Hunter up right now? When we were like this? It just felt . . . I don't know. *Wrong.*

"Thanks," I murmured. Closing my eyes, I willed myself to sleep, to escape my annoyance, escape him. Of course, I was too wound up with irritation—and an aching awareness of him at my back—to have a hope of falling asleep. I was stuck, probably awake until we both got up in the morning.

That was my last thought before my eyes fell shut like lead weights.

Chapter 19

I WAIT IN THE BATHTUB *for the noises on the other side of the wall to stop. The voices fade away eventually, and I count to ten, waiting for Mommy to come and get me. She doesn't come. So I keep waiting and start counting again. This time to twenty.*

I hug my knees to my chest and settle back against the blanket lining the tub, hoping I won't have to spend the night in the bathroom again.

I squeeze Purple Bear, my fingers playing along his soft, well-worn little arms. They used to be plump, full of stuffing. Somehow the stuffing had vanished so that the arms were just flat little appendages of purple fabric now.

The door opens and I peek out from behind the curtain, eager for Mommy, hoping she's come at last to invite me into the bed with her.

Only it's not Mommy.

A man stands there, his hair long and wet-looking. His plaid shirt hangs off his narrow shoulders. It's unbuttoned, open down the front. His soft-looking belly is as white as the bar of soap sitting to my right.

He approaches the toilet, his hand fumbling with his zipper, and I jerk back into the tub, hoping he'll hurry up with his business and leave. Mommy's guests never stay long. I must have made a sound though. The shower curtain screeches on the rail as he yanks it back.

He looms over me. "Well. Who do we have here?"

I shrink away, clutching Purple Bear in front of me.

His knees crack as he kneels down beside the tub. "You Shannon's little girl?"

I nod once.

His dark eyes travel over me, studying my bare legs poking out from Mommy's T-shirt. He leans forward and peers inside the tub like he doesn't want to miss any part of me.

"Not so little, eh. You look like a big girl to me."

His fingers curl around the edge of the tub and they remind me of a corpse, long and thin, white as bone. Several rings flash on them. My gaze fixates on one in the shape of a skull.

If possible I hug Purple Bear even tighter, my arms squeezing around his soft little body. Mommy said he would always protect me. That Purple Bear would keep me safe whenever she wasn't with me.

"What's your name?"

"Where's Mommy?"

"Sleeping." Two bony fingers stretch out and brush my knee. I whimper and jerk my leg back.

He grins brown, furry teeth at me.

I open my mouth, ready to cry for Mommy, but his hand slams over my mouth, cutting off my voice. My air.

There's just the foul taste of his hand. And fear. . .

I WOKE WITH A choked sob, vaulting upright in bed. Strong hands were instantly there, seizing my arms, and I cried out. Turning, I hit at the body beside me.

"Pepper! What's wrong?"

The voice didn't penetrate. I was still trapped in that bathroom, a musty palm suffocating me. *Mommy! Mom!*

"Pepper!" The hands shook my shoulders. "Pepper. It's just a dream. You're okay."

I blinked against the murky, predawn air. "Reece?"

"Yeah." He swept the hair back from my face. "Some dream there."

I nodded.

His thumb brushed my cheek. "You're crying."

I released a shaky laugh and dabbed at my cheeks with the back of my hand, feeling the moisture there. "Must have been something I ate." How could I have been so dumb? The dreams always came without warning. I knew that. I should have known this could happen.

"Something you ate gave you a bad dream?" I heard the skepticism in his voice. "What was the dream about?"

"I don't remember."

"You called for your mom."

My heart clenched. Physically hurt inside my chest. "I did?"

"Yeah."

Yeah. I called for her all right. That night. And later. The night she dropped me off at Gram's I cried. I screamed for her. "What else did you hear?"

He studied me, his eyes gleaming in the gloom. "Want to talk about it?"

"No," I snapped before I could stop myself. "I don't want to talk about when my mom abandoned me. Left me on my grandmother's doorstep like I was some rolled-up newspaper."

He didn't move. Just held still, hands searing imprints on my shoulders. "That happened?"

Yeah, I thought. *That happened.* And other stuff that I would never talk about with anyone. I never had. Mom abandoning me? That was no secret. I could give him that little insight into my colorful history. But not the rest.

I nodded, my voice lodged somewhere in my throat, refusing to surface.

He tugged me back down on the bed, his arm wrapping around me. I stared out at my room washed in the soft purple of morning and wished that his arm didn't feel so good holding me. It wasn't supposed to. That wasn't part of the plan.

"Now you know about my dysfunctional family."

He was silent for a few moments, his hand drawing small circles on my arm. "I understand a bit about dysfunction."

I turned to stare at him. "Okay. Your turn."

He groaned. "Do I have to?"

"C'mon. I showed you mine. You show me yours." It mattered for some reason. Logan had already revealed a lot, but I wanted to hear it from Reece. I wanted him to confide in me.

"Let's see. You know my mom died when I was eight."

"Yes."

"Well, she died because she overdosed on Tylenol. Not on purpose. She had these migraines . . . I remember seeing her pop a few that day. Well, turned out she took a few too many. A lot actually. Her liver shut down in her sleep. She didn't wake up the next morning." He uttered this all matter-of-factly, but I saw in his eyes the anguish he kept banked. What had that been like for him? Waking up and finding his mom still in bed, unmoving. Dead.

"Oh my God."

"My old man was never exactly the warm and fuzzy type before that, but after . . ."

I nodded, understanding.

"Guess we're not that different, after all," he added.

I rested my cheek on his chest, knowing we were going to have to get up in a few minutes and get dressed, but for now, we held each other as his words sank in and made my stomach knot. *We're not that different.* Two people that didn't have the faintest clue about belonging to a normal, loving family.

"No. I guess not."

I HURRIED ACROSS CAMPUS, stopping at the crosswalk for the light. I bounced anxiously in place, burying my hands deep in my jacket pockets. I was already late for Statistics.

"Hey, Pepper! Hold up!"

My head whipped around to watch Hunter jogging toward me. He gave me a light hug. I closed my eyes, enveloped in him.

"Hi! How's it going?"

"Good." He nodded across the street. "Headed that way?"

"Yeah. Kensington."

"C'mon. I'll walk you. I just got out of class."

We crossed the street together. My hand escaped my pocket to flex nervously around my strap.

"I'm looking forward to Thanksgiving. I need a break."

"Yeah, me, too," I returned. "Can't wait to see Lila."

He rolled his eyes. "We'll have to hear about her new boy-friend."

I tsked. "Behave. This one is nice."

"Do I have to be? She changes boyfriends like socks."

"We can't all be devoted to someone for years on end," I teased.

He looked at me with wide eyes. "First of all, it was maybe, *maybe* two years." He waggled two fingers at me. "And we're not dating anymore, remember?"

I grinned, staring straight ahead. Sensing his gaze on me, I slid him another look and my pulse quickened at the way he was studying me. Almost like he had never seen me before.

"What about you? Are you dating anyone?" Two things happened in that moment. First, an image of Reece flashed across my mind. Not that it should. I hadn't seen or heard from him in a week. Not since he spent the night with me in my dorm. Second, I realized that he was asking if I was single. He'd never asked me if I was dating anyone before. Obviously he'd never cared enough to ask. But he cared now.

"No. Not really."

"Hmm," he murmured. "You sound a little uncertain. There's someone. And now your cheeks are pink, so I know I'm right."

I pressed a hand to my face as if I could feel said pinkness there. "No, they're not. It's just chilly."

"Oh, you have a boyfriend." He chuckled.

"Shut it! I don't." We stopped before the steps leading into

Kensington. I stepped to the side, clear of the flood of students passing in and out of the double doors. I stood on the bottom step, which brought me almost to eye level with Hunter.

He smiled, that dimple I loved so much denting his left cheek. "Maybe not yet. But there's someone. I can see it in your eyes."

You. I wanted to shout. *It's always been you.*

His gaze flicked up and down, quickly looking me over. "You look good, Pepper. Did you do something to your hair?"

"Oh. Thanks." I smoothed a hand over my hair, glad I'd worn it down and not in a ponytail. "Yeah. Some highlights." Thankfully my voice sounded natural. Like compliments were something I heard all the time. Reece's voice floated through my mind. *You're beautiful.*

I glanced over my shoulder. "I think I'm late."

Hunter nodded. "Oh, yeah. Sorry. I'll text you. You okay to leave on Wednesday?"

"Sounds good."

"Great." He walked backward several steps before turning and merging into the flow of students.

I watched him go even though I was already late. Staring at his back, I tried to recall whether Hunter had ever paid me a compliment before. Sure, he had always been nice to me, but he'd never looked at me the way he just did. Like he saw me as something other than his little sister's best friend.

Like he saw me.

Chapter 20

EMERSON WALKED INTO MY room, cracking the stem of a banana as I worked on a paper at my laptop. "So no Reece tonight?"

The question hit a nerve. There shouldn't be an assumption that I would be with him just because we'd spent a few nights together. *Should there?*

I wanted to snap that I hadn't heard from him in over a week, so why would she think I would be seeing him again? But that might reveal just how much I wanted to see him again. Instead, I answered, "No. Just trying to get some work done. This is due Thursday, but I have to work tomorrow so I'm getting it done now." I glanced at her.

"Hmm," she murmured, taking a bite from her banana.

I leaned back in my chair and stared at her evenly. "What?"

"Well, you haven't seen him since you took care of him, right?"

I had told Georgia and Emerson all about staying with Reece when he was sick. I just never mentioned the follow-up night when he brought me a cupcake and stayed over. Georgia had been at Harris's that night, and Em got in so late that Reece and I were already asleep. She never heard a sound from next door. Not even when he left in the morning.

I frowned. "I didn't take care of him."

Emerson had looked confused when I explained about nursing him through his stomach bug. Clearly, if there wasn't making out involved she wasn't sure what I was doing with him. Valid confusion. To be fair, I suffered from some of the same confusion. Only Georgia had looked vaguely knowing. Like she understood perfectly what I was doing with him. I resisted the urge to ask her what was behind her meaningful little nod. I didn't need to let on just how adrift I felt.

She arched an eyebrow.

"I just got him some medicine," I denied lamely. *And curled up with him and held him through the worst of his fever.*

"Oh, really?" She looked amused. "The last time Georgia was sick, I stayed far away just so I wouldn't catch it. And we're best friends." She cocked her head. "What do *you* do for some guy you just met?" She pointed a finger at me somewhat accusingly. "You skip work and nurse him like a regular Florence Nightingale."

I shrugged. "I have strong immunities." Not much of an excuse, but it was all I could think to say.

Suddenly my phone vibrated. I picked it up and felt my stomach pitch. *Speak of the devil.*

Reece: Hey. How are you?

What? Had I summoned him with my thoughts?

"Who's that?"

"Just my lab partner," I lied. I'm not sure why I felt compelled to lie, but it was my first impulse. I put my phone facedown.

Accepting my lie, she continued, "So you have no plans to see him again? You don't want to go to Mulvaney's this weekend?"

"No."

"Hm. Just thought you might be missing him."

"Nope." Avoiding her gaze, I returned my attention to my monitor and typed another word. "It's not like we're a thing, Em. I know it and so does he." My gaze flicked to my phone again. *Then why was he texting me?*

"Yeah." She sounded unconvinced. "But the friends with benefits thing can get tricky."

"We're not even that."

"Well, whatever you are." She waved a hand dismissively. "You're done with him then?"

I typed another word. "Yeah. I guess. I haven't really thought much about it—about him." *Only all the time.* "I've been busy. And he has my number anyway." I glanced again to where my phone sat.

"Ah. So you're waiting for *him* to call."

Too late, I regretted saying that. "I'm not *waiting* for him to do anything."

"Okay, okay." She threw her banana peel into my trash can. "Just checking on you, that's all."

"Thanks, but everything's fine, Mom. I'm going home with Hunter for Thanksgiving. That's what this whole thing with Reece was about. Remember?"

"Oh, I remember." She nodded. "I was just curious if you still did." With that parting remark, Em glided back through our adjoining door.

I resumed tapping at the keys, struggling to concentrate on my concluding paragraph. I finally gave up and pushed back from my desk. Standing, I rubbed my hands over my face and paced the small space between my desk and bed.

The conversation with Em hadn't helped. I'd been thinking about him a lot. Especially after he opened up to me and told me about his mother. My mom might have left voluntarily, chosen addiction over me, but we'd both grown up motherless. He was right. We weren't that different. Deciding it wouldn't be wrong to at least reply to his text, I plucked my phone off my desk. His message stared back at me. My fingers paused a moment before typing.

Me: Hey. How's it going?

I hesitated, reading the simple line, making certain it was what I wanted to say. Not too much. Not too little. Satisfied, I hit SEND.

Setting the phone down, I sank back in my chair and reread my last paragraph. Text sent, I was determined to finish this assignment.

And then my phone buzzed. I snatched it up.

Reece: I'm good. Ever since this excellent nurse took really good care of me a few days ago I'm better than ever

Smiling, I typed back, my thumbs flying.

Me: Lucky u
Reece: She tastes good, too. Like cupcake

My face flamed as I typed.

Me: That's what happens when someone feeds her
　　　cupcake
Reece: She just needed one of those sexy nurse outfits to
　　　　make my fantasy complete

I giggled.

Me: Your fantasy involves puke and a nasty stomach
　　　bug???
Reece: It involves you

The smile slipped from my face and my breath caught.
Shit. He wasn't even here, and just like that he made my knees
go weak and my face heat. My fingers trembled over the keys,
unsure how to respond. Then I noticed he had started typing
again. I waited for the words to appear.

Reece: When can I see u again?

My heart raced at the idea of seeing him again. At my place?
Or his? I gnawed on my bottom lip, thinking.

Reece: Can u grab lunch Wed?

I blinked. Lunch out? Not his loft or my dorm. What was that about? Friends went out for lunch. And couples. We weren't a couple, but I guess we could be the latter. Friends. Would that be too weird?

Reece: Hello?
Me: Yes. Wed works
Reece: How about Gino's?

Gino's served the best pizza and calzones in town. The popular pizza parlor wasn't far from Mulvaney's off the strip.

Me: Sounds good. What time should I meet u?
Reece: I'll pick u up at noon, ok?

I frowned. Picking me up made it feel like a date.

Me: It's just lunch. I can meet u there
Reece: I'll pick u up

I stared at the screen, debating arguing. Instead, I just typed okay.

Reece: See u then

Setting my phone on my desk, I looked at the adjoining door. The sound of the television floated into my room. Emerson always studied with the TV on. I took a step in that direction and stopped myself, deciding against telling her about the date. After the inquisition of a few moments ago she would only see this as affirmation that I missed Reece and wanted to see him again or some such nonsense.

It wasn't that. It was simply deepening my education. Our pseudo-date would be a trial run for when Hunter took me out. *If* that even happened like I hoped.

This was just a pretend date. The center of my chest pulled uncomfortably. I rubbed at the spot, willing for the tightness to loosen. Yeah. *Pretend*. As was everything else we had done. Nothing more. Nothing real.

Chapter 21

HE KNOCKED AT A few minutes before noon. I took a final look at myself in the mirror. It was tricky deciding what to wear. We were going for pizza in the middle of the day. It wasn't like getting dressed up for an evening out.

I settled on skinny jeans and a fitted long-sleeved shirt. I opted for my half-boots instead of sneakers like I always wore to class. The hair I wore down. I even tamed the mess of waves with product and a diffuser. A lot of effort for me. I wasn't in total denial. He thought my hair was beautiful and I wanted to live up to that. It was somewhat humbling to know that my ego craved such affirmation. I wasn't so unlike other girls who sought approval. That made me normal, I supposed. A laugh escaped me. Finally. I'd only ever wanted to be normal. To sit at the cool kids' table just for being me and not because I was Lila Montgomery's best friend.

Opening the door, the sight of him hit me like a fist. *God.* When was that going to stop happening. How many kisses would it take for him not to have that effect on me?

"Hey." Okay, did my voice have to sound like I just sucked down helium?

"Hey." His gaze moved over me from top to bottom. "You look really pretty."

"Thanks." I surveyed him in turn. He wore jeans and a gray thermal shirt that hugged his broad shoulders. The shirt wasn't skin-tight, but the corded strength of his lean torso was evident. "So do you."

He grinned.

"Well, not pretty," I corrected. "Good. You look good." *God*. First date fail.

"Thanks. Ready?"

I nodded and grabbed my bag. Pulling the strap across my chest, I locked the door behind me. There were plenty of girls walking the hall and lounging in the small sitting area across from the elevator at this time of day. They weren't subtle in their stares. One girl leaned far back, nearly toppling over the chair to better check out Reece as we waited in front of the elevator.

I'm sure he noticed, but said nothing. Or maybe he didn't notice. Maybe he was just accustomed to being checked out, so he wasn't aware of it happening. He waved me inside the elevator. We didn't talk on the ride down or during the short walk to his Jeep. He opened the passenger door for me, which only bewildered me. The action seemed a bit much for a friend to do for another friend. So what was he doing with me? What was all this about? It couldn't be a real date.

"I'm starving," he said as he pulled out of the parking lot.

"Me, too." Five minutes later we pulled into Gino's parking lot. This close to campus, it was crowded with students.

"Guess I could have picked someplace less busy," Reece murmured after the hostess told us it would be a few minutes.

"They turn tables over fast. Everyone's got class or work to go to."

He nodded and stared out at the restaurant, scanning the red-checkered tablecloths. He actually looked a little nervous.

"Are you working tonight?" I asked.

He faced me again. "Yeah."

"It's nice you have your days free."

"My schedule is pretty much my own, but I like to be there in the evenings when it's peak business. Especially weekends. It's never that busy on weekdays. I think you met Gary. Guy with the mustache?"

"Yes."

"He's been working there since I was in diapers. He can run the place without me."

I nodded. "Seems like running a business would be a big responsibility."

"I like it okay. I've got a few ideas. Been thinking about expanding and adding a second location. Which is crazy when you think that I never wanted anything to do with the place in the beginning. I hated having to come home and work during breaks. It was my old man's thing. Not mine. I guess I didn't like being under his thumb. I was studying business in college when I had to drop out and come home and help out. And now here I am."

Studying him, I asked, "You don't want to go back to school? Finish your degree?"

He shrugged. "I'm running a business now. Learning

through trial and error. And if I went back to school my ol' man would sell off Mulvaney's. It's been in my family too long. I couldn't let him do that. I guess it's in my blood."

The hostess called for us. She led us to a table for two near the window that faced the street. Seated, we opened the menus.

"What kind of pizza do you like?" he asked.

"My favorite is usually the Greek. Love the olives and feta and bits of shaved gyro meat on it. I usually get a slice or two of that—"

"That's one of my favorites, too. Let's get a large." Closing the menu, he added with a grin, "I eat a lot."

"I remember. Pancakes this tall." I floated a hand above the table.

He nodded. "That's right."

"And fourteen meatballs."

"You cheated me on those. I think you just gave me five."

I shook my head. "So unfair. Guys have some kind of super-hero metabolism."

"You should see Logan eat. He'll get a large just for himself and a side of wings and the meatball calzone."

"Teenage boys," I grumbled.

"Yeah, and he plays sports so he has no body fat at all."

My gaze skimmed Reece's chest and arms appreciatively. He was all hard, lean lines and tight muscle. He didn't appear to have an ounce of fat on him either. Recalling that I had stripped down to my panties in front of him suddenly astonished me.

Pushing away the memory, I added, "And your brother has a lot of late night activity, too."

The instant the words slipped out, my face caught fire. I had pretty much just called his brother a man-whore to his face. And it only called attention to what brought us together in the first place—the fact that I had thought *he* was the infamous bartender that slept with every girl to pass through Mulvaney's doors.

Luckily, he didn't take offense. He laughed. The waitress arrived to take our order right then. She froze, an awed smile fixed to her face as she eyed Reece.

"Ah, what can I get for you?" she addressed Reece without glancing at me. I couldn't really blame her. Whenever he was around he was all I could look at, too.

He turned that dazzling smile on her and the waitress's eyes might have glazed over. He ordered our pizza. It took her a moment to look down at her pad. She fumbled with the pen before finally managing to write. "Excellent choice. That's my favorite."

Reece's gaze slid to me and his look made me warm from the inside out. "Ours, too."

She looked at me as though remembering my presence. A stupid smile curved my lips and I looked down at my hands laced together in front of me. *Ours.* That single word ricocheted through my head. It made me feel all kinds of good to hear him say that single word. Foolish, I knew. But there it was.

She asked for our drink orders, and I chimed in with my request.

"I'll have that right out." She beamed at Reece and even sent me a quick, awkward smile—like she knew *I* knew she was imagining him naked.

And then we were alone again.

Reece leaned forward again, looking so at ease I began

to feel relaxed. "So the gloves are off when it comes to my brother, huh?"

"Sorry." I plucked at the edge of my napkin, my sense of ease evaporating.

"It's okay. His reputation is well earned. I tried to stop it in the beginning, but he's eighteen now. He'll start college in the fall. I can't tell him what to do anymore. He's gotta learn for himself." His lips cocked in that sexy half-grin that made my stomach flip every time. "And just hope he doesn't end up a father before his twentieth birthday." He laughed and winced at this simultaneously. The low deep sound rippled over my skin and sank deep inside me. He scrubbed a hand over his short-cropped hair. "Shit. I sound like a father."

He did, and it totally threw me. It didn't fit with my initial notion of him. He really was a nice guy. "I get it. You've had to be more than a brother to him."

Some of the levity faded from his face. He was quiet for a moment before saying, "He was just so little when our mom died . . . and I already told you that our father isn't exactly the type to sit down and talk us through things or comfort us. For bad or good, I've been a parent to him." He shrugged again. "But this year I decided I needed to take a step back."

The waitress set our drinks down and left. I stared at Reece, wondering how many eight-year-old boys would have stepped up to the plate and adopted the role of mother and father for their younger sibling. "I'm sure what you gave him is better than him going without."

He shrugged one shoulder. "It was something. He knows I care about him at least, and he's not alone."

And isn't that everything? I thought of my own mother. I couldn't say that I knew she ever cared about me. Maybe once. Before she started to care about her addiction more.

Almost like he guessed that I was thinking less than pleasant thoughts, he suggested, "Let's talk about something else."

I nodded, okay with leaving the subject behind. Talking about his upbringing only made me think of mine. Maybe that was the downside to us being *not* so different. "Sure."

"Pepper?"

I looked up at the sound of my name and stared at Hunter's face, not registering him at first. It was a strange, bewildering experience staring at Hunter with Reece across from me. Like two worlds coming together that never should have met.

"Hunter." I leaned back in my chair, not realizing until that moment that I had been leaning half across the table, so into Reece and being close to him. "Hi," I added dumbly.

"Hey, how's it going?" His gaze slid from me to Reece and back again. He hovered there, waiting. I couldn't seem to think of a thing to say even though it was apparent he was waiting for an introduction.

"Hey, I'm Reece." Apparently he knew what to say and do. Reece reached out and shook Hunter's hand in a solid-looking grip.

"Hunter Montgomery. I went to high school with Pepper."

"Oh, yeah." Reece smiled amiably. "That's cool to have someone you know around." His expression was innocent. He gave nothing away, like that I might have mentioned Hunter's name a dozen times. *Thank God.*

"Yeah. It is." Hunter's eyes settled on me as he answered Reece.

"We just met a couple weeks ago," Reece added, looking at me with eyes that looked suddenly smoky blue. Probing and intimate. Like he knew what I looked like naked and couldn't wait to get me naked again. "But it feels like we've known each other longer. Know what I mean?"

My eyes flared. I kicked him under the table, wondering what he was doing painting the picture that we were some kind of hot and heavy couple. Even if maybe we were. Sort of. Or not. I didn't know what we were exactly, but it wasn't a couple. That's the only thing I knew for sure, and I didn't need him planting the idea in Hunter's head that I was unavailable.

"Uh. Yeah," Hunter murmured, his eyebrows drawing together.

I still couldn't find my voice. My face felt overly hot and I knew I must be as red as the little squares on the tablecloth.

"Yeah, well, nice meeting you, man." The smile was still on Reece's face and in his voice, but there was a steeliness in his gaze. His meaning was clear. Good-bye and go the fuck away.

"See you later, Hunter," I murmured softly and gave a small wave, eager for him to leave, but not because I was so enamored of my date and wanted some alone time. I wanted the embarrassment to come to an end. I wanted to stop Hunter from concluding that I was involved deeply with the guy sitting across from me.

"Yeah." Hunter nodded and moved back across the restaurant. He reclaimed his seat at the bar with a couple of other guys. I'd seen him around campus with one of them. I thought it was his roommate.

"So that's the infamous Hunter."

I lifted my gaze back to Reece. "This was a bad idea."

"What was?"

"You. Us. This date we're pretending to be on." Reece was silent and I flicked my gaze to Hunter across the restaurant and back to him again. "Did you have to do that?"

"Do what? Make you look desirable?" He looked at me in exasperation. "You should be thanking me."

"What? How?"

"I just took you from one category . . . the-girl-I-never-pictured-naked category, and dropped you into I-wonder-what-she's-like-in-bed."

I blinked and fell silent as our pizza arrived. The waitress placed it on the table between us along with two plates.

"Oh," I murmured, processing this bit of information.

"Now don't look, but trust me when I say he hasn't been able to stop glancing over here."

I leaned forward in my chair. "Really?"

"Yeah. And now it's just about to get better."

I leaned forward a bit more, the steam from the pizza floating up to my face. "Better how?"

He leaned across the table and pressed his mouth to mine. I immediately forgot the impropriety of kissing in broad daylight in a public place. His mouth was warm and open against mine. The kiss branded me. Too intoxicating to resist. I immediately responded. His tongue slipped inside and stroked my own. Nothing around us existed. It was just his mouth on my mouth. My hands reached out, fingers grazing the planes of his face, touching but not quite. It was like if I touched him, he might vanish from me altogether.

A plate crashed nearby and I jerked. Reece pulled back ever so slightly. His lips still grazing mine, he murmured, "Very nice. That should do the trick."

The air *whoosh*ed from my lips and I dropped back in my seat. "What?"

"Hunter can't take his eyes off you right now. You should see his face—but no. Don't look. I wouldn't be surprised if he calls you tomorrow."

Actually I wasn't tempted to look. That was the sad thing. I was too busy staring at the guy I wanted to pull back across the table and keep on kissing.

Which was all kinds of fucked up. I needed to get a grip on myself. Reece wasn't the one. He wasn't *my* one.

Gulping a deep breath, I folded my hands in my lap. "Oh." I wasn't sure how I felt that he had just staged that kiss. I hadn't been thinking about Hunter with my lips locked to Reece's. I should have been. But I wasn't. Had Reece felt anything at all?

His gaze held mine. "Pretty good luck, huh."

"What's that?" Right now, I didn't feel particularly lucky.

"Running into him here."

"Yeah." I nodded, watching as he dug into the pizza between us, serving one slice to each of us.

"Eat up." He took a large bite from his slice.

I followed suit, willing the knots in my stomach to untie themselves.

He groaned, and the sound elicited all manner of wicked feelings inside me. "This is the best."

I resisted the urge to smack him.

"It really is," I agreed.

"Hey." He reached across the table and covered my hand with his own. "It's going to work out. You'll see. You'll get your guy."

My heart clenched a little at his words. Suddenly I wasn't so sure who that guy was anymore.

Chapter 22

HUNTER CALLED THE FOLLOWING day. I'd forgotten that Reece had predicted as much. Or maybe I just blew the suggestion off. When his name popped up on my phone, I practically fell out of my chair. Standing, I took a deep breath and answered, managing to sound calm.

Yes. It was good to see you yesterday.

Yes, I'm well.

Yes. I'm looking forward to Thanksgiving, too. No problem. We can leave Wednesday at eight. My prof canceled my afternoon class, too. That sounds great.

It was a normal conversation and yet there had been a different tenor to it. Hunter laughed too readily. He sounded . . . nervous, asking more than once if I didn't mind leaving so early in the morning. Not that he wasn't always polite, but there was something different in the exchange.

I hated to admit it, but that staged kiss had maybe done some good, after all. He didn't mention it, of course. His manners would never allow that. Nor did he even mention Reece, but Reece and that kiss were there, hanging between us, filling those moments of crackling silence. Reece had been right. Everything was falling into place. If I ever had a chance with Hunter, it was now. Another chance wouldn't come. This was it.

The Monday before Thanksgiving, I found myself bypassing my route home after work and heading for Mulvaney's. I told myself it was just because I wanted to let Reece know he had been right. His staged kiss had done the trick, after all. A simple thanks. That was all. Not because I wanted to see him. Not because he hadn't texted me since our date.

At three in the afternoon, the place was dead. My tennis shoes fell silently on the plank floor. I found him inventorying behind the bar. He didn't notice me approach.

"Hi." I propped my elbows on the bar.

He looked up and smiled widely, immediately making me glad I came. "Hey. Where you been?" He set his clipboard down and gave me his attention. That glad feeling only increased knowing he had noted my absence over the weekend.

"I worked the last couple nights. The Campbells and another family." I needed the money, especially after my car troubles.

"I wondered. Saw Emerson."

"You know her. Never one to miss a good time."

An awkward pause fell. I cleared my throat to fill it. "I owe you a thanks."

"Yeah? What for?"

"Hunter. He called the next day. And he's been texting me off and on."

"Well. There you go." He smiled again, but it seemed less than before. Or maybe that was just my imagination. My ego wanting him to feel something other than happiness for me moving forward with Hunter. "I told you he would call."

"You did." I nodded. "So. Thanks, again."

He looked left and right, as if searching for something to talk about. "You hungry? Want a burger or something?"

"I could eat."

"C'mon." He led me into the back room and shouted over the counter. "Give me a Cyclone Monster and basket of Tijuana fries."

Someone shouted back from the kitchen, acknowledging his order.

My eyes widened. When he turned back around, I said, "Please tell me that's not all for me."

He grinned and my stomach did that crazy little flip-flop. "I'll share it with you."

We sat at one of the tables toward the back. On the same bench, our shoulders brushing. It was uncomfortable being this close to him, not knowing what was okay. Touching, kissing, which we had done so much together before, now seemed like something we couldn't do now. Partly because we were in pub-lic. Partly because none of that was real. Me finally—*maybe*—getting somewhere with Hunter only hammered that home.

"So you're leaving Wednesday with Hunter?"

I nodded. "Yeah. It's a four-hour drive."

"Well, that will give you some quality time with him." He stared straight ahead, in the direction of the kitchen. I stared at his profile. A muscle feathered in his jaw.

I nodded. "Yeah, and I'll be over at his house quite a bit to see Lila. I usually go there after Thanksgiving dinner and hang out. Watch movies. Hunter is usually there unless he makes plans with some of his old friends—"

"He'll be there," he cut in.

"Yeah? Why—"

"He'll be there because you're there." Turning, he faced me, his left arm resting along the top of the table. With the wall to my right and the stretch of his bicep and forearm to my left, I felt caged, like he was closing in on me. "And if his sister wants you two to be together—"

I nodded. "She does."

"Then she'll be a good sister and a good friend and invent some reason to disappear."

I shook my head. "I don't think it will happen like that."

"It will."

I angled my head and studied him, the dark ring of blue around his eyes a stark contrast to the pale blue of his irises. "He doesn't see his old friends often. They might make him go out—"

"I'm telling you. He'll blow them off to be with you."

My chest tightened at the intense way he looked at me, and I heard myself asking, "Is that what you would do?"

He stared at me and I waited, wondering why his answer mattered so much.

"I wouldn't have waited this long for you. I would have already showed up at your dorm the minute I decided I wanted you. I wouldn't leave until I convinced you that you were mine."

"Oh." My skin shivered, imagining this scenario. Reece at my door. Determined. Sexy. Saying things, *doing* things, to convince me I was his. "Maybe he hasn't decided that he wants me then."

"He has. I saw his face at Gino's. He's already gone for you."

Suddenly I realized that we had moved into each other, not touching but so close our breaths mingled.

"Fuck," he rasped and closed that tiny distance, kissing me like it had been forever and not just a week. But this week had felt like forever. I missed this. Missed him. He buried a hand in my hair and hauled me closer, our chests mashed together. His mouth devoured mine and I kissed him back just as greedily.

"Here you go."

I jumped and pulled away. Two baskets of heart attack dropped onto the table before us. The fry cook was already marching away, apparently unfazed by our public makeout.

My chest rose and fell like I had just run a marathon. Reece's eyes were that bright pale blue I was coming to recognize as a sign that he was hot for me. I glanced from the food to him, part of me hoping that he would say forget the food and haul me upstairs with him.

My body didn't even feel like it belonged to me anymore. It was one pulsing ball of nerves, throbbing and aching and yearning desperately for all this foreplay to just reach its most natural conclusion.

It was as though my body lived and breathed for this. For him. I wanted the ache satisfied. But I wouldn't be the one to say the words. I couldn't do that. I couldn't go that far. And there was always the fear, the desperate need to choose the safe path.

All of which meant nothing would happen. Nothing more

than kisses and fondling that made me want to pull my hair out in frustration.

Reece slapped his hands and rubbed them together. "Let's dig in."

Oh yeah. Food.

I picked up a cheese-coated fry.

He grabbed a clump of three. Tilting his head back, he dropped them into his open mouth. I watched him in awe as his strong jaw chewed. "Mmmm."

"How can you look the way you look and eat like this?"

He grinned crookedly and leaned close, the warmth of his body reaching out to wrap around me. "And how do I look?"

I crumpled up a napkin and threw it at him. "Oh, shut it. You know you're hot. Your body is insane."

Grinning in smug satisfaction, he picked up another clump of fries. "I just like to hear you say that. You're not easy to impress."

I frowned. "What does that mean? Am I that difficult?"

"No. It's just that you've set your sights on one guy you met years ago when you were a kid. You don't even glance at the guys who check you out. It's like you don't care what anyone thinks."

He was wrong. I cared what *he* thought. Once I met him, Reece was the only one I even considered when I decided I needed to hone my foreplay skills. He was all that I seemed to see.

Deciding not to debate that point, I warily assessed the burger. "How do I even eat that?"

"You gotta just attack it. It's the only way."

Nodding with resolve, I picked up the massive burger and tackled it with my teeth.

Reece chuckled as I chewed the mouthful and grabbed for a napkin, wiping off the juices from my lips and chin.

"Nice," he said in approval and leaned in and planted a kiss on my lips before I even saw it coming. It was quick and careless, and my heart raced.

Swallowing my bite, I shook my head. "Tell me you don't eat like this every day. You'll have a heart attack before you're thirty."

"Not every day, no. And I work out. Up until I dropped out of college, I played soccer."

"In college?"

He nodded, avoiding my gaze as he gathered the burger up into his hands. I thought back to what he'd told me about his dad. How he'd come home after the accident. He'd given up college—soccer—to take care of him. Out of loyalty and guilt.

"I still play. Coach a boys' team twice a week and play in a rec league on Sundays. I run every morning, too." He looked me over in appreciation. "What about you? You look in shape."

I snorted. "I walk around campus and chase toddlers at the daycare. Nothing more rigorous than that."

"You should run with me sometime."

Normally the suggestion would have made me laugh, but staring into his blue eyes I thought I might actually like to try it.

Picking up another fry, I nodded. "Maybe I'll try."

"You'll get to love it. Your body will miss it when you skip a day."

The back door slammed open right then. I looked up, startled. There was a commotion that sounded like something hitting the wall. A man in a wheelchair rolled into sight. Reece tensed beside me.

The man's hair was long and looked decidedly unclean. He wore a black Pink Floyd T-shirt. Even in blue jeans, his legs looked thin from lack of use. His tattooed arms were muscular as they pushed at the wheels of his chair, propelling him forward.

Reece rose to his feet beside me and made his way across the room. "Dad."

His father's gaze snapped to him and the fierceness of his expression blossomed into outright rage. "There you are, you little fuck."

I jerked like I felt the slap of those words, even though they had been directed at Reece.

Reece's shoulders locked tight, revealing that he wasn't totally unaffected, either.

"Nice to see you, too, Dad. What are you doing here?"

"Thought you could keep me cooped up in that house, huh? Didn't think I could find a way here. Logan drove me over. He's parking the car."

Reece sent me an unreadable look. Part of me knew I should leave, that he was probably embarrassed for me to witness this drama, but I couldn't budge from my spot at the table.

"If you wanted to come here, I would have brought you."

"Yeah. Right." His father held up a crumpled flyer, brandishing it in the air. "What's this, you little shit?"

Was there a moment when he didn't call his son an obscenity? Each word made me flinch and shrink inside myself. Just like when I was a little girl. I couldn't escape it then. All I could do was clutch Purple Bear and shut my eyes and pretend I was somewhere else.

"Looks like a flyer for our Tuesday promotion. Ten-cent wings."

"You're giving away food. You're going to run us out of business."

Reece's sigh reached my ears. "It's good marketing, Dad. We triple our Tuesday night customers. Alcohol sales more than make up for—"

Mr. Mulvaney wadded up the flyer and threw it at his son. It bounced off Reece's chest. "You talk to me before you make a decision like this, you little fuck!"

Reece's hands clenched into fists at his sides, but otherwise he made no move. Logan entered the room, his steps slowing as he took in the scene.

"Logan mentioned you're looking into expanding." Logan's eyes widened and he looked toward Reece apologetically. "How you gonna do that, huh, college boy? I'm not giving you the money."

"I'm not asking you for money." Bright color flushed beneath Reece's skin. "I've tripled profits at this bar in the last two years. If that doesn't convince you that I can—"

"You think you're better than me, you bastard! Think you can do better with this place than I did—"

"No, Dad." Reece's voice sounded suddenly weary. I wanted to rise and go to him, touch him, but I stayed put, knowing that I would only attract attention to myself, and Reece wouldn't want that while he was having it out with his father. It was all so unpleasant . . . so ugly. It reminded me of everything I was running from. Everything I had vowed to leave behind.

"That's right. Just remember that. You don't know shit. I'm not dead yet. I'm still here." Mr. Mulvaney beat his chest with one knotted hand. "This is my place." His barrel chest fell and rose with exerted breaths. Seemingly satisfied that he'd had his say, he glanced back at Logan. "I'm done. C'mon." He rolled past Logan down the ramp.

Logan approached his brother, rubbing the back of his neck. "Look, I'm sorry—"

"It's okay. Go on. He'll be yelling for you."

Nodding, Logan followed after his dad.

Slowly, Reece turned. He moved toward me, but instead of reclaiming his seat he remained standing, his fingers lightly brushing the table, his gaze avoiding mine. "I've got to get back to work." His voice was carefully neutral.

"Reece, I'm—"

His eyes snapped to my face. "What? You're what? Sorry?"

Yeah. I was sorry for him. And I understood. I knew what it felt like when someone you loved betrayed you and stomped all over your heart.

I shook my head. "Why do you blame yourself?" I nodded to where his dad had been moments ago.

"Because if I had been home it wouldn't have ever happened."

"It was an accident. You shouldn't spend your life paying for it."

He snorted. "There's no such thing as an accident, is there? Really? We all make choices. Everything that happens is a result of those choices." His gaze flicked over me coldly. "Just like you made your choice. You're going to be with this Hunter guy. I'm just a distraction until the real thing comes along for you."

His words flayed me. He made it sound so ugly. Like I was using him. I guessed technically I was, but I'd always been up front with him, and he had wanted to do this, too. I thought we were enjoying each other. At least that's what I told myself. Besides, he was the one who initiated things that night he pulled me upstairs after him.

"No," I whispered, but I wasn't sure what I was denying exactly. That Hunter was the end goal for me? He still was. He had to be. I'd spent the last seven years believing in that.

It just felt wrong to label Reece a distraction. He was more than that to me. What, precisely, I didn't know. But definitely more.

The weary look came over him. He waved a hand toward the exit. "Why don't you just go? You really don't know about any of this. You don't know me."

I sucked in a breath and resisted pointing out that I thought I was starting to know him. From the first moment I met him, when he pulled over and announced that he didn't feel right leaving me alone on the side of the road, I'd had a good understanding of him. But I didn't point that out to him. Because obviously he didn't *want* me to know him. It was in every tense line of his lean body and the hard set to his jaw.

"Okay," I murmured. "Good-bye." I pushed up from the table, leaving the half-eaten food behind. Skirting him, I fled the bar, convinced that this time I wouldn't be back. This time he'd asked me to leave. He wanted me gone. It didn't matter what I wanted.

Chapter 23

HOPPING BACK INTO THE car, I handed Hunter his soda and bag of chips as I settled in against the plush leather seat of his BMW. Definitely a luxurious way to travel home. More comfortable than my Corolla. Plus, I didn't have to drive all by myself.

"Bugles?" I questioned, shaking my head with a smile as he ripped into the bag. "Never took you for a Bugles kind of guy."

He grinned. "Don't knock it till you've tried it."

"Oh, I have. I think I was seven when I last ate them." When I lived with my mom we'd subsisted on a steady diet of vending machine fare.

"Well, then you know the wonder that is the tiny Bugle." He held aloft one tiny bugle-shaped chip as if it were the Holy Grail. "Go on. Try just one."

"I'm fine. Really."

"If you can resist, then surely you've never tasted one."

Giggling, I reached inside the bag, grabbed a few, and threw them into my mouth. Chewing the salty, cheese-powder-coated chips, I said, "There. Satisfied? I tasted and can still resist."

"You're simply not human."

Shaking my head again, I unscrewed the cap on my water bottle and took a sip, washing away the taste of Bugles from my mouth.

"Bet you didn't know I liked jerky, too."

"No way. You? Wow. But they don't serve that at the country club," I mocked.

"I haven't been to the country club since I don't know when. Not really my scene anymore, you know?"

No, I didn't. I might have known Hunter all my life, but I didn't really know what he did with his free time. Aside from studying to get into med school and devoting the last two years of his life to a demanding girlfriend.

He looked both ways and pulled back out onto the two-lane highway, leaving the gas station behind. We were soon gliding along the curving road past gorgeous fall foliage. Soon the trees would be shrouded in white, but right now they were a stunning blend of gold, red, and yellow.

We'd been driving two hours but it didn't feel like it. It was fun and easy being with him. We went from regaling each other with childhood stories of Lila to discussing our classes and what we hoped to do with ourselves after college. Hunter was excited when I told him I was considering med school with my psychology degree. If I was going to help people with their problems, having a degree in medicine might make that easier.

My phone buzzed from inside my bag. I dug around in it on the floorboard, expecting another text from Em moaning about having to spend the day shopping with her father's new girlfriend, who was only five years older than herself.

Only it wasn't from Em.

Reece: I'm sorry

My thumb locked, poised over my phone. I hadn't expected to hear from him again. Or even see him. Not unless I just bumped into him on the streets in a freak coincidence. But now he was here, reaching out to me, pulling me back in.

Me: It's ok
Reece: I was a jerk. I shouldn't have told you to go. I
      wanted you to stay

A smile played on my mouth.

Me: Understandable. Your dad just came down on you
Reece: Well. Could have let you finish your food at least
Me: You saved me from the stroke that was sure 2 follow
      that meal
Reece: Wimp
Me: I don't run a half marathon every morning like you
Reece: But you'll run with me

I paused again, thinking. He was asking if we were going to see each other again. Inhaling, I typed.

Me: I thought we had seen the last of each other?
Reece: Do you want to see the last of me?

"Everything okay?"

I jerked at Hunter's question, startled. I had forgotten I was in the car with him. Forgotten he was even here. "Oh. Sorry. Didn't mean to be rude." I typed off a quick reply.

Me: Gotta go. TTYS

Exhaling, I forced a bright smile and returned my attention to Hunter, focusing on him and refusing to touch my phone again.

THANKSGIVING WITH GRAM BROUGHT back a flood of memories. I was hugged so much and smiled so much my cheeks ached. All the residents of Chesterfield Retirement Village were family to me. The place was home, even if unorthodox.

At eight o'clock Thanksgiving night, still stuffed from turkey, dressing, mashed potatoes, yams, and all the other goodies associated with the holiday, I borrowed Mrs. Lansky's car from next door since she hardly used it anymore and headed over to Lila's house.

I didn't even have a chance to push the doorbell before the door was yanked open and Lila locked me in a suffocating embrace with a happy squeal.

Pulling back, she sized me up, assessing me from head to toe. "Damn, you look good! You highlighted your hair. I love it!"

She pulled me into the impressive foyer with its vaulted ceiling. Linking arms with me, she led me into the kitchen, whispering into my ear even though no one was around to overhear. "Whatever you're doing with Hunter, it's working. He hasn't stopped asking me when you're getting here."

"Really," I murmured, heat washing up my neck.

"Uh-huh. He's waiting in the kitchen."

Voices carried from that room, and I knew what I would find before I entered—Lila's parents and grandparents intent over a Monopoly board. Hunter stood at the island, bent over a slice of pumpkin pie as he watched the proceedings.

Everyone exclaimed when they saw me. Hunter straightened, his lips curving in that blinding smile of his as all the Montgomerys surrounded me and took turns lavishing me with hugs. After peppering me with questions about school and my grandmother and forcing me to accept a slice of pie, they returned to their game, and Lila, Hunter, and I headed upstairs for the game room to watch a movie.

I blushed as Lila made a point to sit on the far side of the big, comfy couch, making sure I had to sit beside her brother. Not exactly subtle.

After scrolling through movies to rent, we selected the new James Bond movie.

"Want some Chex Mix?" Hunter asked after it started.

I groaned, rubbing my stomach. "I can't eat for another month."

"I'll have some." Lila pushed PAUSE as Hunter headed downstairs, then directed a hard stare at me.

"All right, so what's the plan?"

I shook my head. "Plan?"

"Yeah . . . you want me to fake a headache so you two can have some alone time?"

I shook my head. "No, no. Don't do that. I want to spend some time with you, too."

"We're shopping tomorrow and doing lunch. We'll have the whole day. This is the only time you two have before you head back on Sunday."

"It's fine, really," I hissed as I heard his returning steps thudding on the stairs.

"Here he comes," she whispered, giving me a knowing wink and settling back into the corner of the couch. She punched PLAY on the remote.

I shook my head at her, hoping to convey that she shouldn't invent some excuse to leave me alone with her brother.

Thirty minutes later, she released an exaggerated sigh. "I'm really tired. Guess turkey really does make you sleepy, huh?" She unfolded her sleek dancer legs that she had tucked under her and rose gracefully to her feet. "I'm going to bed. Need my beauty sleep. Especially if we're going to hit all those sales in the morning. I'll pick up you up at seven, Pepper. Okay?"

I glared at her as she waved good night.

Hunter smiled easily at me. I forced a smile back, willing away my sudden discomfort. I turned my attention back to the movie, but didn't really see anything. Just images flashing on the screen that I couldn't process.

His arm stretched along the back of the couch behind me. I felt it there, the fingers grazing softly at my shoulder. I noted the passing of minutes on the digital clock on the Blu-ray player. Ten minutes. He shifted on the couch. The graze of his fingers was a full-blown touch. Fifteen minutes. His fingers moved, stroking my shoulder in small circles.

My stomach knotted with anxiety, torn between wanting him to make a move and wanting to flee. Was he waiting for an invitation? I couldn't help thinking that Reece would have acted by now. I'd be under him. Or over him. We'd have half our clothes off and his hands would be everywhere. My pulse jackknifed against my throat, remembering how it was with him.

Suddenly I found myself staring at Hunter, studying his profile. Even though his hand stroked my shoulder, he was watching the movie, following the characters through the action scenes. He must have sensed my stare. He turned. I held his gaze.

"Pepper?" His voice fell softly, hesitant and inquiring.

I closed the distance and kissed him. Pushed my lips against his own and serious-as-a-heart-attack kissed him, willing myself to forget Reece in the taste of him.

He was motionless for a second before reacting. Before kissing me back. He was a good kisser. I recognized that at once. He knew what to do. With his lips. His tongue. His hand came up to hold my face like I was something precious and fragile. Even so, I didn't feel it. The zing, the consuming ache filling every inch of me.

Sensation didn't slam through me like it did with Reece. *Had*. Like it *had* with him. I reminded myself of that. *Had*. It was over.

Desperate, frustrated for something to be there between us, for me to feel something—Oh, God, *anything*—with Hunter, I climbed up on my knees and straddled him, never breaking my mouth from his.

He stilled, obviously startled, for half a second before his mouth resumed kissing. He was definitely into it now, groaning when I nipped at his lip, sucking it between my teeth. His hands skimmed down my back, his palms stroking up and down rhythmically.

I tore my lips from his and kissed his jaw, his neck, sucking at the warm skin.

His hand buried in the back of my hair. "God. Pepper. What are you doing to me?"

His words sank inside my mind, forming into a very real question. *What was I doing?*

The answer came back to me, clear and ugly, resounding like a bell in my ears. Using him. Searching for something, desperate to feel with him what I felt when I was with Reece.

Only it wasn't working. It wasn't there. Not with him.

I lifted my lips from his throat and stared down at him, stunned, horrified. He blinked, looking up at me, his deep brown eyes glassy with desire. "Pepper? Everything okay?"

I shook my head, words stuck in my throat.

"Hunter! Lila and Pepper!" Mrs. Montgomery called from the base of the stairs. "We're putting up the desserts. Want any first?"

Annoyance flashed across Hunter's face at the interruption. "No thanks, Mom!" His gaze zeroed back on me. He brushed his thumb against my cheek. "Pepper?"

"I—I need to go home."

"Now?"

I nodded and climbed off him. "Yes. I gotta get up early to meet Lila."

He rose to his feet, one hand stretching out for me like he wanted to touch me but was unsure. "Are we okay?"

I tucked a strand of hair behind my ear, avoiding his gaze. He actually sounded worried. "Yeah. We're good."

"Is it that guy from Gino's? Reece?"

My gaze snapped back to him. "Why do you ask that?"

"I saw how you were together."

"We're not together," I snapped, too quickly probably.

"You're more than friends. I could see that much."

"No," I bit out. "We're not."

He nodded slowly, as if trying to accept that. "Okay. Good. Then I—" He stopped and dragged a hand through his hair. "Then I want to give us a shot, Pepper. I've been thinking about you a lot the last couple of weeks. I know it's tricky considering you and my sister are best friends, but I think it's worth the risk."

This was it. Finally. He was offering what I'd always wanted. A chance to be with him. The rest, the fireworks I'd felt with Reece, they would come. They had to. I refused to believe otherwise.

"I want to try, too," I said slowly, the words withering something inside me. *What was wrong with me?* Where was the elation?

He reached for my arm, slid his fingers down, and captured my hand in his. "Well, all right then. Let's do this. I'm going to court you, Pepper."

"*Court* me?"

"Yeah. Like you deserve."

God. It was like a dream. Those words. From Hunter. Directed at me.

I knew I should say something. "Oh," I managed to get out.

He smiled, seemingly unbothered at my lack of enthusiasm.

Holding my hand, he walked me outside to Mrs. Lansky's car parked in their circular driveway. I unlocked the door.

"I'll pick you up Sunday morning. Eight o'clock okay?"

I nodded, accepting his quick peck on the lips.

He opened the driver's door for me and I slid inside. Buckling my seat belt, I started the car and waved good-bye.

"PEPPER, YOU HOME ALREADY?" Gram poked her head in my room. I didn't bother telling her I'd been home for over an hour and it was already eleven thirty. Gram slept off and on throughout the day like a cat. I didn't know if it was her age, the pain of her arthritis, or the myriad of medicines she took keeping her up all hours.

"Yes, Gram. I got home a little while ago."

She stood at the threshold in her housecoat. The kind that snaps up the front. She still wore one of those. I'm not sure what store even sold them anymore, but she seemed to have an endless supply of them.

Her heavily lined mouth worked in an exaggerated manner before speaking, her tongue darting to moisten her lips. I asked her once why she did that and she said her medication made her mouth dry. "Did you have a good time at the Montgomerys'?"

"Yes, Gram. They all said to tell you Happy Thanksgiving."

"Ah, that's nice. Well, good night, dear." Gram's feet shuffled down the hall, leaving me alone again. I stared at my ceiling, watching the spinning blades of the fan. That sound had lulled me to sleep for so many years. Years when I had lain in this bed fantasizing over becoming Mrs. Hunter Montgomery. And now we were dating. He wanted to *court* me. Take *that*, former cheerleaders of Taylor High School.

Turning onto my side, I curled myself around my pillow, hugging it close. It wasn't a stuffed animal, but I hugged it like it was. Few stuffed animals had ever graced my room. Not since Purple Bear. I was too old to cling to stuffed animals, but the pillow felt comforting and familiar.

My phone buzzed on my nightstand. I reached for it. My stomach fluttered when I saw Reece's name.

Reece: Happy Thanksgiving
Me: Same to you . . .

I bit the inside of my cheek, considering what else to say.

Me: Did you have a good day?
Reece: Yes. My Aunt Beth came over w/a turkey. My dad
           was even almost human
Me: That's good
Reece: What about yours?

I stared at the words on the screen for a long moment, thinking about my day, about kissing Hunter, and how much I should tell Reece.

Reece: How's Hunter?
Me: Good
Reece: You kissed

I gasped, my fingers tightening around my phone. Could he read my mind across miles?

Me: How do you know that?

It didn't occur to me to lie.

Reece: Because that's what I would have done. I did do it. Remember? First chance I got

Me: Actually I kissed him

There was a long pause, and I began to worry that he wasn't going to reply at all. Maybe I shouldn't have been so honest.

Reece: Guess those lessons in foreplay helped after all

Me: Guess so

Reece: Congrats, Pepper. You got what you wanted. Good night

Me: Good night

I dropped the phone on the bed beside me. Turning, I burrowed my face into the pillow and cried great ugly sobs. They weren't the first I had ever cried in this room, on this bed, into this very pillow, but they were definitely the most senseless. I had nothing to cry about. I had come so far and finally gotten what I wanted.

Chapter 24

SUNDAY AFTERNOON, HUNTER DROPPED me off at my dorm with a gentle kiss and a promise to text me later. After unpacking, I fell onto my bed with a sigh, thinking I'd get some homework done, but instead I ended up falling asleep. Apparently the four-hour drive wore me out. Maybe it was all the effort I put into acting cheerful and like I wasn't having any doubts about what I wanted to happen between Hunter and myself.

I didn't feel much better after my nap, either. I still wasn't any more certain about Hunter and me, which filled me with no small amount of panic. For so long I had convinced myself he was the one, the one who would make me right. Make me safe. Make me whole.

If I didn't have that anymore, then what did I have?

Scrubbing both hands over my face, I rose from my bed and sank down at my desk, cracking open my Abnormal Psych notes and telling myself I could actually study when my head hurt from thinking.

My phone buzzed from across the room. I moved to pick it up, glad for the excuse to procrastinate.

Reece: Hey. Home yet?

I smiled, ridiculously happy that he was still communicating with me. After last night, I wasn't so sure.

Me: Yes. Got back couple hours ago
Reece: I want to see you

No mincing words. I hesitated, resisting the immediate urge to type "yes." I needed to consider this. Use logic instead of wild impulse, which seemed to be my only setting when it came to him.

The screen went dark. The phone buzzed again in my hand, a new message from Reece lighting up the screen.

Reece: Open the door

My head whipped around, staring at my door as if it were a living thing. My heart took off, wild as a bird trapped and struggling inside my too-tight chest. In two strides I was there, pulling the door wide. Reece stood before me, phone in hand, those bright blue eyes, brighter even than I remembered, fastened on me.

We moved in unison. He stepped inside, shutting the door behind him just as I scooted back, making room for him to enter. Closed inside my room, we stared at each other, frozen like two statues. Everything slowed. Like someone hit a PAUSE button. Blood rushed, a dull roar in my ears. I imagined I could even hear the muffled thump of my heart.

Then everything leaped to action.

We came together. Phones slipped from our hands and thudded to the floor as we collided. Our mouths fused, lips breaking only to pull our shirts over our heads in a blur of motion. Everything was frantic. Desperate. Almost violent in its fierceness.

"God, I missed you," he muttered, his hand skimming my face, hard fingers burying themselves in my hair and gripping my scalp as his hot mouth crashed over mine.

My hands went for the front of his jeans, yanking open the button snap and tugging the jeans down as he fell over me on the bed, between my thighs. He pulled back to shove them down his narrow hips, cursing when they got stuck at his shoes.

I watched, devouring the sight of him as I anxiously stripped off my yoga pants, my panties, everything.

"Damn it," he snarled, jerking off his shoes and then shucking his jeans the rest of the way off.

Then we came together again, bare skin sliding sinuously against each other. He settled between my thighs and it felt so right, like two puzzle pieces locking together.

He kissed my breasts and I whimpered, arching my spine, wanting more. His mouth closed around one nipple, and I moaned, my fingers clenching his muscular biceps. He shifted his weight and brought his erection directly against the core of me.

I panted, my fingers moving to clutch the back of his neck, clinging, straining against him, pulling him closer as I rotated my hips, needing him inside me like a body needs oxygen.

"Pepper, are you sure?"

God, yes. Gasping, I shifted my hips and pushed up against him. "I want this. I want you, Reece."

His blue eyes gleamed fiercely. He lifted off me and fumbled with his discarded jeans. I almost moaned in pain at the loss of him. All of me felt cold, empty.

And then the warmth was back. He was between my parted thighs, tearing the wrapper off a condom with his teeth. I watched as he rolled it on, fascinated at the sight, the act.

He wrapped an arm around my waist and hauled me closer, holding me steady as he began to sink inside me, his eyes locked with mine. It was a surreal moment, staring into the deep of his eyes, feeling his body joining with mine.

I was ready. My body stretched to accommodate him. It wasn't uncomfortable exactly, but definitely foreign. Still exciting. Gaspy little breaths escaped me.

Just when I thought he was done, that I was filled to capacity, he pushed in deeper.

My eyes flared wide, and I whimpered. Okay, that was a little uncomfortable. He stilled, his biceps tensing, muscles bunching tightly. "Are you all right?"

"Yes. Don't stop. Do it!"

The arm at my waist pulled me closer, mashing my breasts to his chest as he thrust himself fully inside me, wrenching a sharp gasp from me.

"Wow," I choked.

"Should I—?"

"Keep going," I commanded, my nails scoring his back. He rocked his hips against me and I cried out, arching against him.

"Oh, fuck, Pepper, you feel good."

An aching pressure built inside me as he moved faster, increasing the delicious friction and tightening the coil low in my belly. It was like before, when he made me come just by using his hand. Only better. Everything more intense.

I writhed against him, desperate to reach that climax. He hooked a hand under my knee and wrapped my leg around his waist. The next thrust shattered me. I never felt anything so amazing. So good. My vision blurred as he hit that spot deeper. He moved against me, working a steady pace. I dragged my nails through his short hair, loving this absolute freedom to touch him, to love him with my hands. His name tripped from my lips.

"Pepper," he growled in my ear. "Come for me, baby."

I was almost there. Shudders shook through me. I burrowed my head in the warm nook of his neck, muffling my moans. His hand found me, framing my face. A thumb under my chin, fingers splayed over my cheek, he held me there, watching me, peering into my eyes as he moved inside me. "I want to see you."

I nodded jerkily. The familiar burning tightness seized me, made me arch up against him. "Ohh."

"That's it, Pepper." He drove harder into me and I cried out, every nerve bursting. I went limp. He hugged me closer, his lips seizing mine. I groaned into his mouth as I felt his own release follow, shuddering through him.

We collapsed together on the bed, his weight on top of me. As heavy as he was, I didn't want him to ever move. I could stay like this forever.

FOREVER LASTED ABOUT TWO minutes. Reece pressed a kiss to my collarbone that made me shiver and then rose from the bed to dispose of the condom. I found some wipes in my drawer and cleaned myself off, hesitating a moment at the sight of a rusty-colored smudge on my thigh. It startled me, forcing me to confront the reality of what I had just done. With Reece.

I hurriedly wiped the blood away. My face burned as he watched me. I tossed the wipe into the small trash bin, aware of a slight soreness between my legs as I moved. Slipping my panties back on, I lowered myself to the bed, pulled my knees to my chest, and then tugged the covers over me.

"You okay?"

He sat in front of me, his legs going on either side of me so that he could face me and hold me at the same time.

I nodded. "It didn't hurt."

He tucked a strand of hair behind my ear. "It gets better."

I felt my eyes widen. "Really? 'Cause that was pretty amazing."

Grinning, he kissed me. "It was all you, baby."

I doubted that. I could never have as much fun alone as I had with him. I doubted I could have as much fun with any-one. That thought made me frown. Panic fluttered inside me. Reece—*this*. It wasn't the plan.

"Hey. No frowns." He tapped at the edge of my mouth. "Do I even want to know what you're thinking?"

I swallowed. "How can this work, Reece?"

His smile slipped away. The glow ebbed from his eyes. "Wow. You don't waste any time. I'm getting the brush-off already? No time for afterglow." He remained sitting in front of me, his legs stretched on either side of me, but he dropped his arms. No more hug.

"I'm sorry."

"Yeah." His voice bit out the single word. "Me, too."

"I don't want—" I stopped, struggling with what to say. There was a lot that I didn't want to happen in this moment. *I didn't want him to hate me. I didn't want to lose him.*

He laughed harshly. "You don't know what you want, Pepper. That much is clear."

I shook my head, a lump the size of a golf ball inside my throat. "I do. I've always known that. That's why this"—I waved between us—"can never be."

"Oh. Yeah? Then do me a favor and explain it to me. Why is Hunter so important? Why does it gotta be him? 'Cause that's what this is about, right? You fuck me but you still want to be with him."

I flinched and glanced away, my gaze landing on the pictures across the room. The one of me with Lila and Hunter. That was supposed to be my future. With the Montgomerys. With Hunter. Or someone like him.

"You know my mother dumped me and left me to live with my grandmother."

I flicked a glance back at him. He nodded once, his jaw

clenched tightly, waiting for me to continue. "Well, that was after three years of living with her. She lost the house the year after Daddy died. Then we slept on the couches of friends. But that got old. They got tired of us. And she just kept getting worse . . . doing more shit. Anything good, she lost."

"Except you. She kept you."

My eyes stung. I nodded, blinking back the burn. "Yeah. She kept me. It was the two of us. Surviving in motel rooms. Sometimes sleeping in the car. She'd do whatever she needed to get her next fix."

He touched my face, his thumb brushing over my cheek. "What happened to you, baby?"

I inhaled. "Nothing. She always kept me safe. Or tried to anyway. She would leave me in a closet or bathroom. I'd hide in the tub with my stuffed animal. Purple Bear. I had him forever." I smiled in memory. "My father won him at a carnival for me. I'd lost everything but I still had that bear. And Mom. Whenever she stuck me in a tub or closet while she got high with some loser, she told me Purple Bear would keep me safe until she came for me."

I stopped now, because I couldn't really talk about what happened next. I'd never talked about it with anyone before.

"But it didn't keep you safe, did it?"

I shook my head, choking down a sob. "No."

"What happened?"

My voice got really small. "He found me in the tub." My fingers pressed over my lips. "I wasn't quiet enough."

"Who found you?"

I shook my head slowly, seeing the flash of a skull-faced ring. "Some guy. One of Mom's . . . dates."

"What did he do, Pepper?" His whisper was in direct contrast to his face, which was hard as stone, his eyes like ice chips.

I rocked back a little on the bed, hugging my knees closer to my chest. "He made me get out of the tub." I sucked in a deep breath, bracing myself. Soundless tears rolled down my cheeks. I dashed them away with my hand, reciting the events of that night as matter-of-factly as possible—as though they had happened to some other girl and not me. Now that I had started, I was determined to say it all. Finally. "And then he made me take off my shirt."

Reece's arms wrapped around me again, holding me, and in that moment it was like they were the only thing keeping me together. Keeping me from breaking into pieces. My fingers dug into his forearms, clinging to him as words rushed from me.

"H-he unzipped his pants and started playing with himself in front of me . . . l-looking at me. He told me to touch it, but I wouldn't." I shook my head, lips pressing into a firm line as I recalled the man's expression. Angry. But also excited that I was defying him. He wanted me to fight him. "He told me to take off the rest of my clothes. I tried to get away. He grabbed me, tried to pull down my shorts. I fought back and he just laughed and slapped me. Things got really crazy then. I screamed. Went a little hysterical." I searched Reece's gaze, shaking my head almost apologetically. Like I should somehow have kept my cool. "I was just a kid."

He nodded, blinking eyes that looked suspiciously moist. "What happened next?"

I shrugged like it wasn't a big deal. "Mom came in and freaked. They fought. He slapped her around, but she got him out the door, and then she just came into the bathroom and stared at me. I never saw her look like that before. Even at Dad-dy's funeral she had never looked so . . . wrecked. We packed up our stuff in the car and drove. I fell asleep in the backseat, but when I woke we were at Gram's."

I stopped at this part because as hard as it was to tell him what happened to me in that bathroom, this was actually harder. This was the part that was etched in my mind, burned into me with a red-hot brand.

"I was actually excited at first. Mom and Gram didn't get along, so we didn't see her that much. She took me to the door. Hugged me and . . . said good-bye." I couldn't breathe as I remembered this. The feel of my mother's hands on my arms as she bent down and stared at me, her green eyes eerily bright in her thin face. "She told me she couldn't keep me safe anymore." The tears rolled freely, unchecked and silent on my cheeks.

Reece sighed. "It was the best she could do—"

"No," I snapped. "The best she could have done is get the help she needed. Beat her addiction."

He cupped my cheek gently. "She got you to someplace safe."

"Safe?" I laughed at that. It was a harsh and ugly sound. "Funny you should say that."

He arched an eyebrow.

"When she was walking away, she suddenly turned around. She ran back and grabbed Purple Bear from me. She ripped him. Tore him apart right in front of me." I could still see all the tufts of cotton floating in the air.

"What the fuck?"

I continued bitterly, remembering how watching her

destroy that bear felt like she was murdering a part of me. "She told me Purple Bear couldn't keep me *safe*. Just like she couldn't. That I should never expect that from anyone. That I needed to look after myself now and never count on anyone."

He was silent for a moment, processing. "She was trying to help—"

"Yeah. I know she was trying to teach me a lesson in self-reliance. As screwed up as it was. But I was a child."

Reece held me, his hand brushing my back in smooth sweeps. I let him. For a little while anyway, I let his hand and arms, his strong body, comfort me, knowing it would be the last time. He made small hushing sounds near my ear.

"I know you've been hurt," he started, his voice low in my ear. "So have I. Maybe we can help heal each other."

I broke away, peering at him in bewilderment.

He watched me, waiting as I studied him. As I observed a person every bit as damaged as I was. No one lost their mother at eight and lived with a man like his father and came out whole.

I turned and reached for my shirt and pulled it on over my head. Facing him again, I spoke evenly. "Ever since my mom left me I've had a plan. I know it sounds ridiculous to you, but Hunter was part of that."

"That's bullshit." He stood. Indifferent to his nakedness, he grabbed his clothes and started getting dressed with hard movements. "You've built some kind of fairy tale around him. I guess the experience with your mother didn't teach you shit."

I flinched. "What's that supposed to mean?"

He stopped and glared at me. "You don't want Hunter. You're still looking for your purple bear. Someone to give you a sense of security. You don't get it. That doesn't exist. As wrong as your mom was about a lot of crap, she was right about that. Bad shit happens, and there's not always gonna be someone there to protect you from it."

I shook my head. "So what? I'm supposed to just flip a switch and walk away from a good thing and embrace . . ."

My gaze raked him.

You.

I didn't say it, but we both heard it. He understood. His gaze scoured me, blazed a path across my features, missing nothing. Seeing more of me than I had ever revealed to anyone. All my flaws.

He made a disgusted sound and moved for the door. Opening it, he stopped and stood there, staring across the room at me. "You can't even see it. I'm the safest thing you'll ever find."

And then he was gone. I was all alone.

I WAS LYING IN the same spot on the bed when Emerson and Georgia found me. They took one look at my ravaged face and surrounded me on the bed like clucking hens. Between choked tears and hiccups I told them everything. Well, everything except my fucked-up history and why I couldn't be with Reece.

"I don't understand." Georgia pushed the hair back off my shoulders and crossed her legs Indian style. "Why can't you give him a chance?"

"You did sleep with him," Em reminded me. As though I could forget that. "You must care about him."

I looked between the two of them helplessly. I couldn't

bare myself to the bones twice in one day. I couldn't take doing that all over again. "Just trust me. It wouldn't work."

"Okay." Georgia held my hands between us, nodding gently. "Then we support you. Whatever you decide, we're here for you."

"Damn straight," Em agreed. "You just tell us who to punch in the junk and we're on it."

I laughed, wiping at my runny nose. From Emerson's relieved grin, that was clearly her goal. "No. Don't hit anyone."

My phone buzzed from across the room. I jumped up to grab it, my heart a stupid traitor in my chest, lifting with the insane hope that it was Reece.

Evidently it was going to take my heart some time to catch up with my brain. Why would I even want a text from him? Especially after I just broke up with him. Um. Not that we had been official or anything but it sure as hell felt like a breakup.

I scanned my phone. The message wasn't from Reece.

Hunter: Miss u already. Dinner tomorrow?

Guilt pinched at my heart. While he was missing me I had been with Reece. I shook my head. Hunter and I hadn't declared ourselves exclusive. And it had been just one time with Reece. And now it was over. Time to move on.

Dutifully, I typed a message back to him.

"Who is it?" Emerson asked as I set my phone back down and sank onto my swivel chair.

"Hunter. He wants to know if I want to grab dinner tomorrow night."

"What did you tell him?"

"Yes."

Emerson and Georgia exchanged glances. Clearly, they thought I was crazy, and I couldn't disagree with them. Reece's words played over and over in my mind. *I'm the safest thing you'll ever find.* What did he mean by that? Trying to sort it all out made my head ache.

I felt unhinged. I finally had what I wanted. The guy I'd waited almost a decade for, and all I could do was think about someone else. Someone who was just as broken as me.

Chapter 25

DAYS SLID INTO WEEKS. The weather grew colder and the first week of December saw our first snowfall. I lost myself in school, work, and Hunter. Meeting at the Java Hut most mornings became habit. True to his word, he was courting me. For the first time in my life I had a boyfriend.

Dinners out. A few movies. Study dates in the library. He was the perfect gentleman. Whenever the thought crossed my mind that he was maybe a little boring—or that *we* were—my mind drifted to Reece. I shouldn't compare them, but I always found myself doing so. They were different. Reece was passion. Reece was risk. Reece and me? Well, that was never happening.

Besides. He wasn't coming around anymore. He'd moved on just as I had. If I felt especially bitter and a little nauseated when I thought about him moving on, resuming his life, seeing other girls, I told myself it would pass. Eventually.

Em saw Reece at the bar—unnecessarily reminding me that he looked good. Well, to quote her: *damn* good. He had acknowledged her. Maybe they talked. I don't know. I changed the subject. I was afraid to ask. Afraid to know what Em told him. As candid as she was, I was sure I wouldn't like it.

My boots thudded over the sidewalk as I hurried toward the Hut. I was running a little late to meet Hunter. The pavement was swept clear of snow but a thin layer coated the shrubbery and lawn like fine powder.

I snuggled my chin deeper into my favorite cashmere scarf. It was a gift from Lila last Christmas, and more than I would ever have spent on myself. Turning the corner, I spotted Hunter waiting out front. He looked good in his dark overcoat with an ash-colored wool scarf draped effortlessly around him. He was one of those guys that looked good in a scarf. A pair of girls passing him on the sidewalk sent him a long glance. He didn't even notice. His attention was fixed on me as I approached.

"Hey," I greeted him, my breath fogging lightly in front of me.

"Hey there." He leaned in and kissed my cheek.

"You didn't have to wait out here. It's freezing."

He pulled open the door for me and I stepped into the cozy warm interior, immediately inhaling the aroma of espresso beans and fresh-baked pastries. Christmas music played softly and several festive wreaths and green garlands hung about the place.

Tugging off my gloves, I got into line.

"Let me guess. The usual latte and scone?" he asked beside me.

"Am I *that* predictable?" Smiling, I narrowed my eyes on him in mock annoyance. "That's not such a good thing, I think. We've only been dating a little while."

"But we've known each other forever," he reminded me.

"I suppose. But a girl likes to be a little bit of a mystery."

His gaze scanned me. "Oh, you mystify me plenty, Pepper." The way his eyes rested on my mouth killed the light-hearted moment. I knew what he was thinking. It wasn't hard to read his mind when he looked at me like that.

Since returning from Thanksgiving—*since Reece*—the extent of our making out had been kissing. Nothing more. The other night at his place he'd slipped a hand under my sweater. My reaction? Darting off his couch and inventing some excuse to get home. It wasn't hard to figure out the question on his mind. *Why was I so frigid?*

It just felt too soon. Too fast.

You took things fast with Reece. Shaking off the annoying little whisper, I looked straight ahead, willing the line to move. That's when I noticed the girl moving away from the cashier and off to the side to wait at the bar for her drink. She was hard to miss.

With sleek blond hair that fell to her waist, she was stunning. She wore a black fitted leather jacket, leggings, and heeled boots that reached her knees. Emerson would die for her jacket. The boots, too. I was still admiring her when Reece joined her.

My Reece. No. Not mine.

OhGodOhGodOhGod.

Everything slowed and ground to a halt. Except the two of them. Reece and this beautiful girl. He'd obviously just paid for their drinks. They didn't touch, but their body language was familiar as they stood comfortably side by side. She leaned toward him as she talked, touching his arm.

He stood in his usual casual manner, one hand slipped halfway inside the back pocket of his jeans as he listened to her, watching her like he used to watch me. Intent and focused. As if whatever she was saying was riveting.

"Pepper, the line moved." Hunter took my elbow and guided me forward.

My chest ached. Air felt too thick to drag into my raw lungs. They wouldn't be able to leave without seeing me. Closer up in line now, we were just a few feet away from them. Panicked, I jerked around.

I was freaking out, but I had never counted on seeing him again. Stupid, I guess, thinking that he limited his life to the bar. Of course he did other things. He ran every morning. Played soccer and coached a boys' league. Fixed the Campbells' sink and whatever else broke in their house. He was out there, coexisting in the same world with me. I should have anticipated this moment. Just because I quit going to Mulvaney's didn't mean I was never going to come face-to-face with him again.

"Pepper?" Hunter stared down at me in concern, his forehead creased. "Are you okay?"

I nodded, commanding myself to get a grip. "Yeah." Feeling calmer, I inhaled and turned back around, hoping that Reece and the gorgeous girl had slipped out the door by now.

Reece stood directly in front of me. "Hi, Pepper. How are you?"

His voice sounded exactly as I remembered. Deep. Calm and even. His face revealed none of the intense emotions that had been there the last time I saw him. He looked relaxed. Politely interested.

"Hi. I'm good. How are you?" Was that croak my voice?

He nodded. "Good."

Check yes for useless pleasantries.

He reached out and lightly brushed the arm of the girl beside him. "This is Tatiana."

Oh my God. Her name was Tatiana? Only supermodels and Russian ice skaters were named Tatiana. Which one was she?

"Hi." She smiled warmly. I detected no accent.

Reece's gaze traveled to Hunter, reminding me that it was my turn. "You remember Hunter?"

"Yeah. Hey, man." The two shook hands, and the moment was even stranger than the last time at Gino's. Hunter, my now-boyfriend, shaking hands with the guy I'd kicked out of my dorm room minutes after taking my virginity. I just didn't think a latte was going to cut it for me. I needed something stronger. Like hemlock.

Reece's gaze drifted back to me. "Well, see you around. Take care."

I nodded numbly. "Bye. Merry Christmas."

He hesitated, his gaze unreadable as it locked with mine, lingering. "You, too, Pepper."

And then he was gone. With a hand on Tatiana's back, he guided her outside. I couldn't resist sneaking a look behind me as they departed and passed along the front windows. They made a beautiful couple, and that only made me want to throw up.

When I turned, it was to find Hunter watching me, a thoughtful look on his face.

I flashed him a pained smile and stepped up to the cashier.

I ordered my scone and latte. "See," I said as we moved over to the bar. "You do know me well."

"I want to."

Something in his voice drew my attention. He looked at me searchingly, his brown eyes probing. Like he wanted me to say something. Or do something.

I placed a hand on his chest and leaned in to give him a peck on the lips. He surprised me by pulling me closer and kissing me more exuberantly than he ever had in public.

When he pulled back, he said, "I want to know you. If you'll let me."

A sudden lump formed in my throat, making it impossible to speak. My latte and scone appeared at the bar and I stepped forward to claim them, wondering if I could even make that promise with any honesty. Because something was becoming increasingly clear to me. No matter how much I tried to pretend otherwise. No matter how much I tried to deny it.

Reece had ruined me for anyone else.

CLOSING THE DOOR ON Madison's room, I moved on to Sheridan's bedroom at the top of the stairs. The seven-year-old slept, too, her thumb plugged into her mouth. We'd had a full evening. Both girls were wiped out. We'd colored and played Candy Land and hide-and-seek. All before dining on pizza and Rice Krispie Treats in the shape of Christmas trees. Satisfied that both were settled, I headed downstairs. The Campbells' new puppy had its paws up on the coffee table in an attempt to chew on the corner of my notebook. Smiling, I scooped up the little fur ball and cuddled it for a moment as I admired the twinkling Christmas tree. I toed one of the bright packages and addressed the puppy. "All these shiny boxes, and you go for my stuff? I can just hear myself telling my prof now: but the dog ate my homework."

The sweet little beast slapped my nose with a too big paw and licked my face.

"Aw, don't try to sweet-talk me. Mrs. Campbell says you have to go in your crate after the girls go to bed." I walked through the old farmhouse, past the kitchen and down the short hall into the laundry room where they kept the crate. Once inside, the puppy immediately began to cry.

I wagged a finger at his face peering at me through the cage door. "Now stop that. You know the drill by now."

I closed the laundry room door so I didn't have to hear the little Lab's whimpers and took my place on the couch. A week before break and I had a paper due. That's why I took the babysitting job when Mrs. Campbell called. Hunter had wanted me to go out with him and some of his other premed friends, but this way I figured I could at least knock out my first draft.

It had nothing to do with the fact that I had decided I needed to break up with Hunter. At least that's what I told myself.

I sighed heavily. I couldn't take it anymore. I cared about him too much. He was so good. I just didn't appreciate him like he deserved. I didn't want him. Not like I wanted Reece.

I could admit that to myself now. I wanted Reece. Wrong or right, there it was. Not that it mattered. He'd moved on. Even if I hadn't been terrible to him, even if the idea of going to him didn't *still* fill me with all my old anxieties, there was Tatiana now.

No. I wasn't breaking up with Hunter to run after Reece. Sadly, that ship had sailed. I was doing it because it wasn't fair to stay with Hunter feeling the way I did. Hunter wanted me. All of me. And I couldn't do it. I couldn't give him that. I couldn't give him me. I had to end it. I was just waiting for the right time. The right words.

Pushing thoughts of Hunter and Reece aside, I forced myself to concentrate on my notes and write. An hour went by. I was halfway through my draft and making progress when I laid my head down on the couch to rest my aching eyes. Just for a minute. Maybe if I was lucky, Reece would be waiting for me in my dreams.

I WOKE TO A faint popping sound.

Pushing up on the couch, it took me a moment to remember where I was. I coughed, covering my mouth as my waking brain struggled to grasp why the room was so gray. The lights of the Christmas tree sparkled through the opaque air.

Smoke.

My heart jumped to my throat. I vaulted to my feet and looked around wildly, trying to process what was happening.

I heard the pop again.

Fire.

The smoke billowed thickly from the kitchen. I hurried that way, peering within, thinking that I needed to hurry and put out whatever was burning.

That's when I saw that the stove was engulfed in flames that were spreading to the cabinets. The heat reached me where I stood, singeing my face. I immediately forgot about trying to put out the fire myself. I didn't even know if they had an extinguisher in the house.

The kids. They were my only thought as I rushed for the stairs, charging through the rising smoke. I coughed violently, remembering that in the event of a fire you should crawl on the floor where the smoke was least dense.

Except the girls were on the second floor. I had no choice. I was going up.

I scrambled up the stairs, gasping and coughing my way through the haze. The smoke alarm went off then, loud and shrill. I prayed it was actually wired to a system that alerted the authorities and not just a warning for the inhabitants of the house.

I ran into Madison's room and grabbed the two-year-old. She resisted at first, groggy and confused from sleep. Holding her tight, I kept moving, talking so she could recognize my voice, "It's me, Maddy. We've got to get out of the house."

Sheridan was already awake from the alarm, sitting up in bed with eyes wide in her little face. "C'mon!" I grabbed her hand and pulled her after me. When we reached the top of the stairs, the fire was a living, breathing beast below, snarling for us.

Sheridan pulled back in fear. I tightened my grip on her small hand, determined not to lose her. "We have to do this. Don't let go of my hand!"

Maybe it was the panic in my voice, but she stopped pulling away. Madison buried her face in my sweater and tightened her thin arms around my neck. Holding them tightly, I descended the stairs. Just a few more steps to the front door. *We were going to make it!*

Somehow I had the presence of mind to grab my bag off the table right beside the front door. Unbolting the lock, I hurled us out into the fresh air, leaving the heat and smoke behind.

I made it several yards away from the house before passing Madison to her sister. My eyes had teared so badly it was hard to see, but I managed to recover my phone from my bag. Over the girls' sobs, I dialed 911. This far outside the city, I knew it was going to take them a while to get here. I only hoped there was something left of the house when they arrived.

I'd just finished giving the address to the operator when Sheridan screamed loud enough to give me a heart attack. I dropped to my knees on the cold ground and grabbed her arms. "What? What is it? Are you hurt?"

She pointed to the house. "Jazz! Jazz is in there!"

I looked in horror back at the burning house. Oh. God. The puppy. I just acted. I shoved the phone at Sheridan. "Wait here! I mean it. Stay with your sister. Help is coming."

I sprinted back into the house, convinced that I could do this. There was still time. The laundry room was on the other side of the kitchen. I could reach it. I could save the dog.

Dropping to my knees, I began crawling through the smoke. I knew the floor plan well. Coughing, I reached the room quickly and had the cage door open in a flash.

The puppy whimpered but came to me readily. I stuffed him inside my sweatshirt. When I turned around, ready to crawl back out, the fire had spread even more, a great wall ahead of me. In the blink of an eye, it had consumed half the living room, eating up the walls like some kind of red-orange river.

Oh God. Was this it? I'd lived my whole life afraid to make a move because it might be the wrong one, and now I would die in a fire before I even turned twenty?

I'd said good-bye to Reece and kicked him out of my life for what? To end this way? No. *Hell no.*

I moved, dragging myself over the floor, choking for breath. I clawed one hand after the other. The puppy was still, a warm little body inside my sweatshirt, and I wondered dimly if it was too late for him. Had this all been for nothing?

My entire body felt like lead as I struggled through the black smoke. My head throbbed as I wheezed, my lungs withering, dying for a taste of oxygen. I turned my face, searching, suddenly confused. Which way was the door?

Oh God. *So sorry. I'm so sorry.* I'm not sure who the apology was for. Myself? Gram? My friends? Reece?

Reece.

Yes. I wished I could tell him I was sorry. Sorry about running. From us. From all he had offered me. That was my biggest sin, I realized. My greatest regret. Running from love. *I'm the safest thing you'll ever find.* Suddenly I understood what he had been saying. He had cared about me. Maybe even loved me. He was the real thing. Better than any plan or fantasy I'd created in my head. And I'd pushed him away.

My arms gave out. I slumped to the carpet, collapsing on my side, still coughing, my chest tight and aching.

"Pepper!"

I flinched.

"Pepper!"

Cruel mind. Maybe this was my hell, to imagine Reece's voice so close.

"Pepper!"

I forced my head up and peered through the haze. I made out the shape of someone through the smoke and flames. Just a glimpse and then he moved away. But I recognized that voice. Reece . . .

"Here!" My voice came out a pathetic croak.

Life surged inside me, desperate for one more chance. My body fought back up to its hands and knees.

I cried out again, "Here!" I was louder, but it still wasn't enough. Panting, I pushed myself to keep going, praying I was headed in the right direction. I was making progress until I bumped into something hard. I peered through the fog, registering that it was the Campbells' grandfather clock. Flames ate at the top portion of it. Suddenly it started to crumble. I tried to back away, but it came down, landing on me and pinning me across my hips. It was only a matter of moments before it was engulfed in fire. And me with it.

Something groaned and I heard a crash behind me. A glance back revealed that a section of the ceiling had collapsed. It wouldn't be long before the rest of it caved in. I was going to burn to death. And Reece was in here somewhere searching for me.

He would burn, too.

Throwing back my head, I screamed with everything I had left. To save Reece. To save *me*. My voice ripped from my raw throat: "Here! I'm here!"

It was enough.

Reece emerged, charging through the smoke, his face sweaty and red where it wasn't covered in soot. Squatting, he pulled me free and swept me into his arms. Cradling me to his chest, he didn't bother to crawl. He ran. The fire roared all around us as he cut a straight line for the door.

We burst out into the night. The sudden cold was a shock on my scalded flesh. Reece carried me to where the girls waited. Once there, he dropped to his knees, still clutching me to him.

The girls surrounded us, crying and exclaiming. I still wheezed, starved for air. All of me hurt. My lungs, my eyes, my skin.

"Pepper." Reece turned my face and examined me. "Are you all right?"

I nodded once and even that motion hurt. "Are you?" I tried to assess him in turn, to see if he was hurt, but my eyes continued to blur with tears.

"I'm fine."

Something stirred against my chest and I remembered the puppy. I tugged at the hem of my sweatshirt, and the girls saw Jazz. They squealed and grabbed him.

Still unable to catch my breath, I fell back on the ground.

Reece's face loomed over me. "Pepper? Pepper?"

He sounded so panicked. I wanted to tell him everything was going to be all right. That I was fine. I wanted to thank him for coming, for giving me the strength to keep going, to keep fighting.

I wanted to say all these things. All these things and more. But I couldn't. I couldn't catch my breath. My hand drifted to my chest, as though I could find some switch there to help open up my oxygen-starved lungs.

There was no switch.

I wheezed, terrible little sounds escaping my lips as I struggled for more air. Spots danced before my eyes, and I hated that most of all. The edges of my vision grayed. I could barely see Reece anymore. My gaze strained, as if struggling to memorize his face. Overheated and marred with soot, it was the most beautiful thing I had ever seen.

I could hear him, though, screaming my name again and again. Could feel him. His hands on my arms, my face.

My vision went dark, and just before that darkness rolled in on my mind, I got out two words. Just two words. But they were good ones. I hoped he heard them.

"Love. You."

Chapter 26

OUCH. IT WAS MY first thought when I came to. Ouch and then: *Dear God, that really hurts.*

I moaned, and the simple action only made my throat hurt more. I quickly sealed my lips, stopping the effort.

"You're awake!"

I opened my eyes to witness Reece lurching from a chair beside me. My gaze flicked around me—hospital bed?

"Where am I?" I asked in a voice as gravelly as sandpaper. I winced and he grabbed a cup of water and held it to my lips. I drank deeply, letting the water flow over my raw tongue and throat as he replied.

"In the emergency room."

"The girls—"

"They're fine. They're with their parents. The house is gone. Some kind of faulty wiring in the kitchen. Old house. We're lucky it didn't happen when the Campbells were in bed. They might not have gotten out."

My head felt like it weighed two tons, but I lifted it to

glance down at myself. The movement made me aware of the tubes running into my nose. I reached up to touch them.

"It's to give you oxygen. Don't mess with it. They had a full oxygen mask on you earlier. They said you'll need to keep the tubes in for a while to help your lungs recover."

My hand fell away. I licked at my dry lips and fought to swallow against my raw throat. He reached for the cup again and handed it to me over the bed guard. I sipped and handed it back. "You came. H-how did you know?"

"I heard the alarm down the road. And then I saw the black smoke in the sky. I didn't know you were there until I found the girls in the yard." His jaw clenched. A muscle feathered in his cheek. His eyes blazed down at me. "You went back for a dog? What the fuck were you thinking? You could have died, Pepper! I watched the paramedics work on you and . . . I thought . . ." He stopped, his voice choking. I had never seen him like this. Not even when he told me about his mother. Not even when his father showed up and made a scene at Mulvaney's.

I held silent, letting him yell at me. I deserved it. For tonight and more.

He ducked his head, leaning his forehead on the bed guard as though he needed a moment to compose himself and stop from strangling me. I reached out and ran my fingers over his hair.

He lifted his head. His eyes gleamed with moisture and his voice was quiet as he continued, "I thought you were gone, Pepper. It was bad enough to lose you the first time, but to lose you like that? I couldn't have dealt with that."

I choked on a sob. It tore through my ravaged throat, but I couldn't have stopped it if I tried. Another hoarse sob followed. "You're the reason I'm alive. I heard you and that made me fight. You were there, somewhere, and I knew that. I had to get to you."

He reached for my face, and that's when I noticed his bandaged hands.

"Reece!" I gently took them between my hands. My eyes flew to his face. "This is from saving me."

"They're just minor burns. From when I lifted the clock. I'll be fine."

I blinked long and hard before opening my eyes to look at him. "God, we could have died tonight. It could have ended like that." A sob welled up in the back of my throat. I swallowed it down and moistened my lips. "I understand what you meant now. Bad shit happens. I thought picking Hunter . . . I was being smart." I shook my head. "My safe choices didn't matter tonight though. Did they?"

A stillness came over him. "So what are you saying?" His question hung heavily on the air.

"I know you're with Tatiana now, but—"

He shook his head, his expression bewildered. "I'm not."

"What?"

"It was just a coffee. We're old friends."

"Oh." I blinked.

"You're with Hunter." It was more of a question than a statement.

Tears welled up in my eyes. "But it hasn't been right. It hasn't been you. I can't . . . I haven't been able to—" I sucked in a deep breath. "I can't be a real girlfriend to him when all I can do is think about you."

"Ah, shit, Pepper." Still holding my face, he lowered his forehead to mine. "I'm not going through this again with you just so you can run when you get scared that I'm not like some ideal you built up in your head. I love you. I'm fucking *in* love with you, but it's all or nothing. I won't do this again unless it's going to be like that."

Now I was crying, choking on my sobs. "I know. I want that. It took me so long to figure that out, but I know now. *You* are the safest thing I'll ever find." I deliberately repeated his words, holding his gaze and letting them sink in. "Because you love me. Because I love you."

Then we were kissing. Both of us a mess. Oxygen tubing running up my nose. Neither one of us cared.

He pulled back and stared at me for a long moment before a slow grin broke across his face. "I heard you say it the first time, you know, but this time it's even better."

I blinked. "What first time?"

"Right before you passed out. Wasn't sure if you meant it. Could have just been your oxygen-starved brain."

"I remember saying it. I meant it. And I mean it now."

He kissed me again. "I love you. Ever since you walked into Mulvaney's looking like it was the last place you wanted to be." A corner of his mouth lifted. "And ever since you explained so matter-of-factly that you were looking for lessons in foreplay."

I rolled my head on the pillow with a groan. "Please. Don't remind me of that."

"C'mon." He kissed my grimy cheek. "It's good stuff. We can tell our grandkids about it someday."

I lifted my head and looked into his eyes, warmth blossoming through me at his words. "I'd rather tell the one about how their grandfather carried their grandmother out of a burning building."

He grinned, but there was such seriousness in his eyes, such depth that I felt like I was looking at forever. "That will be a good one, too."

"I think we're going to have a few to choose from."

"Of course we will. We'll never be boring."

At that moment, my roommates arrived. They yanked back the curtain, a nurse fast on their heels. Their eyes widened when they saw Reece hovering over me, his hands framing my face.

"Hey," I greeted them with an awkward wave.

"Are you okay?" Georgia rushed to my side, looking me over.

"I'm fine."

"And what's this?" Em nodded at Reece. He released my face but now held my hand, fingers laced with mine.

He looked at me, waiting for me to answer. "My boyfriend."

"Thought you had one of those already," Georgia murmured.

"Yeah. Who should be here any minute," Emerson volunteered with a pointed look at our joined hands. "We called him on our way here."

"I'm already here."

All eyes swung to where Hunter stood by the curtain, looking composed. He stepped closer, his forehead knitted with concern as he eyed me up and down, not missing my hand linked with Reece's. "Are you okay?"

That was so very Hunter. Worried about my welfare first. "Yes. I'm fine."

His shoulders relaxed. I hadn't been aware of the tension there until that moment. Nodding as if satisfied with my answer, his gaze shifted to Reece. Reece's hand tightened around mine as though he feared I might let go. Not that I ever would. Not anymore. Not again.

Hunter studied him for a long moment, like he was trying to reach some kind of decision. "If you hurt her—"

"I won't," Reece answered swiftly, with certainty, as if he knew exactly what question was coming.

I blinked at Hunter, bewildered. I hadn't even broken up with him. "How did you know—"

"I've always known. I just thought your feelings might change. You might start to feel something more for me. God knows you seemed determined to ignore whatever it was you had with Reece."

Emerson snorted from where she and Georgia had moved to lurk discreetly. "Ain't that the truth."

Hunter glanced at her and then looked at me fondly, a small smile playing on his lips. "I guess when it's real it doesn't ever fade away."

I shook my head. "No. It doesn't." God knows I had willed it to. "I'm sorry. You deserve better."

"I'll find it." He looked at Reece again and then back to me. "And thanks to you, I know what I'm looking for now." He leaned down and kissed me on the cheek. "I'll see you later, Pepper."

I nodded as he walked away, confident that I would see him again. Of course. He was Lila's brother, and he was still my friend.

"Wow," Em breathed. "What a day. Save the lives of two children. Nearly burned alive. Break up with your boyfriend. Get a new one. What's tomorrow gonna be like?"

I smiled up at Reece. "I doubt I'm getting out of bed."

Two weeks later . . .

Bing Crosby crooned softly in the background as Gram wished us good night. Reece and I shared a smile and settled onto the couch together. We were all alone after spending the day with Gram and all her friends. The old ladies loved Reece. Which made them not too different from young ladies. He flirted with them outrageously and they reveled in it, goosing him every chance they got. Obviously they just wanted to feel his nice backside for themselves.

Reece slipped a hand under the throw blanket and rubbed my feet.

"Ah, that feels good." I leaned back into the couch cushions.

"You deserve it, all the baking and cooking you did. I think you fed twenty people."

"*We* fed twenty people. You helped," I reminded him.

"It was fun. And was I *not* going to spend Christmas with you?" He looked at me like the very idea was crazy.

I smiled drowsily as I snuggled back against the comfy couch cushion. His fingers worked magic on my feet. The pads of his fingers slid beneath my loose pajama bottoms, skimming over my knees and traveling up my thighs, creating delicious friction on my skin and working another kind of magic on me.

I sighed Reece's name as he touched the edge of my panties. His fingers found me, slipping inside. I gasped, arching my spine. "What are you doing?"

"Making love to my girlfriend on Christmas."

"Ohh. But now? Here?" I glanced back toward the hall where Gram had disappeared to her room.

He slipped his hand free from my panties and came over me, kissing me hotly as he tugged my pajama bottoms off. "After the day she had today, she's not waking up until tomorrow morning."

I moaned as he guided me to straddle him. In a quick move, he freed himself from his own clothing and entered me. I threw back my head at the full sensation of him inside me, so glad that I'd gotten on the pill so we didn't have to stop in search of a condom. I rocked against him, holding him tightly to me. My fingers clenched on his shoulders as we moved together.

He dragged his mouth down my throat, leaving a burning path on my skin.

I clutched him closer, riding him faster. "I love you, Reece," I whispered hoarsely as I broke apart, splintering into pieces.

His hands tightened on my hips. He followed me, his body straining into mine. He muffled his cry into the crook of my neck, but I felt its force ripple through me. We held still, locked together for a long moment, enjoying each other.

He lifted his head and stared down at me, a slow smile curving his lips. "I love you, too."

I smoothed my hand over his forehead and down the back

of his skull, chafing my palm over his short hair, never tired of feeling the velvet scrape against my palm.

A mischievous smile played on his mouth. "Wait here." Arranging his clothes back in place, he jogged down the hall. I pulled my pajama bottoms back on and was sitting on the couch, waiting for him to return. When he did, it was with a small box wrapped in Christmas paper.

I pointed at it with a frown. "What's that? No fair. We already exchanged presents."

"I have one more for you. I wanted to give it to you alone."

"You shouldn't have done that. I didn't get you anything else."

He looked solemnly into my eyes. "Yes. You did. You do. You give me something every day."

My throat thickened with emotion.

"Now c'mon." He thrust it into my hands. "Open it, would you?"

I stared at the box and then back at him. He sat anxiously, his hand tapping on his knee. Smiling, I kissed him, beyond amazed that I had him in my life. And horrified that I had almost let him walk away.

I tore into the package. It was just a plain brown box, the kind you find at any office supply store. Turning it, I opened the lid, and peered inside. My hand closed around papers. Pulling them out, I scanned them uncomprehendingly for a moment. And then the words registered.

I dropped the papers and gawked at him. "We're going to Disney World for New Year's?"

He nodded and I screamed. Just like every kid in those

commercials, I freaked. Throwing my arms around his neck, I hugged him in a death squeeze.

Pulling back, I rained kisses all over his face. "How . . . why . . . ?"

"I remember you telling me about the Montgomerys going all the time and that you had never been. You had that poster in your room, and it just felt like something you really wanted to do."

"And now I am going to do it. With you." I shook my head, emotion clogging my throat. "You're the best boyfriend ever."

Yeah, he loved me. Totally and completely. Even knowing my past and all my hang-ups. That was huge in itself, but he got me. He understood me.

He cupped my cheek, that sexy smile of his taking hold of me. "This from a girl who only wanted foreplay from me and nothing more."

I turned my face to kiss his palm. "But now I want all of you. Everything."

He pulled me onto his lap and wrapped his arms around me. "Good. Because that's what you got."

About the Author

Sophie Jordan is the international and *New York Times* best-selling author of the Firelight series and Avon romances. When she's not writing, she spends her time overloading on caffeine (lattes preferred), talking plotlines with anyone who will listen (including her kids), and cramming her DVR with true-crime and reality-TV shows.

Don't Miss NEW BOOKS from your FAVORITE NEW ADULT AUTHORS

Cora Carmack

LOSING IT A Novel
Available in Paperback and eBook

FAKING IT A Novel
Available in Paperback and eBook

KEEPING HER An Original eNovella
eBook on Sale August 2013

FINDING IT A Novel
Available in Paperback and eBook Fall 2013

Jay Crownover

RULE A Novel
Available in eBook
Available in Paperback Fall 2013

JET A Novel
Available in eBook
Available in Paperback Fall 2013

ROME A Novel
Available in Paperback and eBook Winter 2014

Lisa Desrochers

A LITTLE TOO FAR A Novel
Available in eBook Fall 2013

A LITTLE TOO MUCH A Novel
Available in eBook Fall 2013

A LITTLE TOO HOT A Novel
Available in eBook Winter 2014

Abigail Gibbs

THE DARK HEROINE A Novel
Available in Paperback and eBook

AUTUMN ROSE A Novel
Available in Paperback and eBook Winter 2014

Sophie Jordan

FOREPLAY A Novel
Available in Paperback and eBook Fall 2013

J Lynn

WAIT FOR YOU A Novel
Available in eBook
Available in Paperback Fall 2013

BE WITH ME A Novel
Available in Paperback Winter 2014

TRUST ME A Novella
Available in eBook Fall 2013

Molly McAdams

FROM ASHES A Novel
Available in Paperback and eBook

TAKING CHANCES A Novel
Available in Paperback and eBook

STEALING HARPER An Original eNovella
Available in eBook

FORGIVING LIES A Novel
Available in Paperback and eBook Fall 2013

DECEIVING LIES A Novel
Available in Paperback and eBook Winter 2014

Shannon Stoker

THE REGISTRY A Novel
Available in Paperback and eBook

THE COLLECTION A Novel
Available in Paperback and eBook Winter 2014